The
Dominant
Blonde

The
Dominant
Blonde

Alisa Kwitney

 AVON BOOKS   *An Imprint of* HarperCollins*Publishers*

HarperCollins books may be purchased for educational, business, or sales promotional use. For information please write: Special Markets Department, Harper-Collins Publishers Inc., 10 East 53rd Street, New York, NY 10022.

FIRST EDITION

Designed by Shubhani Sarkar

Library of Congress Cataloging-in-Publication Data

Kwitney, Alisa, 1964–
    The dominant blonde / by Alisa Kwitney.—1st ed.
    p.   cm
ISBN 0-06-008329-8
1. Swindlers and swindling—Fiction. 2. Ex–police
officers—Fiction. 3. Missing persons—Fiction.
4. Seaside resorts—Fiction. 1. Title.

PS3611.W58 D66 2002
813'.54—dc21   2001053753

03   04   05   06   WBC/RRD   10   9   8

This book is for Mark, my husband and best dive buddy

Acknowledgments

I would like to thank my mother, Ziva, for early encouragement; Natasha Bobkova, for Russian phrases and the creative distraction of two very determined small children; Holly Harrison, Alexis Sinclair, Kevin Jones, and Susan Taylor-Gol, for barbless criticism and good advice; Opal, for everything I always wanted to know about blonding and carnival in the Caribbean; Sgt. Jim Cowan of the NYPD Scuba Patrol, for giving me the gory details; Gary Collins at Pan Aqua, for filling in the blanks in my memory; Peter Bennet, president of the Diver Alert Network (DAN), and Dan Nord, for taking the time to teach me about recompression chambers.

The
Dominant
Blonde

1

Before you trust a man, Lydia's grandmother used to say, you have to know three things: how he spends his money, how he holds his drink, and how he loses his temper.

Despite this advice, Lydia had gone on dating one extravagant drunken disaster after another. But now, one year after her grandmother's demise, Lydia knew she had found a man of whom her nana would have approved.

A beer or two only added to his genial good mood.

He was generous to a fault.

In four months, she had never once seen him get mad.

And, as an added bonus, Abe Bohemius was the first man who had ever suggested that she go on vacation with him and not broken up with her two days before the date on the nonrefundable tickets.

This time, Lydia thought, I just might've gotten it right.

Resting her luggage at her feet, Lydia paused to savor the sea-salt, flower-musked breeze. Back in New York City, the gray-faced hordes were tunneling through the subways on their way home from work. Here, sky met sea in an expansive wash of vivid blue.

Lydia turned as the sun shifted and a shadow fell across her face. Looking up, she saw that she was standing in the shade of a great, dark bird, hunkered in apparent misery atop a flagless pole. With a rusty squawk, the bird launched itself into the air, giving two flaps of its enormous wings before swooping low over the sprawling wood dining hall and veering off toward the treeline. A few tourists, eating watery fish stew out on the verandah, put down their spoons and pointed.

"Hey," Abe called over his shoulder. "How you doing back there?"

Lydia pressed her hands into the small of her back and took a deep breath of heavily vegetated humidity. "Just a little rest break."

Abe turned, shading his eyes with his hand as he inspected their surroundings. There were damp patches under his blue silk shirt. "So what do you think, Lyd? This paradise or what?"

"Or what." Lydia smiled. Abe smiled back in perfect misunderstanding.

The brochures for Neptune's Rest had promised a resort of sugar-white beaches and jewel-like waters of incredible brightness and clarity, as well as gardens as fragrant and lush as bridal bouquets, and aggressively tame parrots who would eat the mango right out of your hand. The photographs and text had also implied, but not stated, that you and your lover would be having some wild monkey sex in a hammock.

What the brochure's idyllic pictures and lyrical descriptions had concealed was the odd, ramshackle aspect of the place, and the vague air of neglect and sadness that afflicted everything from the palm trees, which listed at acute angles to the ground, to the male-pattern baldness of the thatch-roofed huts.

"You okay? Still need to take a breather?" Abe smiled at her, all dark eyes and white teeth.

"No, no, I'm okay. It isn't far, is it?"

"Nah. We're in cabin D-10. This here's the B line of cabins, so we're probably just over there somewheres. You ready?"

Following Abe's sweaty back, Lydia allowed the resort some leeway. After all, she and Abe did not exactly resemble the sleekly oiled models who had draped provocatively over each other in the brochure's various settings. Abe was handsome, but in a swarthy, furry, barrel-chested fashion. She, despite being a blonde and a size ten for the first time in her life, had a face that showed every line from thirty-one years of concerted worrying.

Abe stopped to inspect a small sign, half-hidden behind a tiki torch. "Damn. This says G line. We must've gone too far."

"Let's ask someone."

"Lydia, I got a map. You don't need to—"

"Excuse me." Lydia spotted an islander, dressed in the resort's navy blue uniform, walking swiftly along another path. "Excuse me," she called. "Hello?" The man kept walking.

"Yo! Hey!" Abe whistled loudly.

The young man, who had a round, almost babyish face and sleepy eyes, ambled over. "I didn't realize you were calling me."

"We can't figure out where's our cabin." Abe showed him their keys.

"That way, sir. By that palm tree over there."

"Great. Thanks." Abe stuffed a dollar bill into the man's front pocket. The young man looked down at it.

"Thanks, but tips are not—"

"What's your name, kid?"

"Thomas."

"Thomas, you look in on us in half an hour or so, I got some diving questions for you."

Thomas looked uncomfortable. "I'm afraid I'm not really the most expert—"

"Don't worry, I'm an old hand. Fact is, I don't really want a site crowded with other tourists. You can show me some of the spots where the locals dive, right? When you're done with whatever it is you're doing. Here, take this, we can negotiate a sum when you drop by, okay?" Abe patted another, larger bill into the young man's pocket. Lydia, looking away from Thomas's shuttered expression, saw that the strange bird was still circling far overhead.

"That isn't a parrot, is it? What kind of bird is that?"

"That bird? I don't know the name in English, ma'am."

Lydia peered at the sky. "It almost looks like a vulture."

"Ah, yes. 'Vulture.' I believe that is the word. Excuse me?" Thomas smiled, then loped swiftly away. Lydia, suddenly recalling that the island of Epiphany didn't have any native languages other than English, snorted with laughter.

Abe hefted his suitcase up. "Something funny?"

"Just happy, I guess." Lydia looked at her bag, bent from the knees, and hauled it into her arms.

Abe looked at Lydia for a long moment, as if bringing her into focus. "You want me to take your bag?"

Lydia tried to peek around the burden in her arms. "Oh, no, that's quite all right, you did warn me not to schlepp all these shoes . . ."

"Ah, you girls always pack too much stuff. Here." Abe deftly snatched the duffel out of her arms.

"Thanks!"

"Wouldn't want to tire my girl out her first night here." Abe set off across the uneven ground, bouncing along on his short, muscular legs, her bag slung over his shoulder like a dead carcass, his own suitcase rolling obediently behind him.

§

The cabin looked as if someone had airlifted it straight out of Camp Wahiki-Liki, "An Authentic Indian Experience for Urban

Youth." As summer camp had been the location and the occasion of some of the worst experiences of Lydia Gold's life, she could not say that this was a welcome discovery.

But this was not meant to be a luxurious holiday, Lydia reminded herself as she unpacked the third pair of shoes from her deflated purple bag. This was meant to be seven days of exploration and adventure. She and Abe had chosen to be here instead of lazing around some lavish Caribbean resort. That was the kind of place you went to bake yourself cancerous in the sun. The tiny island of Epiphany was the kind of place you went if you were a dedicated scuba-diving nut, and wanted to spend most of your time staring at fish on their own level.

Or, to be more precise, this was the kind of place you went when your boyfriend wanted an adrenaline rush, and you wanted to show him that you weren't the most physically timid human on the planet.

Given her druthers, Lydia would have chosen luxurious lethargy. First of all, it would have been less expensive. Scuba diving seemed mainly to consist of elaborate preparations involving the purchase of special gadgets and gizmos to be worn, inserted, ingested, or installed.

Lydia's secret fantasies were more bacchanalian. She wished she could have seen at least the start of the carnival revels, due to begin the day after she and Abe were booked to go home.

It wasn't that she was lazy or debauched, Lydia told herself. But this was the first time in her life that she had been slim enough to consider the kind of vacation where you wore a swimsuit all day long, and Lydia wanted to be that Cosmo girl, complete with barefoot sunsets, blue martinis, and Middle Eastern sex techniques. And if Abe Bohemius wasn't exactly the feast she'd conjured for herself in the long, hungry midnights of her imagination, then he was the first not to leave a bitter aftertaste in his wake.

No, he was more than that. He was the first man she'd ever dated who had taken care of her when she'd gotten her period, offering to rub her back and fill her hot-water bottle.

He was the first man who had ever told her she was beautiful. Not pretty, not sweet, but beautiful.

He was honest enough to admit that he worried that she might be smarter than he was. She had been worried about that, too, but suddenly, when he'd said it, she'd looked at him and realized she could imagine him waking up in the dead of night to appease a wailing infant.

So what if he didn't read much. She read enough for both of them. Or possibly too much. What had Yeats's mythic passions and D. H. Lawrence's pagan rites given her aside from the mistaken impression that sex could impress itself upon the spirit as well as the flesh?

There was a knock on the door. Lydia looked up from her unpacking; Abe had already gotten up.

"Who is it, Abe?" No answer. Lydia glanced over to where Abe stood in the doorway, his silk shirt unbuttoned to the waist. She could not see around him to the person on the other side. There was a brief, businesslike consultation about times and equipment before Abe pressed some money into the unseen visitor's hand. Then the door slammed shut.

Lydia hung her white cotton sundress in the narrow closet. "Who was that?"

"That young guy we just met. While you're busy getting certified, Thomas says he can show me around, take me to some of the best dive sites."

"You think he's experienced enough to do that?"

"You kidding? Out here, they all dive from the time they can walk. Nothing else for them to do." Abe bent over his suitcase, inserting his right hand and feeling along the lining.

"Did you lose something?"

Abe whipped his head around. "Ah, just making sure my suntan lotion didn't leak into my shorts."

Lydia, who double-bagged all her lotions, went back to her own suitcase. "So where am I going to be while you're off checking out the island's hidden treasures?"

Abe zipped his suitcase closed. There was a click as he locked the zipper shut. Maybe the maids weren't so trustworthy on the island, Lydia thought. "You? You'll be out doing your first certification dives." Abe caught Lydia's look of distress and tweaked her under the chin. "You nervous about tomorrow?"

"Completely terrified."

Abe laughed. "Don't think about it. You've already done it all in the pool."

"The ocean's different."

"Course it is. It's better. Lemme ask you something. What'd you do in a swimming pool when you was a kid—laps? Dives? Fancy jumps offa diving board?"

"I used to sink to the bottom and pretend I was a mermaid."

"There you go. A born diver. You're gonna be a natural."

Lydia smiled. "You're so good for my confidence. Think you can keep saying that for the next twelve hours?"

"You know me. I'll keep telling you how great you are until you believe it." Abe brushed up behind her to impart a light pinch on her rear.

"Hey, watch those hands, mister."

"Baby, believe me, I was." Abe seemed about to say something else. He turned Lydia around until she faced him. "Tell me something. You been happy with me these last few months?"

"You know I have."

"Good." Abe pressed Lydia into a warm embrace, and she fought the urge to pull back. His back was still sweaty and there was something a little too urgent about his touch, as if he were trying to reassure himself about something.

As if he knew that she loved him with steadfast loyalty and grateful affection, but not with adoration, and not with the intensity that he seemed to feel for her.

Suddenly ashamed of herself, Lydia hugged Abe back fiercely. She wished she could tell him that he could relax. She wished she could tell him just how good it was, for once, to be the one more loved. His adoring glances had given her confidence. His assumption that they had a future imbued her with a sense of her own worth. She would have given anything to pay him back in the same coin.

Instead, she promised herself silently that she would do everything in her power to make Abe happy, even scuba diving, even if it meant accidentally drowning herself off the pokiest island in the Caribbean.

2

In the beginning, when the business had been unfamiliar, badly organized, and always on the verge of some sort of crisis, Liam Mac-Nally had been filled with a sense of exhilarated calm. But, as so often happens in life and love affairs, it turned out that the early, nervy, unsettled time was the happiest. What came after was the long, leisurely disenchantment as Liam learned something about himself: He wasn't cut out to be in one of the service professions. There was something about tending to people's needs on their vacations that felt essentially unmasculine to him.

Which was ridiculous, thought Liam as he turned off the small boat's engine. What was unmanly about taking people out on a boat and guiding them through a dive? It was the kind of job men had in Hemingway novels. Except a Hemingway hero didn't have to explain over and over that no, this activity was not included in the resort's flat fee, and no, he couldn't take anyone scuba diving in the ocean who hadn't taken a pool orientation first. Yes, that was an extra fifty dollars. Yes, he did feel it was essential. Even if that other club didn't require it. Maybe they had more insurance. Liam couldn't afford it if someone drowned.

Liam had no idea why he wasn't happier. This was, after all, the life he had chosen, the blissful, stress-free, permanent vacation of a job he had dreamed of back in the days when scuba diving had meant inserting himself into the rubbery bondage of a full dry suit and sub-merging himself in the fecal stew of the Hudson River, searching for the unpleasant conclusion to a missing persons case.

It was impossible that he could be having a *second* midlife crisis at the age of thirty-five.

"Okay, everyone, let's go through an equipment check. Anyone need any assistance?" Liam glanced around at his small group of first-timers: a plump, tanned thirteen-year-old boy with a thick gold chain around his neck; a slender, brunette executive type with state-of-the-art equipment; and a big-boned blonde struggling with the zipper on her hot-pink dive skin.

"Here. Allow me." Liam gave the zipper a slight tug and it sailed over the blonde's generous breasts. He was already moving away when she stopped him with a tentative hand on his arm.

"Thanks! Uh, excuse me? But is this the way the life jacket goes on?"

Swallowing a sigh, Liam turned back to the owner of the throaty, little-girl voice. He had the feeling that this one was going to be trouble. She had the look of a low-ranking animal trying to appease the pack leader: large, doe eyes opened so wide the whites gleamed, a glossy-pink smile of fear.

Liam gave her his warmest professional smile.

"Okay, now, this part slips on just like a vest—remember?"

"I'm sorry. I'm just a little rattled."

Liam adjusted the chest and waist straps. "Everyone gets nervous the first time. So—Lydia? Is that your name? You may recall that this is actually called a buoyancy-control device, because unlike a life jacket—"

"Oh! That's right!"

"Unlike a life jacket, this can be adjusted so you can get under the water—otherwise there's no dive, right? And then, once you've descended as far as you plan on going, you can add a bit more buoyancy to the suit—is that comfortable?"

"I think so. Wait—something's digging into my thigh."

The brunette, seeing all the attention Blondie was getting, wanted to be checked over from bum to bristols, too. Keeping his expression neutral while he rearranged the lady's air tank, Liam wondered how the geekiest boy in high school had become the kind of man women seemed to find attractive. What was it that had been so wrong with him then, and what was it that was right with him now? Was it merely a matter of age bestowing confidence, or was it something less admirable? Had he learned to play a part so well he'd forgotten it was an act?

"I don't need any help, I don't think," said the boy with a slight accent.

"No, I see you've done very well by yourself."

"You were occupied." His flat, dark gaze skimmed over the two women, and Liam felt himself reprimanded. He cleared his throat and jumped up onto the bench near the boy.

"All right, shall we get started? Good. Now then," Liam said, paying particular attention to the boy, "the scariest part is getting in. But this here is just ten to fifteen feet of water we'll be in—you might even think of it as just another dip in the pool, though you might find some fish got in."

There was some weak laughter, mainly from the women. The boy, who was much calmer and more self-possessed than Liam recalled himself being at that age, sat and looked at him with a kind of placid intensity. Christ, thought Liam, what is this kid, twelve years old? Thirteen? At his age I'd have been beside myself with excitement at the prospect of scuba diving.

At fourteen, he'd have shown less emotion than this pampered-looking child, albeit for very different reasons.

Liam stood up, and gestured for the blonde to go first. It was best to let the nervous ones get things over with as quickly as possible. Miss Monroe here would probably need about ten minutes to talk down into the water. You didn't want to leave the other two paddling like ducks while she dithered endlessly up on deck. "Are you ready?"

The blonde grinned at him with a flash of unexpected humor. "Is anyone ever ready for something they haven't done before?"

Despite his promise to himself not to flirt, Liam leaned closer to the warm cocoa-butter smell of her skin. She wasn't his type—she sounded like a six-year-old with a sore throat—but there was something game about her, and he liked that. "You look like a lady with a spirit of adventure. Why not just say screw it and jump in without even thinking?"

"Like this?" To Liam's surprise, the woman turned abruptly and jumped into the water, her face mask and snorkel still perched on her forehead. Instantly inhaling a wave, she sputtered and coughed for a moment, and then remembered to inflate her vest.

"Are you all right down there?"

Adding to his surprise, the woman laughed. "You know," she said, "I think I am."

"Then give me the signal."

The woman belatedly gave the arm signal that she was not in distress. Laughing himself, Liam turned his attention to the disgruntled brunette.

§

It was late afternoon when Lydia returned to her cabin, exhausted, and yet unable to lie down. The big, sinfully attractive

Irish guy had been right. The scary part was getting in—not only jumping off the boat wearing what felt like a ton of equipment, but also sinking underwater breathing through a big silicone plug in your mouth while waves slapped you in the face mask.

But once she'd settled down on the sandy bottom, Lydia had felt much calmer. Reassured by the transparent ceiling of water only twelve feet overhead, she'd knelt in a circle with the other two beginners and watched the dive guide. He nodded to one novice diver after the other, until it was Lydia's turn to pull back the strap of her face mask and allow some water to seep inside, so she could demonstrate that she could successfully clear it without panicking and drowning herself.

It had taken Lydia what felt like a small eternity of blowing through her nose before she could see again. Blinking back the slight sting of salt from her eyes, she watched as a preternaturally poised teenage boy cleared his mask in half the time it had taken her.

But on the second dive, Lydia felt she had proven herself. She had been paired off with the other woman, a trim brunette who had seemed incredibly cool and efficient, up until the moment when her spare regulator had begun to free-flow, sending a plume of bubbles rushing furiously to the surface. Lydia had been the first one to calm the woman, looking deeply into her eyes, miming that she should continue to inhale slowly and regularly from her main air source as the guide tapped the spare regulator on his thigh, stopping the flow. For a moment, she thought he seemed surprised when he looked at her, as if in recognition of a kindred spirit. She had to admit, she was a bit surprised by herself. She had never really thought of herself as a cool head in a crisis.

After that, the lanky dive guide had seemed to treat her with a kind of relaxed camaraderie, as if she'd joined his team somehow. It was deeply flattering. She wondered briefly whether, had she been unattached, their relaxed banter might have turned to flirtation. As it was, she'd treated him as if he were her long-lost big brother. He probably didn't get that treatment very often. For all she knew, that was what he'd found most attractive.

Stripping off her wet dive skin, Lydia glanced at the clock. Five-thirty in the afternoon. She wondered what time Abe would be getting back. He'd been a little odd when he'd left her in the morning, so sweetly apologetic about leaving her on her own for even a moment that she'd almost had to push him out the door.

Lydia's grandmother had always said, "When a man is too nice, there's something not so nice going on." Unfortunately, she'd said this to Lydia when she was only sixteen and in love with Jack Havers, the cruelest boy in the eleventh grade, so it hadn't made much of an impression. Now, nearly twice as old as she'd been back when Jack had begun his campaign of suspicious friendliness, Lydia felt a momentary pang of doubt. Was it possible that Abe was doing something he didn't want her to know about—gambling, say? Or was he arranging something he just didn't want her to know about just yet?

Lydia ran the shower for ten minutes before accepting that tepid was the only temperature she was likely to achieve. Standing under the desultory trickle, she closed her eyes and allowed herself to wonder: Was he planning to propose?

Because there was *something* going on, Lydia could feel it. She didn't want to permit her past to make her suspicious, but there was some barely restrained excitement in Abe's usually slumberous eyes, some secret knowledge that had him bouncing on the balls of his feet, poised to leap out across some great, life-changing divide.

On the one hand, Lydia thought, it was entirely possible that this kind, straightforward, unpolished gem of a man might be setting up some unforgettably romantic proposal, with hidden musicians and horse-drawn conveyances and ring boxes buried in the sand.

On the other hand, he might be scheming to stash drugs on her person so she would smuggle them, unknowing, back into the States.

No, Lydia thought, that's ridiculous, Abe is not like that. And if her judgment had been a little off in the past, well, that was because all those other times, she was always blind in love with some man who wasn't completely sure he was in love with her.

This time, the opposite was true.

Wrapping the threadbare hotel towel around herself, Lydia sat down on the edge of the shiny peach bedspread and wondered what she would do if Abe did intend to propose.

What she felt for him was not the passionate certainty of romance novels. But passion was deceptive. Lydia could name at least six painfully brief and oddly impersonal encounters, each of which she had mistaken for a romantic bolt from on high. The most recent of these had thrown her into a four-month bout of the blues.

Because this was what the glib movies and books never seemed to mention about being single. They described some heartache, true, but not the humiliation of being too heavy breasted for your brides-maid's dress, and frantically sewing a brassiere into the lining the night before your brother's wedding. Your *younger* brother's wedding.

The protagonists of romantic comedies surely did not make the mistake of staying up past midnight with the bride's blue-eyed brother in the hotel disco. They did not allow one slow dance too many to lead to just one nightcap too many back in his room. The quirky-but-lovable heroine of fiction never had to experience sitting across from the bride's brother at breakfast the morning after, chin rubbed scarlet by his stubble, while he steadfastly refused to meet her eyes. Or as his sister, the bride, stopped glowing long enough to stare at her with steely contempt.

One more man, badly chosen in a moment of passion, but this one would haunt her through the rest of her life.

And then there had been that other little mistake in judgment. The professional one that had sent Lydia home with her tail tucked between her legs: Please, Daddy, sorry I wasted all your money on graduate school, but now I don't have housing anymore, so may I move back in, please?

All through the stifling heat of June, July, and half of August, Lydia had felt like the eternal adolescent, back in her old bedroom with its fading lavender paint, back to her old job at the family salon, trimming ten identical Upper East Side bobs a day. As young women did not often frequent the Chrysalis Salon and Day Spa, Lydia's world became a forest of aging female heads. Her mother, who had the tendency to confide in strangers as if they were friends, made sure that each of her daughter's new clients knew the history of Lydia's unfortunate love life.

And then there was Abe, a man walking into the gold-and-marble-interior salon and spa in broad daylight without apology or excuse, asking for the half-day rejuvenation with haircut, pedicure, and aromatherapy seaweed treatment for water retention. He hadn't really been her type, even after she'd trimmed the ridiculous late-eighties mane of hair off his thick neck, but then he had grasped her wrist and told her softly that her mother was right—she did just need to find a guy to appreciate her.

He'd woken her up. Like Sleeping Beauty. Or perhaps more like Rip Van Winkle. She found that she had changed during her long hibernation. The bad news was that she had a faint new worry line between her eyebrows and five gray hairs. The good news was that she was two dress sizes smaller. In celebration, she dyed her dirty-blond hair the shade it had been when she had been a toddler visiting her grandmother in Miami Beach.

Four months after her blonding, Abe had hinted that this vacation might be the time and place for them to decide on their future together.

"Can't you get him to propose before your cousin's wedding in April?" Lydia's mother had asked.

"Mom."

"Because then you could show off your ring at her reception."

Was there a ring? Combing her fingers through her hair, Lydia wandered over to Abe's suitcase. She touched the rough canvas-and-leather exterior, pretending to wrestle with the question of whether or not to invade Abe's privacy. The truth was, Lydia was only looking for the right justification. Wouldn't it be kinder, she told herself, to find out Abe's intentions here and now? It would give her time to consider what to say. It would give her time to prepare her response.

The real question, of course, was simple enough: Was it enough to love the man, even if she wasn't actually in love with him?

For Lydia, who had never felt loved enough, there was no simple answer. I can't decide this theoretically, she thought. I have to touch the ring. If I see it, I will just know what to say to him when the time comes.

Lydia let her fingers slide over the lock that held the zipper in place. Her own suitcase, although a different brand, had a similar key, and Lydia had seen a news program that demonstrated how one suitcase key could pretty much work all suitcase locks.

The key fit perfectly, and Lydia thought she ought to tell Abe that the lock was useless.

Well, all right, there was no way to do that without giving herself away. Lydia could see that the art of deception probably took some practice.

Unzipping the top of Abe's suitcase, gliding her hand across his Hawaiian shirt, his safari-print shorts. A veteran of spy novels, she ran both hands smoothly over all the inside seams.

There was a bulge in an inside pocket of the suitcase.

A box. It *was* there.

Knowing that she was committing the most unromantic act in the world, she listened for the sounds of someone approaching the cabin and then let her fingers explore the ring box. Why am I doing this? Lydia wondered, aware that she was destroying the fantasy proposal she had carried around in her head for years—the moment of shock and wonder and elation when the man you had chosen chose you out of all the women in the world.

Well, there was a kind of shock, wonder, and elation. It was just arriving a bit prematurely.

Sinking to her knees, Lydia decided not to remove the box. What if she forgot exactly where it belonged and ruined everything? Yet it might not be a ring. Perhaps it was a pin, or a necklace. It might be earrings. A boyfriend had once given Lydia earrings, back in high school. But then he'd gone and ruined it by confiding that his mother had picked them on her own.

Mothers always like Lydia.

With trembling fingers, Lydia pressed the little button that opened the catch. Leaving the box in its pocket, she sucked in her breath and withdrew a ring.

Not a diamond. Something else. In the dim light of the cabin, the large gem seemed almost black, but held up to the bedside lamp, it glittered a deep-ocean blue.

A brilliant-cut sapphire, large enough to make Lydia blink. Not what she would have chosen, but hadn't Princess Diana . . .

That was not a good marriage to think about.

Oh, Lord, Lydia thought, there *is* a ring, an incredible ring, and I still don't know what to say to him.

Trembling, Lydia slid the cool, strange, solitaire onto her finger.

Then, without warning, the doorknob rattled.

The door! Abe was at the door! Panicking, Lydia tugged at the ring on her finger, only to find, to her abject horror, that it would not come loose.

Abe walked into the cabin to find Lydia smiling brightly at him, stark naked, her hands sunk wrist deep in her own suitcase.

"You're back already! Hope I didn't leave you alone too long."

"Not at all!"

"I just . . . Thomas just showed me some great sites. But I hurried right back to my baby." Abe came up behind her and nuzzled her neck. "How come you're all naked?"

"I'm looking for just the right panties," said Lydia, tugging more discreetly at the ring while pretending to rummage through her underwear.

"So whaddya think—should we dress up tonight?"

"Um." Lydia felt the ring pop off her finger and slide into the jumble of her underpants just as Abe planted a kiss on the curve of her neck, his hands sliding under the towel to cup her breasts. Lydia felt a prickle of terror rise over her skin. What if Abe meant to propose tonight?

"Don't do it," she blurted out.

"Do what?" Abe gave her breasts a friendly squeeze.

"Don't dress up." Lydia stepped out of his embrace. "Let's just start out the holiday casual, you know, leave room for a big romantic evening later on."

"Yeah, okay. So now you get your pretty little butt on into the bathroom and—"

"No, I'm ready!"

"Lyd, you're naked."

"I mean, as soon as I get some clothes on, I'm ready." She grabbed an oversize T-shirt from her case and threw it over her head.

"You're not gonna put on any makeup?"

"Hey, we're on vacation." No way was she leaving him alone with that suitcase.

"Yeah, but I thought you girls always—"

"You're implying I need it?"

"Baby, you just suit yourself and I'm happy." Abe held out his hands in mock surrender. She could tell he was thinking there was no use arguing with a woman. "Well, if you aren't gonna shower, maybe we should just . . ." Abe, walking past his suitcase, suddenly paused. "Hey," he said, frowning slightly, "Were you looking for something in—"

Lydia launched herself across the room and stopped his question with a kiss.

Hours later, as the shadows lengthened in the small cabin, Lydia lay, fretting, trapped in the bed with her lover's heavy arm slung across her body. The ring was still in her suitcase. Please, God, she prayed, let him leave me alone, if only for five minutes, so I can get the damn thing back in its box after breakfast.

But the next day Abe was particularly solicitous as he escorted her to their first open-water dive together, and so the strange stone remained buried between Lydia's underwear and her brassieres, like a grain of sand embedded in an oyster.

3

Twenty years earlier, before Liam's red hair had darkened to brown and he'd gained enough weight to stop looking like a freckled skeleton, he'd been the class clown. Girls had liked him, but only as a buddy. He'd learned a lot about what the fair sex really wanted, but hadn't had a lot of opportunities to put his knowledge into practice.

But then Liam had grown into his spidery frame, and although he himself saw only a kind of average, bony-faced guy in the mirror, the kind you see on every street corner in Ireland, it had been years since a woman had treated him like a comrade in arms.

The way the blond woman had. He'd actually been looking forward to seeing her again. Blondie had turned out to be surprisingly laid back, despite his initial misgivings. He'd probably invite her for a drink later, without worrying that she'd take it as the beginning of some high-octane holiday romance.

He hadn't realized she was with someone until she'd come up to him and said, "Need my help saving anyone's life today?" Liam had checked her weight belt and been coming up with the perfect response when a compact rottweiler of a man had slung his arm around the blond woman's shoulders, knocking her slightly off balance.

"How's my girl?" The question seemed aimed at Liam. Liam looked at the blonde.

"Just a little nervous."

"Ahh, you'll do great." The boyfriend's dark eyes gleamed wetly with good humor. "Those first dives were nothing, just like diving in the pool. Baby stuff. But this, this you're gonna love." Turning to Liam, he said, "You tell her, there's nothing like the thrill you get first time down. You get eighty, ninety feet down, you feel like you're in another world."

"Actually, we'll only be going as deep as fifty this afternoon."

"Only fifty?"

"That's enough for the beginners. Besides, that's where the wreck is." The little boat had been sunk there especially for divers such as these, novices who wanted more adventure than was healthy for them. Still, the fish liked it.

"We going inside the wreck?"

"No, not today. Inside it's deeper, and someone could get stuck. We'll just look around the outside this morning."

"Way I calculated it, I could go at least sixty and still not need to come up till I ran low on air."

Liam knew better than to argue with the man's sense of his own expertise. "Your girlfriend's not ready for a deeper dive yet, and neither are these others. Most of them still need another dive after this one before they're certified."

"But the way I figured—"

"You figured wrong."

"I still don't see—"

Liam sighed and felt the stiff weariness of too much lifting and too little sleep all down the length of his spine. "There's plenty of time for deep diving later on," he reminded the man. "You're here for the week, are you not?"

"Yeah, yeah, of course we are." The shorter man smiled again, showing a lot of white teeth in his olive-skinned face. "Anyway, you're the boss here."

"Don't worry, I'll make sure you enjoy yourself."

"Sure thing, Captain. Whatever you say."

There was something a little too quick about the man's capitulation, but Liam decided to take it at face value. Lots of decent women were stuck with obnoxious losers. Still, he'd have thought Blondie would have more taste. Turning away, Liam busied himself with getting the remaining tanks out of the hold, making sure that they were all full of air before distributing them to the passengers. After three straight weeks of torrential rain, the sun was finally shining, and the air was filled with the familiar predive smell of diesel and saltwater mingled with cocoa butter and skin. Most of the tourists were looking fairly contented as they sat in the back of the small boat, slathering themselves with their expensive sunscreens and beginning to check their diving equipment. Not that most of them knew what they were doing. Liam figured at least two people would come surging back out of the water, realizing too late that they had neglected to turn on the air in their tanks.

Blondie's boyfriend, for one. And the gingerhead with the sunburned shoulders and nose, who'd complained about the cheese-and-bologna sandwiches Liam had prepared. A vegan, for Christ's sake. You can eat the bread, can't you? Liam had inquired.

"Yes, but that's hardly——"

"So eat the bread."

Liam lugged the last tank of air up into position before pausing to take stock of his passengers. There was the executive brunette who'd freaked out the day before, the idiot vegan, the sleekly organized Argentinian couple. Perched in the front of the craft, an old, barrel-chested guy and his jaded grandson were both looking fairly competent as they pointed out landmarks along the shoreline and discussed a fold-out chart of tropical fish.

And there was Blondie, nervously checking her dive watch again. Blondie's boyfriend intercepted Liam's glance and flashed him a brief, mirthless smile, as if to say, Yeah, one delicious slab of girlflesh, but it's on my plate, buster. Liam thought she might be a dish, but not to his taste. Too short, too stacked, and too trussed up in that black one-piece swimsuit. All in all, she had the utilitarian glamour of a 1940s starlet waiting for a martini, a husband, and a ranch house.

But he'd kind of hoped they'd continue palling around. Ah, well.

Now Blondie's boyfriend was ostentatiously zipping her hot-pink dive skin up in front, while giving her some piece of advice that was making her look distinctly queasy. At least she wouldn't be shivering from cold halfway through the dive. All too often, Liam had to convince his customers that no matter how hot it was on the surface, there was always a chill twenty feet below. Blondie's boyfriend had refused to listen. He seemed to feel that Liam was calling his masculinity into question by insinuating that he might lose body heat. Well, let him learn the hard way, so long as he didn't wind up hyperventilating and requiring time in a recompression chamber, which was bad for business. Maybe that carpet of body hair would keep him comfortable.

Liam pulled on his own blue short-sleeved suit, wincing as he hit something in his left arm, the one he'd impaled three years earlier on a rusty stanchion in zero-visibility water.

"Are you okay?"

Liam turned to face the long-limbed brunette.

"Yeah, I'm fine."

"Because I've taken first aid." The lady smiled with impeccably made-up lips and marked a place in the book she had been reading. There was a body, bleeding very neatly, on the cover.

"Thanks. I'll remember that." Liam smiled and moved over to help the Argentinian couple, leaving the brunette to her literature. A lot of women thought a holiday fling with the hired help was a pleasant extra, less exotic than a swim with the dolphins but more entertaining than the ubiquitous nightly limbo contests and steel-drum bands.

Liam didn't have it in him to provide the additional service. Last year he'd glutted himself on well-tended career types, and now highly-strung Manhattanites were as unappealing to him as pre-mixed piña coladas.

The only problem was the faint remnant of County Wicklow in Liam's speech. Still audible after two decades in Boston, the accent tended to act as a kind of dog whistle to most Americans. They pricked up their ears, alerted, curious, compelled. Unable to completely lose his brogue, Liam used it to his best advantage, deepening it when the occasion warranted. Although Liam was aware of this, he felt it could hardly be called an affectation, as it had become second nature to him.

Without trying, Liam knew he could easily attract yet another driven jobnik who lived out of her desk and her health club and had nothing to talk about when stripped of the particulars of her narrow life. In her own world, the lady would doubtless be intelligent, insightful, even charming. On a boat in the Caribbean, she was as vapid as a teenager, clutching her glossy book and her fruity drink, hoping for a fling with someone who would appreciate her Pilates-honed abdominals, ideally a corporate VP also on vacation who might call her back home for dinner at some pricey Thai place on the Upper East Side, but if not, hey, the dive guide's probably good for a laugh.

Come carnival next week and Liam would probably have to hide out on the boat to escape being molested by hard-edged lawyers on three-day benders.

Liam helped the vegan get his tank turned on, and was about to address the group when the blonde came up again, breathing a bit too heavily.

"Um, excuse me . . . ?"

"Liam."

"Um, Liam, is it okay if I stick with you? Abe went ahead and started his dive a little early."

"He did *what?*"

"He started his dive." Blondie raised her eyebrows and her shoulders in an exaggerated show of helpless affection. Like they were all in love with the guy and had agreed to put up with him.

"Shite." Liam dragged a hand over his face. This was just the kind of thing Martin was waiting for, some idiot who had to go and drown himself on Liam's boat.

"But I was wondering, isn't he supposed to always have a buddy?"

Liam forced himself to smile calmly. "Indeed he should, just in case he cuts himself on a rock and starts bleeding, or runs out of air, or goes deep enough to get nitrogen narcosis and tries to hand his regulator to a fish." Liam took a deep breath. "Hey, I don't suppose good old Abe happened to tell you where he was planning to dive? And how deep?"

The blonde shook her head. "He didn't mention it, no. He just said, 'Look, you'll feel safer with the paid guide the first time anyhow, and I'll meet you back at the boat at four.' Where could he have gone for a deep dive around here?"

"This is the ocean. You can go deep just about anywhere."

She thought about it. "You say the only wreck's fifty feet down? Is there any other interesting diving around here?"

Shite. She was being smarter than he was. And Liam knew he couldn't just let Abe take his chances, because if Martin Thorne got wind of this, the man would spin the story like Rumpelstiltskin.

As owner of the island's one resort, Martin enjoyed knowing that just about everyone on the island worked for him, directly or indirectly. So far, Liam had been keeping the relationship indirect. He was an independent contractor despite Martin's repeated attempts to make him an employee.

If Martin decided that Liam was at fault for losing this diver, it just might tip the balance. One major screw-up like that and Martin would get Liam right where he wanted him: on the payroll and under his thumb. Liam cursed under his breath.

"What's your name again?"

"Lydia."

"Well, Lydia, there's a pretty well-known tunnel in the reef that divers take all the way to a hundred and twenty, and I'll bet a whore's underwear that's where we'll find dear old Abe has gone for a dunk."

"Is it—is Abe in danger?"

"Not if he remembers to get out at a hundred and twenty."

"How much deeper does it go?"

Just thinking about it made Liam's head hurt. "Deep."

§

Lydia fought down a brief wave of fear that chilled her skin and made her heart leap into a trip-hammer rhythm. Before this, she had done only yesterday's two open-water dives. Aside from that, all her experience had been gained in the calm, albeit unsanitary waters of a Manhattan YMCA.

Yet surely this was no reason to slow Liam down with her misgivings. After this last excursion, she would be a certified scuba diver.

And she was good in a crisis. She knew that now.

Attach air tank to buoyancy-control device. Hope it won't fall off sixty feet below, leaving her to die ignominiously on a vacation meant to be her first real bid for freedom. Lydia could just imagine her mother at her funeral, leaning over the coffin, her handsome, plump features livid with grief, her lips soundlessly mouthing the ancient Jewish litany of grief, the *See What You Get When You Don't Listen to Your Mother.*

Underneath her bare feet, the sway of the boat seemed to grow more pronounced. Calm and controlled, Lydia reminded herself. Let the lissome lasses have the hysterics.

"All right," she heard Liam say behind her. "I'm set."

He was standing there, suddenly close, buoyancy-control device and air tank hastily donned over bare skin. If she just turned her head and took one step back she would be leaning on the firm comfort of his chest. Not that she would consider such a thing, she was just free-associating, the way you do when you're trying not to think about bloodied boyfriends floating unconscious somewhere like so much expensively attired shark bait.

"I'm set, too."

Liam looked puzzled, then smiled with professional charm. "You're going to stay here and explain why we'll be starting the morning dive a little late." Lydia noticed that Liam had attached an extra pony bottle of air, in case his first tank ran out, or in case Abe's did.

"I'll have to go down to one twenty to start, then work my way up along a grid, like this." Liam sketched a zigzag pattern in the air, then rested his lean brown hands on her shoulders, and even through the thick layer of padding and nylon, Lydia felt the contact.

She looked up into the startling silver of his direct gaze and thought, If it weren't for Abe, I would think that clench in my stomach wasn't all fear. Lydia thought about putting a mask on her face and falling underwater and corrected herself. Mostly fear. At least seventy-five percent. But damn it, she wasn't going to let the fear decide. As Abe always said, *Remember, you're the hero of your own story.*

Lydia cleared her throat.

"But you said it was never safe to dive alone. I thought—I could be your buddy."

"We'll be buddies some other time. Just you inform the other passengers, all right?" Hoisting himself up so that he was sitting on the edge of the boat, Liam put one hand to his mask and fell backward into the water.

Lydia turned to look at the other passengers, a few of whom had overheard Liam's last remark. The lanky brunette businesswoman who'd panicked when her regulator began seeping air underwater looked up from her novel with an expression of irritation.

"The afternoon dive has been postponed," Lydia announced loudly, and then climbed up on the bench to reach the rail before following the captain with a loud splash.

Fighting a temporary wave of disorientation, Lydia held her nose with her left hand and blew gently, clearing her ears while using her right hand to pull the cord that released air from her vest. Some ten feet below her, Liam was descending at a quicker pace, and Lydia's heart began to accelerate. What if he didn't see her? What if she was lost, alone beneath the waves?

Breathing deeply, Lydia forced herself to stay calm. You're the crisis girl, she reminded herself. Don't get freaked out just because you're twenty feet underwater. Twenty-five. Thirty. At forty-five feet, just as she was beginning to despair, Liam looked up. With only his eyes showing through the mask, it was hard to read his expression, but Lydia didn't fool herself into thinking that he was happy.

For a long moment, as she descended the last ten feet to hover in front of Liam, Lydia forgot to breathe. Liam grasped Lydia firmly by her upper arms, breathing in and out himself, and Lydia began to relax, and remember. At her first calm exhalation, she thought she detected something approaching a smile light Liam's pale eyes, behind the Plexiglas. Then, gesturing at a dark gap in the coral some five feet below them, Liam waited for her response. The kick of panic in her belly urged her to shake her head no. The thought of Abe alone down here prompted her to gesture with her right hand, finger to thumb: Okay. Still keeping one hand reassuringly on her upper arm, Liam swam down to the cave entrance by her side, his long body barely moving as it cut swiftly through the water. Lydia felt how slow and clumsy she was by comparison, moving her arms too much, using up precious air with excess motion.

When they were abreast of the tunnel entrance, Liam tapped her watch, then held out three fingers. Lydia understood. Could she wait for him that long? The cave was probably very, very deep. It was safest for her to stay here. Alone. But just for a few minutes. Liam put his hand under her chin, looked deep in her eyes. He was searching, she knew, for signs of panic. But she felt oddly resigned. A fish, large and flat and gaudily striped, blew silent kisses as it swam past her. It was beautiful here, peaceful. Lydia nodded yes, then remembered to gesture okay. Her decision, once made, frightened her, but she thought, If I panic now, I ruin Liam's chances of locating Abe. Lydia forced herself to breathe deeply, the sound of each exhalation echoing in her ears like Darth Vader's evil, asthmatic gasp.

Liam eased himself into the cave with steady grace, gave her one last okay sign, and then undulated away, the careful, measured kicks of his fins barely creating any bubbles.

All around her, the world was a clear blue-green, which seemed peaceful until she glanced down at her bright-pink nylon-sheathed legs and realized that they, too, were now aquamarine. I'm deep enough down that things are losing their colors, Lydia thought, and her heart kicked up a notch. Lydia kicked her legs slowly, looking up at the wall of graceful coral cities, then glancing down at her depth gauge. She'd dropped ten feet without noticing. For a moment, she couldn't spot the cave. Forcing herself to take a few deep breaths, her heart still beating wildly, she brought herself back up into position.

A person could lose all sense of reality down here, Lydia thought. There was only the sound of her own stentorian intake of air, and the sudden regard of a moray eel, its beady gaze oddly appealing as it darted out from a crevice before vanishing again into another hole. Off to the left, a plume of bubbles erupted from behind a stand of coral, and Lydia thought she saw a flash of something pale surging up through the water.

And then everything was very still.

Lydia took a deep breath and for a single, terrifying moment looked away from the wall of undersea vegetation and gazed out at the perfect, fathomless blue of inner space. With a lurch in her chest, Lydia felt an unfamiliar panic take hold of her, the panic of losing her grip on reality, of becoming unmoored from herself. I could be anyone, Lydia thought as she floated. An astronaut, cut adrift from the world. A fetus unborn. An invertebrate soul in a dense, liquid heaven.

Oh, shit. These were not good thoughts to be having, all on your own, thirty feet down, where you could kill yourself by doing something as simple as holding your breath on the way to the surface. This was why she'd hated getting stoned, the two times she had tried it in college. Except that then, when she'd told herself it was all in her mind, it had all been in her mind. With a cold rush of fear, Lydia thought, How long has it been? Am I running out of air yet? She checked her watch. Seven minutes. What was she supposed to do now?

She was about to lose the one man who wanted to marry her, before he'd even had a chance to propose. More to the point, she couldn't just wait here while two men died. And just as she began to ease her head and shoulders into the tunnel, she saw Liam, swimming up toward the light.

Alone.

4

Lydia glanced around the antiseptic opulence of the hotel manager's office, trying to make sense of it all. She was sitting on a red velvet chair in her damp dive suit, shivering in one of the hotel's only air-conditioned rooms. Liam had put on a T-shirt over his swim tanks and was talking with two nattily attired officials who wore almost identical expressions of cautious sympathy. One of the uniforms was explaining something that had to do with commercial divers and island policy, but Lydia found it hard to follow. Something about it being an awfully big ocean, but with the water temperature what it was, a person could conceivably survive for quite some time on the open sea. The other uniform added that there was a hyperbaric chamber on the other side of the island, so that Abe could be recompressed if he was found suffering from the bends. Liam stared at both officials as if he knew something neither man was saying. Then there was a pause and everyone seemed to look at her expectantly.

Lydia cleared her throat. "I don't understand—how long do you expect it's going to take until you locate Abe?"

The young policeman also cleared his throat. "Miss Gold, we cannot in good conscience give you a timetable when it's altogether possible we won't find him at all."

The hotel's representative, older and more polished, came to his rescue. "Of course there is an excellent chance that we will be able to rescue your boyfriend, Miss Gold. And the resort is doing everything in its power to help. Captain MacNally here states that he went back down"—the man glanced down at his steno pad—"three more times and searched extensively, though without a satisfactory result. Now we have a helicopter out to survey the surface, as well as an underwater search team led by one of our most experienced divers, Martin Thorne. They'll search for Mr. Bohemius until well after dark."

"What happens then?"

Liam picked up a hotel towel and settled it over Lydia's shoulders. He steadied her for a moment with his hands while answering, "The divers will take a rest, and the search will resume in the morning."

"But all those hours when nobody's searching—"

"Lydia, nobody's going to give up too soon. I can promise you that. We are all very aware that Abe could still be alive out there."

"He could, couldn't he? What you said before—what those gentlemen said—what with the water being as warm as it is, you said that a person could survive quite some time, right?"

Liam paused, his gray eyes regarding her with startling directness. "The water is about eighty degrees, Lydia, but eighty-degree water wants to make your body temperature eighty degrees, too. And that's assuming that he made it to the surface."

Lydia looked down at her left knuckle, which was bleeding from some scrape she didn't recall receiving. "You don't think he made it back up, then?"

"He might have run into trouble but made an emergency ascent, just breathed out a big lungful of air all the way to the top, and as long as he didn't black out before hitting the surface—well, it's possible."

"But if he did black out . . ."

Liam met her eyes as she looked up at him again. "We'll keep looking. That's all we can do."

Lydia's heart turned over in her chest. "I'm still not sure I completely understood what they were saying before. If you don't find him tonight . . . do you think Abe still has a chance? You might find him tomorrow."

Liam walked over to a small reproduction table where a crystal decanter of whiskey and two glasses stood, like props. With the air of a doctor administering a vaccine, he poured out a glass and handed it to Lydia. "I suppose there's always the chance for a miracle."

"Oh," she said.

"But we intend to search for a full three days," offered the policeman. "In cases such as these, we believe in doing everything possible to recover the body." The concierge shot him a dark look.

Lydia sipped her whiskey and shivered underneath the ceiling fan. The policeman scribbled something down in his notebook. At least, she thought it was the policeman. Both he and the concierge wore vaguely nautical insignia, complete with braided trim and jaunty hats.

"Did Mr. Bohemius have any close relatives we should contact?"

"His mother's dead. His father moved to Israel. He's got a sister, Kira. She lives in New York." And Kira would have to be told. A wave of distress washed over Lydia at the thought. Dark-haired and slender and lively, Kira had become something of a best friend to Lydia over these past few months, and now Lydia felt as if she had somehow betrayed the younger woman. Kira and Abe were unusually close for grown siblings. Abe had explained that the two barely ever spoke to their remaining family in Israel. He and Kira had rebelled against his father's strict Orthodoxy, which had grown more extreme after their mother died. "I'm putting my brother in your care," Kira had joked on more than one occasion. What would Lydia say to her now?

"Do you know the father's name and address?"

"I'm sorry, no."

"How long were you two involved, Miss Gold?"

"Four months." Why were they asking so many questions? Behind her, Liam stood in his short-sleeved scuba suit, almost as still out of the water as he was in it.

Misconstruing her glance backward, Liam put a warm hand on her shoulder. "I think that might be enough for now, gentlemen. The lady's just had quite a shock."

"Of course." The policeman—or was it the concierge?—stood and smiled awkwardly down at Lydia. "We will do what we can, Miss Gold."

After another stiff apology from the second uniformed man, Liam was allowed to usher Lydia from the hotel office and out onto the path leading to her cabin. The smell of the tropics, with its faint undertone of decomposing vegetation, lodged in the back of Lydia's throat.

"What can I do?"

Lydia shook her head and then looked up. Liam seemed very quiet and very intent, raking back the unfashionably long hair that kept falling into his face. Lydia thought he'd be glad to be asked to perform some service—fetch some whiskey, find some Valium. There was something disquieting, however, about his pale eyes. All traces of the earlier boyishness and laughter were gone from his expression now. His eyes seemed to carry the knowledge of what corpses looked like underwater. Lydia thought, He knows what Abe probably looks like now.

"I'll just go to my cabin."

Liam walked alongside her with no comment. He took the key from her hand and opened the door, and suddenly Lydia realized she'd left all her dive gear, and Abe's, on the boat.

"I forgot to bring Abe's——"

"It'll be brought to you." He seemed to be waiting for something.

Lydia smiled at him weakly, feeling as though she were carrying an egg around. In her chest. "You've been so very nice . . ."

Liam came forward two steps, took her by the elbows. His eyes were long and gray and very intent on hers. "You don't have to be so polite, you know. It's all right to scream. It's all right to scream at me."

Lydia stared at him. "Scream at you? Why?" She read the answer in Liam's steady, stoic gaze. He was the captain, he was assuming responsibility. In lieu of God or Fate, she could hold Liam accountable. In the face of such complete, admirable male stupidity, Lydia was at a loss for words. In the end, she simply told him, "I'm not the screaming type." Which made it sound as if she just whimpered in bed. Oh, hell. Lydia tried again. "I just need to be alone . . ."

"Are you sure about that?" He loomed over here, a presence so strongly, comfortingly masculine that she felt an impulse to collapse in his arms. His very long, sinewy arms, corded with muscle, relaxed at the shoulder.

She had forgotten the way physical attraction, like a badly trained golden retriever, keeps jumping up and will not be made to sit in the corner and out of the way.

If he stays too long, Lydia thought, I'm going to make a complete fool of myself. Where was her grief? She kept feeling that she had just forgotten it somewhere, left it behind like a handbag in a restaurant. There was that same drop of terror in the chest: You have misplaced something vital. "I appreciate your concern, but . . ."

Liam rubbed her upper arms, as if restoring circulation. You could tell he touched people, for a living, in his line of work. There was a wealth of sensate knowledge in the way he placed his fingertips against her flesh. "You know, this isn't a time for social niceties. You get to cry. You get to rant. You're allowed to lose control."

Lydia tried to summon grief, picturing Abe going deeper and deeper into the tunnel, somehow dislodging his regulator and breathing out a last gasp of bubbles as he sank down into a softer, darker place.

Liam's hand was on the back of her head, stroking. Lydia realized she was breathing with her mouth open. She had drooled a little on Liam's chest.

"I'm sorry."

"Don't be."

Shamefully, horribly, Lydia felt herself flush. "I'm fine," she murmured, pulling away. She stepped into her cabin.

"If there's anything I can do . . ."

"Thanks." Lydia shut the door and leaned her back against it, closing her eyes. She had drooled on him. She was an animal. Worse, she was a slut. Animals weren't to blame when they went into heat. How could her body react to him like this? Perhaps it was a reaction to death, an instinctive impulse toward life and regeneration.

Or maybe she was just a tramp. It was one thing to have dated and bedded one too many men in the search for true love. It was another thing to find oneself attracted to a new candidate moments after the old one had met his untimely end.

Not that Liam was a viable choice; it was so clear that he was a registered emotional independent, down to the unshod soles of his well-shaped feet.

Oh, God, please let me stop having these thoughts. As if in answer to her prayers, Lydia suddenly remembered the ring. *At least now I don't have to worry about getting it back before Abe proposes,* she thought, choking back a laugh. Then something, some feeling, dislodged itself and Lydia found herself crying at last, hanging red-faced over the edge of the bed until her chest hurt and her nose began to run.

You got your ring, she congratulated herself. You were so worried about it, and now it's all yours.

Feeling inside her suitcase, Lydia located Abe's ring. The color of the Caribbean, it rested in her palm with a surprising weight.

Abe, she thought, I would have said yes.

But somehow it didn't lessen her feeling that she'd betrayed him.

5

Liam came down from his room wearing faded blue jeans, a clean white T-shirt, and a look of bleak preoccupation.

Hearing the screen door slam shut, Liam's business partner, Fish, looked up from his inventory, smiling with the benevolent calm of the Buddha. "Bad day?"

"Guy died."

"Ah." Fish put aside the catalog of masks and snorkels and pulled out two shot glasses and a half-empty bottle of scotch from beneath the front desk. "Drink?"

"Why the hell not?" Liam threw the liquor back, savoring its warm burn down his throat as Fish poured himself a drink. Watching the older man, Liam noticed that his thick, poet's shock of black hair, which would doubtless outlast Liam's own, was even more disordered than usual, and there was a telltale flush on those cherubic cheeks. On the countertop, a small mountain of ash lay beside the ashtray, and there was what looked to be a fresh burn on the Formica. "Lookin' a bit rough there," said Liam. "You're not already toasted, are you, Fish?"

"What time is it?"

"Two o'clock."

"Then I'm almost certainly not drunk yet. Since drunk is a relative term, after all. Ask me again in an hour—looking back, you'll find that at two, I was relatively sober." Fish raised one eyebrow. "Why? There something you need me to be sober for?"

"Fish, I just told you someone died."

"That's a good reason *not* to be sober." Fish poured himself another shot. "Well? Are you going to tell me what happened?"

"Give me a cigarette first."

Fish, who could be relied on not to make inane comments about the fact that Liam had quit two weeks earlier, found a damp pack of Marlboro ultralights and shook a slightly bent cigarette out of the pack.

Once he'd had a good, long drag of nicotine and tar, Liam settled himself on a stool and explained about Abe, who'd thought he had a new system for calculating the dive tables, and had found the key to Davy Jones's locker instead.

"You're so sure the shmuck is dead?"

"Unless he's sprouted gills and a tail, the shmuck is dead."

"So why aren't you out searching with Martin's team?"

"You know I don't do that anymore. Besides, I'm near my limit. If I go down again, I'll probably come up bent."

"Huh. You keeping my smokes now?"

Liam threw the pack back, and Fish shook out the least bent cigarette in the pack and lit it. "So. How's the girlfriend holding up?"

Liam thought about Lydia's hopeful brown eyes, which had gleamed like a spaniel's when she'd asked, "Do you think Abe still has a chance?" She reminded Liam of Lady, the cocker spaniel from that old Disney film, the one who managed to get beaten up by a pair of Siamese cats, took the blame for the broken furniture, and was promptly muzzled and thrown in the doghouse.

She was the sort to love with canine devotion despite whatever kicks and blows the world might send her way. In that respect, she was like Liam's own mother—there was that same infuriating mixture of bravery and naiveté. Christ, what do you say to a woman like that—"Your man's fish food, lady, but cheer up, you might be prying him out of a tuna can one of these days?"

"She must be a hell of a girl," Fish commented, bringing Liam out of his reverie, "to keep you thinking on your reply so long."

Liam laughed, coughing out cigarette smoke. "She's the kind of girl who would go around with the kind of guy who walks big dogs on short leads and gets into fights with traffic cops."

"And she blames you."

"Me? No way."

"So you're blaming yourself."

"Christ, no, why should I do that?" Liam rocked his chair back so that it teetered on two legs. "Martin will be only too pleased to do that for me."

"Ah, Martin. He's only jealous."

Liam kneaded the back of his neck with one hand, trying to work the kinks out. "Yeah, well, what if jealousy makes him take out an ad in the *Island Gazette* saying, 'Liam MacNally's Dives Don't Always End on Land'? We're already in the red. Any less business and I won't be able to afford to keep you on."

"You can't afford me now." Fish looked up from polishing a mask, a twinkle in his dissolute teddy-bear eyes. "I just doctor the books so you think you can."

"You doctor the books so I think I can afford all that booze you drink while I keep buying tuna fish for dinner. And what's Martin got to be jealous of, I'd like to know? The size of my dick? He just about owns the whole island."

"Maybe he's jealous of your not owning anything but the thing you really want. Maybe he envies your kind of freedom."

"That would explain much."

"Maybe you envy *his* kind of freedom."

"We are not going to work for him, Fish."

"Maybe not." Fish lit another cigarette and stared out at their expensive stock. Then he gave a sigh and poured himself another shot.

Liam settled his chair's front legs back on the floor with a thud and ground out the remains of his cigarette. "You think maybe you should lay off that stuff for a while, save a few brain cells?"

"Too late for that. By this point, this stuff is what preserves the few memories I've got left."

For a moment, Liam thought of Fish as he had been three years earlier in New York City—a spindly, potbellied derelict, albeit one possessed with a certain elfin charm. They had sat side by side in the local hard-drinking Irish pub on more than one occasion, but hadn't spoken till the night when Liam had managed to injure his arm, swallow what felt like half of the East River, and locate a head but no body.

"Hey, Irish," the older man had said over his shoulder, "for once you look like you need a drink as badly as I do."

"Mister, you just don't want to bother me tonight." Liam stared at his Guinness and wondered what parasites might currently be swimming their way up his intestines.

"Ah. And are we using alcohol this evening as an anesthetic, or as an antiseptic?"

Liam had turned his coldest stare on the older man. "Listen, buddy, today I found a fucking head. My partner thought it was hysterical. Just kept laughing and laughing. Back at the barracks, someone wrote 'Liam MacNally Gives Good Head' on my fucking locker. Last week, I had to dive into a water tower to pull out a newborn infant, and this week I'm a fucking headhunter. I think I've probably got bilharzia from drinking the city's sewage, and I've just severed some kind of tendon in my arm because I couldn't see one fucking foot in front of my face."

And then, still looking into the old man's blotched and filthy face, Liam had watched the derelict raise one eyebrow ever so slightly, a daring look, both sarcastic and compassionate.

"So you ate a little shit at work today?"

Liam burst out laughing.

Fish had continued regarding the younger man steadily. "Don't be so hard on yourself, son. You nearly died tonight."

Perhaps it was the novelty of being called "son"; perhaps it was the fact that, until Fish spelled it out, Liam had not admitted to himself that it could just as well have been his heart that had gotten speared in the fetid murk.

A week later, Liam received a phone call and went by the police station to put up bail for Fish, who had been arrested for drunk and disorderly. He allowed Fish to shower in his apartment and learned that the older man had been a high school English teacher who'd been caught exchanging pornographic E-mails with a fourteen-year-old girl.

"Her grammar was so good," Fish lamented. "None of my, students ever spoke like that. Now, how was I supposed to guess a teenager would know the subjunctive?"

Their friendship was doubtless some sort of unhealthy co-dependency, and most of Liam's cop friends tried to talk him out of it, sensing that their friend was drifting away from their fraternity. But, as Liam's ex-wife, Altagracia, once observed, it was a case of the blind drunk leading the emotionally lame. Fish moved into Liam's Brooklyn apartment right around the time that Liam's latest girlfriend, Brianna, had departed, leaving a blow-up sex doll in his bed. She'd also left a note, explaining that she'd found her own replacement to save him the trouble of making any unnecessary conversation, but she had gotten it all wrong.

It wasn't that Liam had wanted sex without some deeper connection. It was that he hadn't felt capable of climbing out from under the baggage of how women saw him. Capable. Confident. Laid back. In control. Above all, one of the good guys, someone who would pull over on a dark highway and fix your tire. None of them knew about the anger. Even Altagracia had commented that he never really lost his temper.

But you don't lose your temper if you're afraid where you might find it.

Freed from the burden of feminine expectations, Liam enjoyed plenty of conversation with Fish—early memories of Ireland, the decision to pull up stakes and move to America when he was ten, his parents' breakup when he was twelve.

Liam's sole omission was the reason his parents had divorced. That information remained in a sealed record with the juvenile court.

Other than that, he censored nothing in his conversations with Fish. He spoke of his fears, his hopes, and his abiding dream—a move to someplace beautiful and unspoiled, a chance to enjoy work, with time left over for reading and thinking. A chance to live for the day, for who knew which would prove to be one's last?

Four years later and Liam was still surprised that they'd actually done it. But life on a small tropical island wasn't quite as simple as they'd anticipated, and if Out of the Blue Diving was to survive independent of Martin Thorne and Neptune's Rest, they needed to attract more than just occasional cruise ship detritus.

Accustomed to Liam's long silences, Fish wiped the corners of his eyes on the hem of his batik shirt and returned to taking inventory. After a while, he cleared his throat. "So, how's the bereaved blonde doing? In need of some Irish comfort?"

Liam shook another cigarette out of the pack, then let it slide back down, not deigning to answer.

Fish smiled unrepentantly. "Not your type, then?"

"Not my type."

Fish made two more notations. "Bet you wind up banging her, though."

"You're a cynic, Fish."

"And you're an idealist. But you'll still wind up banging her. First you'll tell her, 'Listen, honey, I'm not in the market for a lover, I'm more in the way of needing a friend,' and she'll go wild for that. Then you'll tell her, 'I've been married, and I've learned that for me, that's not a permanent state. I like relationships when they're about people and emotion, not about mortgages and commuter tickets.' And then Blondie will nod, and say, 'Absolutely, I understand,' and then you'll go at each other like a couple of dingoes."

Liam took another swig of the whiskey. "Christ, you make me sound like some kind of gigolo Boy Scout."

"If the condom fits . . ."

Liam stood up. "You're a foul man, you are."

"Not at all. A fool man, perhaps. And it has always been the fool's prerogative to speak the truth. Going out to join Martin's search party?"

"Go to hell."

"Don't slam the door on the way out," Fish called out behind his departing friend.

§

Lionel Fish, former teacher of English at Stuyvesant High School, often wondered just how much Liam really understood

about himself. Oh, Liam was intelligent enough, but he had a predis-
position for performing heroics, and in Fish's opinion, heroism
always involved a certain amount of stupidity.

Still, thought Fish, standing up and pausing with his arms braced
on the desk, there was something truly lovely about a man who
thought he was a hedonist, living for the pursuit of pleasure, when it
was perfectly clear to anyone with eyes that he was a romantic,
searching for some more elusive form of joy.

Fish had to admit, he had come to savor the unfolding of Liam's
life. Perhaps this was what it was like to have a child. You got to
watch the character form.

Shutting the door of the shop, Fish paused at the foot of the stairs
that led up to his private room. In the beginning, he and Liam had
thought it made perfect sense to share the two-story cabin, and each
had a bedroom upstairs, but after Liam had begun shtupping all
those tourists, Fish had begun to reconsider the arrangement.

To Fish's way of thinking, there was nothing more depressing
than hearing other people make love while you were lying alone in
bed with a Graham Greene novel. It was enough to make a man feel
old. But then Liam had stopped bringing women home. At first, Fish
had thought Liam might be going to the women's cabins, but then
he'd realized that Liam had undergone a change of heart. It certainly
wasn't the women who'd lost interest. They all looked at him as if
he'd been sent by central casting expressly to star in their holiday
romances.

It was the face that hooked them first—that chiseled, rugged,
workingman's jaw, that idealist's high forehead, lined with concern,
those painfully direct gray eyes. Then there was the stance. He carried himself like a soldier, but with a maverick glint in his eye and a
curl of self-mockery in his smile.

Fish paused on the stairs, out of breath.

He wondered how many of the women who used to march up and down these stairs knew anything of Liam's past. Did he just draw out their stories, or did he let them hear a little of his own?

Probably the former, although if Liam did reveal anything, he probably revealed it in shorthand. Skinny, clever, little old man of a child, the kind you're likely to beget from a youthful, combustible passion. Loud nights at the local pub, screaming matches in the kitchen, bottles breaking and clothes flying out the second-story window. Just like the movies, but without the Irish fiddle playing in the background.

The only person Fish knew who had heard the rest of the story was Altagracia, Liam's frighteningly pretty ex-wife. She'd repeated some of the facts to him with a newscaster's emotionless, well-timed cadences—the move to New York and what was meant to be a better life, the slow escalation into more serious violence. The thirty-year-old father's anguished confessions to his twelve-year-old son: "I'm not like this, Liam, really I'm not. She just has this way, your mother, of goading and hounding me into it."

Father's cut lip. Mother's bruised arm. And, finally, the last argument, the one Liam would never discuss.

"Why do you want to know?" Altagracia had inquired. "You planning on adopting him?"

"No," Fish had replied. "I plan on teaching him."

Freed from the constraints of classroom and syllabus, Fish had organized his tutorial to include generous amounts of alcohol, judicious applications of marijuana (infused into a batch of chocolate chip cookies), and, most of all, a healthy dose of literature. Biding his time, Fish had begun to fill Liam's almost empty bookcase (a few Florida detective novels, a restaurant guide) with a little Hemingway to start, to show where all that hard-boiled, plain-speaking aesthetic had begun, adding some of Yeats's lyrical Irish magic to keep the machismo from coming to a boil. After that, who knew? Chekhov maybe. James Joyce. Hell, even Jane Austen. The man would grow.

But now, in the fourth year of what Fish thought of as their field trip, he was beginning to wonder about his prize pupil. Initially, Liam had done so well, inventing a new life for himself out of context, but he soon became distracted with a series of the most boring women imaginable. Women who were all business, as goal oriented in leisure as they were out of it—women utterly devoid of inner fantasy lives. Eventually, even Liam had become disenchanted, and had traded his promiscuity for chastity—two sides of the same romantic coin, in Fish's opinion. Only true romantics went to those extremes—swive every woman in sight or save yourself for Miss Right. It did not bode well, Fish thought, for Liam's emotional maturation. And this obsession with Martin Thorne! Wasn't it enough to have one surrogate father? Must Liam go around collecting them, bad ones to rebel against as well as ineffectual ones to nurture him?

His surrogate son was caught between rebellion and perfectionism. No possible good could come of that.

Mounting the last few steps, Fish tried to remember if he'd finished the whiskey. Upon reflection, he felt there was still a good half bottle left downstairs for when Liam returned, flustered and aggravated, from meeting up with Martin. Because Martin would not let Liam risk his life and play the hero, because Martin looked at Liam and saw a rogue lion, one that needed either to be tamed or chased out.

As Fish gained the entrance to his room, he heaved a sigh and felt the slight twinge of a cramp in his chest. Perhaps it was a sign that he needed to begin walking along the beach again, for exercise. Or possibly even cut down on the booze. Or cigarettes. The cramp tightened with a second breath. All right, possibly I should cut down on both booze and cigarettes, Fish conceded. Although switching to red wine might do the trick; that was good for the heart, wasn't it?

Strange how red was usually used to signal danger. In the red, Liam had said, as if they were approaching a dangerous tide of financial trouble. The truth was, their little dive shop was swimming in a veritable Red Sea of money problems. Martin was not the bad guy. Martin was their lifeline. Without his resort, there *was* no business.

And if Liam did not progress to where he could see that in life, as in literature, "hero" and "villain" are relative terms, what would happen when he learned of the deal Fish had just made with Martin?

6

Martin Thorne had always reminded Liam of the great white hunters he'd seen in films of the thirties and forties: solid, elegant, attractively weathered, a genteel expert in the sport of death. Such a person, in Liam's opinion, demanded to be provoked. In Martin's presence, Liam found himself constantly tempted to mischief. Like a certain cartoon rabbit, he just wanted to plant a big wet one on that austere British kisser and watch the steam erupt from those well-trimmed ears.

Now, as Liam's motorboat approached Martin's larger ship, Liam tried to remind himself that he didn't have to respond to provocation. If Martin insinuated that Liam could have prevented the idjit from going overboard, Liam would remain calm. If he tried to pull rank, Liam would maintain his sense of humor.

The chatter of the motorboat drowned out the sound of Martin's voice as he leaned over his larger ship's side to throw down the ladder. As Liam killed his engine, he watched Martin's lips continue to move until his hearing cleared and he could make out the words.

". . . as you should know, MacNally, since you've already been down five times today, by your own count. You're tired and worn down."

"Not me," said Liam as he secured the little boat to the larger ship. "But if you need a rest, I'll spell you."

"We're all tired, MacNally." Martin held out his hand and helped Liam over the side of the ship.

"That's why I came, Martin. Thought you might need an extra hand."

Martin threw back his head and stretched. Well into his fifties, his hair turned as much silver as gold, the older man still had the lean, sinewy build of an athlete. The lion in winter, Liam thought. "We've got Pete and Joey from the other side of the island. They know what they're doing. Thomas and Pascal are coming 'round next shift."

"None of them has my experience."

"I'm not arguing with that. But I don't want to see you bent, MacNally."

Liam began to prepare his tank. "Think it'll look bad for the resort?" The waves began to slap against the ship. The water was growing choppy.

"Christ, you're a cowboy. Listen, Liam, there's a helicopter and another boat out searching the surface. But if he's still down there, he's a corpse. We find him today or tomorrow, that doesn't make a lot of difference."

Liam strapped on his tank. "It does to me. He's one of mine, and I want him found."

After two hours of searching, Liam stretched out on the deck of the boat and slept. When he opened his eyes again, a rip of vibrant color glowed against the darkening sky. Liam rubbed his eyes and began to haul a fresh tank into position.

"No way, MacNally. Time to head back."

"The other guys are still out there."

"The hell they are. That's a fresh team. You go on, Liam, head back to shore and get some food in you."

Liam spat into his face mask to clear the glass. "Thanks all the same, but I think I'll have the one last look 'round."

Martin looked like he was about to argue, but then just sighed instead. "You'll want a glow stick and a torch. It's going to be pretty dark down there."

"I'm used to the dark, remember? I'm the guy used to dive in liquid stool."

"You used to dive in thirty feet of liquid stool. This is the ocean. It goes a bit deeper than that."

Liam sighed. "Just give me the torch, Martin, and quit the pissing contest."

Martin affixed the small cyalume tube to Liam's tank and bent it, breaking the seal so that the green liquid began to glow. It looked eerily phosphorescent, like a child's Halloween toy. "One dive, no more. And wait till I get suited up."

"You've got to stay with the boat."

"You're not going down this tired, in the dark, without a buddy. That leaves me."

The two men lowered themselves down the ladder and plunged into the dark slap of the ocean without looking at each other. They made eye contact only briefly before descending beneath the surface, and then they were swimming with the current, toward the tunnel.

Just before they reached the coral mouth, Liam and Martin passed two of the other divers heading back up, toward the boat. Nothing. No sign of the missing person. In the glow of Liam's torch, he could see the translucent bodies of tiny shrimp dancing through the current. Behind him, he saw the white beam of Martin's flashlight and the green glow of the cyalume that marked the position of his tank.

And then they were at the small coral cave, and Liam felt the slight change in water temperature as he began his descent.

At eighty feet, Liam's dive computer gave a sharp pinging tone, signaling that it was time for him to begin his ascent. Liam turned and looked at Martin. Should they go for it? Silently, the older man acceded. They could hang at fifteen feet for a while to allow the nitrogen to leave their bodies. The men continued to follow the tunnel's winding route downward. Ninety feet. One hundred. Liam's computer was pinging again and again. *Ask not for whom the bell tolls.* At one hundred and twenty feet, the legal limit of sport diving, the beam of Liam's flashlight dimmed perceptibly and he felt Martin's hand on his arm. Liam knew what that meant—let's go back up.

Liam shook his head. His batteries might be low, but they still had Martin's light. And according to the navy tables, which were designed for fit young men and therefore allowed for less of a safety margin, Liam figured he still had a few minutes to spare. He would go to one fifty, where the tunnel curved, then head back.

Behind him, he could hear Martin banging on his tank with his flashlight, trying to get Liam's attention. Ignoring him, Liam continued down. At one hundred and fifty feet, Liam felt a violent tug; Martin, his eyes enraged behind his mask, was pulling at the back of his hood. Shaking him off, Liam accidentally knocked against the older man's arm, and there was a clank as Martin's flashlight dropped down the tunnel into the inky blackness below. With only two glow lights on his tank to make him visible, Martin was now effectively blind.

Liam's light was still about half strength, but for how long?

Suddenly aware of the closeness of the tunnel, Liam felt the faintest tinge of claustrophobia. How deep were they? In this darkness, they could slip down fifty feet while fumbling around and hardly even notice it. He longed for his old Aga mask, which he'd worn in the freezing cesspools of New York's waterways. The Aga had a built-in microphone. If he'd had it, he could have told Martin to grab on to his belt. Instead, Liam felt for the other man's arm, found his hand, and guided it to his waist.

Martin's fingers closed around Liam's belt and Liam began to swim upward. The single, weakened beam of Liam's flashlight was all that stood between them and the endless night of the ocean. As they emerged from the cave, Liam felt his chest expand with the freedom, but he also felt the persistent tug of the current pulling against him. Martin began to feel heavier, his kicking slower and less efficient. For the first time, it occurred to Liam that Martin might really be tired. How many dives had the older man already done this day?

At fifteen feet, in silence, the two men stopped their ascent. Liam's computer suggested that he hang underwater for another fifteen minutes to ensure his safety from the nitrogen that had built up in his bloodstream. Unfortunately, Liam had almost run out of air with the extra effort of hauling Martin along. Martin, who had not started out with a full tank, was the first to break the surface. Liam had never ever seen the man nonplussed before. Now Martin seemed swelled with anger.

"What the hell did you think you were doing down there?" Martin, having spat out his regulator, now pushed his mask down so he could relieve the pressure on his forehead.

"I know my limits, Martin."

"You don't know mine!" Martin swam over to the ship's rope ladder and paused for a moment. "The next time you decide to push your own personal envelope, MacNally, you just might think who you're dragging down with you."

"You didn't have to follow me."

Martin heaved himself up the ladder, paused, and then continued climbing. Seeing how tired the older man was, Liam felt a stab of guilt. "You didn't have to follow me!" he yelled up at the deck.

A wave rolled up and smashed him in the face.

§

At nine o'clock, Lydia opened her cabin door to a handsome, silver-haired older man standing with an almost military bearing. For a moment, she thought he was the chief of police. Then she saw that his pressed navy shirt bore the resort logo.

"Is there any news?" Lydia felt that she was acting a part, gleaned from a hundred old books and movies. Did this man feel it, too?

"I'm afraid not, Miss Gold. But we'll resume searching at first light."

Funny how they tell you not to have hope when you do, Lydia thought, then encourage you not to lose it when you don't.

"Miss Gold? Lydia? My name is Martin Thorne. Do you feel well enough to answer a few questions about what happened?"

"I did already. To the police. And the hotel." Lydia clasped her hands together in her lap, and Abe's brilliant-cut ring caught her eye. It was eye-catching. It was flashy. It weighed on her hand like a burden of guilt. She had meant to wear it as a memorial to Abe. Now she wondered if she were just pretending to be someone she was not.

"I understand that, Miss Gold. However, there are a few more questions that need answering, if you're up to it."

Lydia looked up into Martin Thorne's Prussian-blue eyes. He looks, she thought, altogether too Aryan for my comfort. "Will it help you find Abe?"

"It might, but . . . Forgive my bluntness, but do you think you might speak a bit more freely now that Captain MacNally is not by your side? Please don't misunderstand me. I don't mean to imply that Captain MacNally was criminally negligent, but I do wish to ascertain from you——"

With a slight bang, the door slammed open and Liam walked in, his chest heaving slightly from exertion. When he saw Martin there, Lydia watched him startle, then resolutely bring his focus back onto her.

"I was just coming back to make sure you were all right when I heard you had a visitor. Hello, Martin."

"Hello, MacNally." Martin regarded Liam with a look of pure British imperialism, assurance mingled with paternalism. "I hadn't expected to see you here so quickly."

"As I recall, I wasn't the one who was hurting." Liam walked over to Lydia and Martin released her hands. "You all right, then?" Before she could answer, he turned to Martin. "I think she's under enough stress at the moment, without you coming 'round to ask her a lot of leading questions."

"They're questions that need to be asked, upsetting or no."

"You know I run a tight ship!"

Martin lifted his gaze, unintimidated by Liam hovering over him. "I know you are impulsive. No man can run the whole show on his own and still be aware of everything that's going on, Liam. It's not a criticism of you. But as part owner of this resort, it's my reputation on the line when one of the boats we charter loses a passenger."

"There are always risks, Martin. You're just sore because you don't own me, like you do the rest of the help around here."

"Liam, don't do this to yourself. You know there has to be an inquiry. There is a history to consider here. There was that Australian woman last year, and now . . ."

Oh, Lydia thought. This is what they're really arguing about. Or does it go even deeper?

"Sheila's suicide has nothing to do with how I take care of my passengers."

Martin's face was set and merciless, although he made a slight gesture of conciliation with his hands as he spoke, as if to smooth away the roughness of his words. "It does when the suicide takes place off your boat."

"Is this about what happened earlier, Martin? Because I think it's damned unprofessional to carry over a personal grudge—"

"This isn't about that. Not unless you bring it into the pot."

It was uncanny. Lydia felt as if she was watching actors enacting a scene from her own life, albeit one she'd never had the courage to perform. She, too, had felt responsible for someone's suicide, and it was like wearing an albatross necklace; you felt you had to go around repeating your story, asking for an absolution that you never quite believed. How much more horrible to have someone actively blame you.

Liam's voice cut through Lydia's thoughts. "So what exactly do you feel I should have done to prevent Sheila from taking those pills?" Liam sounded almost hoarse with surpressed emotion. "Tied her hands to the wheel?"

"You should be aware when a woman is that depressed, and you should damn well keep your pants zipped around her."

"You bastard! For your information, I never touched Sheila."

Lydia cleared her throat. "I'm sorry," she said deliberately, "but I'm a little confused. Mind if I ask what's going on here? What does this have to do with finding Abe?"

Liam turned to her, his face flushed, his eyes glittering. Martin, his face the same tanned teak as before, showed no outward response to Lydia's intervention. Remembering Nick's overdose and her own feeling of responsibility, Lydia's sympathy lay with Liam. It was clear that he had spent hours alone defending himself from similar accusations made in his own mind.

The older man, for all his weathered, high-status charm, left her with a vague feeling of rebelliousness. He was the type of person who found her type of person brassy. He would never let his heart overrule his head, would never give in to a craving at midnight. Around him Liam suddenly seemed less sure of himself. It was like watching a partisan confront a general—her sympathy was all with the former. Even if Martin was right and a second crew member would have made all the difference, it was still not Liam's fault. Abe had chosen his fate.

As if sensing that her allegiance had shifted away from him, Martin took a step toward the door.

"I see it truly was a mistake to bother you at this time, Miss Gold. If you will forgive me, I'll show myself out." With a curt nod to Liam, Martin departed, leaving a resounding quiet behind him. Lydia felt responsible as the silence stretched out, Liam's gray eyes shaded with equal parts irritation and concern. She felt she knew his mind. He wanted to rant about Martin, to defend himself, but thought it inappropriate behavior under the circumstances. Liam raked his hair back in exasperation, but an instant later it flopped back over his high forehead, very carelessly aristocratic and some ten years out of date. Lydia wondered what it would be like to cut it. It was the kind of silky, slippery hair that would show up any mistake in an instant.

I shouldn't even register how attractive he is, Lydia thought. But she did, and there was no way to fight it. It was like telling yourself not to think of a certain tune when it was lodged in your mind.

"He blames you," she said.

"Oh, yeah."

"Is that why you thought I would blame you, too?"

A muscle jumped in Liam's jaw, just like in the movies. Lydia knew she had scored a point of some sort, but what was the game, and what had she won? Liam shook his head, as if clearing it. "Yes. No. Christ, I don't know. I should probably go, too."

"Are you sure you don't want to talk about Sheila?"

"Any reason why I should?"

"No reason. Maybe instead I'll tell you a story. Last year, when I was in the final months of social-work school, one of the patients I saw at the clinic died of an overdose. His name was Nick Beringer, a clever, handsome, bone-thin twenty-eight-year-old. And a heroin addict." Lydia drew in a deep breath, walked over to the window, and addressed her story to the night sky.

"Nick just loved deducing my thought processes from the questions I asked him, and in telling me at each session what clues I'd failed to observe, what mistakes I was making. Finally, I lost my temper. If he was so clever, I said, why didn't he prescribe his own cure?"

"Shit." Liam came up beside her, patting his shirt pockets as if checking for something, maybe cigarettes, then stopped. "So he killed himself?"

"A week later. Nick had been an addict for many years and he'd never OD'd before. So I wondered, was that his cure? Had I goaded him into doing it?" The only person who could answer those questions was Nick, and in her dreams he sat in her office, mocking her with silences.

"Some people hit the self-destruct button early on, and it's like a timer's ticking, and then one day it goes off. There's nothing you can do about it."

"Maybe not." Lydia smiled at him.

Liam leaned against the window frame, a creature of fit, lean strength, and to Lydia he seemed like a visitor from a different planet. "I guess that's a lot of bullshit. If you're the right kind of person, you see someone in distress, and you want to help, you try to help, and if you fail, you feel you're to blame. It's romantic nonsense, really, but it's a built-in flaw."

Warmed by Liam's inclusion of her in his noble romantics' club, Lydia didn't tell him the rest of it: how she'd dropped out of graduate school and left behind all her friends there, how her life had pretty much fallen apart after that.

"It's pretty late. I should let you rest."

Lydia didn't argue. She thought, Oh, I know what you want. You want me to say, No, stay, have a drink. You want me to draw you out. In high school and college, most of Lydia's best friends had been guys who didn't know how to talk to other guys. It was only after going to work as a hairdresser that she'd spent her days surrounded by women and gay men.

Liam wanted her to coax him into conversation, but he was afraid to look as if he was making a move on her. And yet something in the quiet air between them, fraught with confidences and regrets, promised that, if he stayed, something would happen. Something that would start out as compassion and wind up in a tangle on the sheets, with the big black bird of remorse looming, like a vulture, from the bedpost.

"Liam—what happened with Abe—it really wasn't your fault. It was Abe's decision to dive alone. He broke the rules, and he's paid the price." Lydia could feel Liam glance up at her as her voice broke on that last bit. "Look, I'm tired, and I think you really do need to go now." She looked up.

"Lydia—" He was on the verge of reaching out to her.

"Go." She pushed him out the door, realizing only afterward how rude she'd just been. Not that it mattered. He wasn't the type to stay up late over a woman. He was the type to lose sleep over whether or not he believed he'd done the right thing.

Lydia showered and went to bed, even though it was only nine o'clock. As she slid between the cool, stiff sheets by herself, she thought guiltily of Abe's sister. But better to call her in the morning, surely.

It was far too early to sleep. If she fell asleep now, she'd probably be up in the middle of the night, pacing the creaky wood floor of her cabin.

Lydia surrendered consciousness almost instantly.

7

At three-thirty in the morning, Lydia emerged from the humid heat of her cabin onto the beach, where the waves softly lapped the shore. A few electric tiki torches on the beach path illuminated the shallows, which the half-moon silvered with ripples of light. Farther out, the shadows swallowed the shapes of the boats Lydia knew were moored nearby.

When she closed her eyes, Lydia could imagine she was a child back in her grandmother's condo, sleeping on the folding couch next to the duck-shaped lamps and the vase of silk flowers, listening to the rhythmic rustle of the ocean outside. Veteran of a dozen Miami trips to visit her grandmother, Lydia knew there really wasn't anything that could harm her if she waded in—well, nothing worse than a jellyfish, at any rate, and the dive guide would have mentioned if the currents were washing those ashore. She knew the odds against being eaten by a shark. Scientists who went down waving chunks of bloody fish couldn't always attract the shy creatures. So if the dark sea conjured up a few ancient fears, well then, Lydia felt she could accept that. Better to feel that than to feel this faintly damning sense of relief, and the guilt that attended it.

Turning toward the lights on the beach, reassured by the calmness of the waves and the closeness of the dive shop, Lydia walked into the cool water up to her knees, then sat down.

No one was forcing me to marry him, she thought. So why do I feel that his death has released me from some obligation?

Lydia swam out a bit, still in water no deeper than her knees were she to stand, and kicked her legs in place. She felt the thin cotton of her tank top and boxer shorts become saturated. Even though she knew there was no one around at this hour, Lydia sat up once with a splash to glance around at the empty dining hut and dive shop before lying back again. Absolute solitude, the warm night and the sea that had swallowed her lover—almost as good as absolution. The corrosive regret that had been scouring Lydia's conscience for the past two hours finally eased into a bittersweet sadness. The ring on her finger glittered beneath the waves. A sea change. He doth suffer a sea change. What Shakespeare had really described was someone getting his face nibbled off by fish. A wave of nausea crept up Lydia's throat.

Think of something else. Think of Atlantis, a kingdom beneath the ocean. Think of mermaids turning to sea foam after a thousand years. Would Abe have liked her to think of him surrounded by mermaids? Would he have liked to have seen her almost naked beneath the stars? They might have made love like this tonight, had he lived. Though probably they would not have. Abe was not really the most enthusiastic lover she'd ever had. It was part of what had made her feel he really loved her, and didn't just want to screw her for a while, like some others she could mention.

Not that there were any problems in that department. He made love to her an average of twice a week and was always very careful to make sure that he didn't hurt her. Sometimes a little too careful. But at least he didn't do the standard male impression of a rocket hurtling intently toward some distant target. She had read descriptions of the moment of climax that suggested some fusion of lovers' spirit and flesh, but in Lydia's experience, when push came to shove, you were pretty much on your own. At the critical moment, men always seemed locked inside their own pleasure. Abe had been different. He'd always seemed aware of her, focused somehow on her reactions, which meant she didn't wind up feeling so strangely bereft afterward, leaking tears onto the pillow while pretending to sleep.

She hadn't hungered for Abe deep down in her womb. But that didn't mean anything. She'd hungered for her lousy brother-in-law, and look where that had gotten her.

Was it wrong to be thinking negative thoughts about someone so recently deceased? Lydia tried to think about Abe in a more spiritual manner, and failed miserably. Abe had been a sturdy, physical, no-nonsense man who worried less about mortality than he did about dinner. Perhaps it was a result of having been a paratrooper in the army, living life on the edge. He had been a bit of a throwback. Yet Lydia had liked that he was old fashioned. He never fiddled with bits farther aft that she'd rather not have fiddled with, and always insisted on making sure that she enjoyed herself in bed as much as he did. Which meant he kept going and going until she was sore and obliged to moan her way into a little respite. But Lydia didn't count this as a mark against Abe. Men never seemed to understand that the female orgasm wasn't a creature you captured with a net. It was more like a unicorn, and securing it required more magic than cunning, more passion than skill.

So far, the only man who'd succeeded in snaring that particular unicorn was the one who lived in her imagination.

A sudden sound brought Lydia to her feet. False alarm. The wind was picking up, and just to her left, she could hear the rhythmic slamming of boats tied up at the dock, and behind that the steady, lulling shushing of the waves. She couldn't make out any figure standing in the shadows. A second panicky thought raced through her: Was there an undertow? Lydia stood up and saw that she was still only waist deep. Settling back under the tropical stars, Lydia felt an unexpected wave of sadness wash over her. The salt of her tears mingled with the salt of the sea, and she didn't really know why she was there, only that she'd wanted to be out on the great black waters that were carrying Abe away, wanted to submerge herself in the vast strangeness that seemed to have overtaken her life.

Abe, she thought, I did care for you. Just not enough. And then she knew what she could do to feel closer to his spirit.

Taking a deep breath, Lydia let the waters close over her face.

§

At first, Liam thought that the nicely curved creature washing up out of the dark waves looked a bit like a sea nymph—Nereid, that was. Naiads were what you found in your lakes and streams. Of course, Liam admitted, he had consumed a fair bit of Fish's scotch.

Sitting in the shadows of the dive-shop porch, contemplating both the murderous innocence of the sea and his twentieth, and definitely last, cigarette, Liam felt a very expatriate Irish mood on him. Yeatsian phrases like "murderous innocence" and "blear-eyed wisdom" bobbing about in his consciousness, Liam thought the woman seemed elemental as she flashed, fishlike, before sinking back into the ocean without a trace.

And didn't come up again.

When she did surface, gasping, her magnificent full breasts heaving for air, Liam had flicked his burning cigarette away and was already racing toward the surf, and by the time she had begun to submerge herself again, his strong overhead strokes had carried him to within a hand span of her drowning form.

Grasping the woman around the chest and hauling her backward onto his chest, Liam felt the slippery weight of her drenched clothing as she desperately tried to flip herself out of his embrace.

"Don't you fight me," he warned, surprised by his own flash of anger.

"Get off me! I'll scream!" The woman thrashed wildly, and Liam had to struggle to contain her arms without hurting her.

"I'm saving your life, you silly wee bitch. Are you drunk, or just stupid?"

"Just stupid," she gasped as she stopped fighting him. Liam finally realized whom it was that he held. "How about you, since you're trying to keep me from drowning in less than five feet of water?"

Stymied by her calm response, Liam tightened his grip and said neutrally, "A wee bit drunk." As often happened when Liam felt the need to charm or cajole, he instinctively deepened his brogue. "All our talk of suicide—I thought—you're not killing yourself?"

"Of course I'm not! I was just—I wanted to be under the water just for a second. To be closer to him. To Abe."

Liam leaned back into the water until her head fell back onto his shoulder So comforting to be giving someone comfort this way. "It's just a black night tonight. It will pass."

"That's what we Jews say. 'This too shall pass.' "

'Is that meant to be taken in an optimistic or pessimistic sense?"

'Both."

The woman started to say something in her softly husky voice, sounding like Lolita after her third pack of cigarettes. Ridiculously sexy, it was. He felt the lady's softly rounded bottom brush against the front of his shorts, and became aware of the generous spill of smooth, sun-kissed flesh barely contained by one small, very wet tank top. After a moment, Liam belatedly tried to focus on what she was saying.

"I'm sorry, I must've drifted for a moment there. You have a nice voice."

She moved her hand under the water, splashing a little. "Oh, please." Liam realized he'd overstepped himself. He'd been obvious, and now she couldn't pretend that things were innocent between them. Pretense was so important early on. You had to leave the woman the emotional room in which to lie to herself about how much she knew about what was going to happen next.

Liam tried to rescue the situation by claiming innocence himself. "Why 'Oh, please'? What's that supposed to mean?"

"I think you can let me go now."

"Not till you tell me what you meant by that."

"Don't you think it's pretty tacky to start hitting on me, given the situation?"

Liam released her arms, surprised, and the woman drifted away. "I wasn't hitting on you."

The woman stood up, realized her clothing was transparent, and sank back down again. "Maybe it's a reflexive thing with you. You probably got into the habit of flirting with women and forgot how to relate on any other level. Listen, I think I should probably be getting back now . . ."

Ah. An opening. "But you don't want to do that, do you? Why not swim with me?"

She hesitated.

"It's safe enough. No reflexive flirting, I promise." Because he didn't want to leave it like this. He felt like a fool, and a clumsy one.

"Okay. But not too far out."

They swam out over their heads and then struck a line parallel to shore. The woman swam with even, health-club strokes, moving her head around a little too much, bending too much at the knee. After about five minutes, she gave a small grunt of pain and then slowed, switching to a breast stroke. Liam stopped to tread water.

"You all right?"

"Yes," she panted. "Fine."

"Do you have a cramp?"

"Ouch. A little one."

"Here," Liam moved behind her, supporting her with his body. "I'll bring you back in."

"Thanks."

The silence stretched between them as Liam swam, holding Lydia firmly against his chest. "How's the cramp?"

"Better, I think."

They were silent again. Liam felt an odd reluctance to reach the beach. He also felt a persistent stab of guilt, although he was sure he hadn't really been flirting with her before. "Is this the first time you've lost—I mean, have you ever lost anyone close to you before?" There. That seemed the right thing to say.

"Not really. My grandmother, but that was different." The water splashed between them as Liam hauled her forward.

"Neither have I. Not personally. I've seen death plenty, though. Used to dive for bodies, back in New York. Guns and bodies. Sometimes cars."

"Cars?"

"People lose a lot of things in New York Harbor." Liam stopped, treading water again. He couldn't see the woman's face, but he could feel the tension in her body. She was trying not to touch him, but the waves kept rocking her body back against his, pushing her into the long, flat cradle of his chest and legs.

Liam pulled the woman into shallower water, stopping when the small waves lapped at his chest and her throat. He kept one arm out, supporting her; they were still a fair way from the row of cabins where they'd started. "How's the cramp? Better? So, as I was saying, some of the guys who tried out for the unit were used to the meanest sections of the city. Some of them had even been shot. First off, they were absolutely disgusted by the prospect of putting their bodies into that filth, even with a full dry suit. So that got rid of some of them. The rest, if they passed the pool physical, and managed to put up with one of us hassling them underwater—pulling their mask off, spinning them about—they got a trial tour of duty. Most couldn't take it. Give them bloodshed and mayhem, sure, but ask them to pull a week-old body out of the drink—suddenly their stomachs don't feel so good."

"All right, I'm convinced, you're the man."

"I'm not braggin'! Christ, people are always on at me to tell them about my time on the unit, and I can't be bothered, and here I am telling you and you just think I'm boasting."

"I'm sorry. It's just that we're not moving anymore, are we?"

"I wanted to see if you could swim on your own."

"Oh." She tried, but then gave a little moan of pain. "Worse than before."

"Here, lean back."

After a moment, she rested her head back into his shoulder. Liam started swimming again. "So tell me more about being a diving cop."

"About corpses or cars? Ah, that wasn't quite the thing to say, was it? I'm sorry, I was trying to distract you and I'm acting like—"

"Shh. Tell me about your job."

Hazily, Liam wished his ex-wife could see this. She'd always said he was so bad at comforting her, that he turned every touch into foreplay. It wasn't a character flaw. He had just been so young and so in love. He wasn't a selfish person. Liam gently rocked the woman in his arms and felt the long sigh she gave all the way down to his toes. Fish was mad to think he'd wind up banging her, even if she did look like a modern version of a fifties B-movie queen.

Except you could tell she'd turn into the kind of woman who'd gain ten pounds with each kid, although she'd also probably look just fine in the morning. She looked good now, her eyelashes long and surprisingly dark even without her warpaint on. Women who wore too much makeup were usually a bit tense in bed, in Liam's experience. Clearing his throat, Liam began talking again.

"And you get to taking a pride in your skill, right? In the beginning, you dread finding what you're looking for. But in the end, you start believing it's a game."

"So why did you stop? Why aren't you out looking tonight?"

Why wasn't he? Christ, because he was drunk. Because he'd been reckless. Because he'd made a decision to pursue a dream and acknowledging that he missed the old life seemed too much like admitting failure. "I took a vacation with my wife." Liam felt the woman in his arms startle, and chuckled. "My ex-wife. I took her to Ireland. We stayed near Dingle." There, he thought. Now let's go back to pretending you're distraught and I'm saving you.

"What happened then?" She sounded wary.

"She told me that I was really with her for the first time since we'd gotten married. She said back home I'd always be half there, half underwater somewhere. Half watching TV with her, half talking with her, even half—well, you know. Said she hadn't understood the difference till I came back to myself in Ireland."

"And then?"

Without really thinking about what he was doing, Liam moved very quietly back into the deeper water, so the woman's feet couldn't touch. So she would let him hold her. It was nice doing this, reaching out to someone. Helping them, even if they weren't on the verge of topping themselves. "And then we came back to New York and there was—TWA Flight 800. The first day, our sonar located wreckage, it was already late, but we dove anyway. One of our team ran out of air and had to make an emergency ascent—from one hundred and thirty feet down. We pulled up body after body and by the time we finished it was growing dark. And when we came back to shore, there were the families, just standing there, waiting. And the press. 'What'd you find? What've you got? Why aren't you doing more?' All this while the families watched us."

"You must've been angry."

"I was. I spent so much time being angry I forgot about my wife. I wasn't even half there anymore. So she left." The dark shadow of a cloud drifted past the moon, and Liam floated for a moment in silence. "Don't let the anger get the better of you," he said out loud.

The woman in his arms stirred. "I'm not angry."

"Ah, well, yes. When it comes to most things, men get angry. Women get sad." That sounded like something Hemingway would have said. The problem with me, Liam thought, keeping them both afloat with a few lazy motions of his strong arms, is that I haven't fully integrated my Yeats with my Hemingway. Then the woman turned in his arms to ask him something, put her foot down and sank like a stone.

"Help! Help!" She was flailing and swallowing water, not having realized they were in over her head. Liam pulled her head out, cursing himself and apologizing, and swam her toward shore.

"Sorry, sorry. Shit, I'm a fucking idjit, are you all right?" They were chest deep and Liam turned her in his arms. She looked different wet. Her hair looked dark, like her eyes. She looked younger by moonlight. Yet sharper somehow, more knowing. He searched her eyes until he realized he was wanting to kiss her, and knowing how wrong that would be, Liam tucked her head into his shoulder. "I'm an idjit," he repeated, and she sighed and pressed closer into his arms, her nails digging into his shoulders a little. After a moment, Liam realized she was crying.

"Oh, God," she said, "what's wrong with me?"

And then—this part was really quite a blur, and the next morning Liam could not quite recall exactly how it had come about—he was holding her, her head to his shoulder and then she sort of trembled and—and bit him, a long, gentle bite that shot electricity right through him. He thought she might have groaned, too. But then she said, "No, no," and began to lurch clumsily out of the water. She was running as soon as her feet hit the beach.

Liam thought about it lying in his bed later and wondered if he'd been too drunk to recognize whether or not she'd been willing. His skin burned with shame. Surely that bite had been—but she had run, so perhaps not. Could he be the sort of man to get a raging erection from a woman biting him in self-defense? And even if she'd been the willingest woman in all creation, what was he thinking, going after her like that, the night she lost her fiancé? It was just the kind of thing Martin would think Liam would do—seduce a woman to cheer her up. Come to think of it, Fish seemed to have a similar impression.

Except, if he hadn't been seducing her, why had he just told her more about himself than he'd told any living person, save Fish? Liam thought, I'll just have to deal with it in the morning.

He fell asleep trying to remember her name.

8

There was a crashing thud over Fish's head as Liam landed near, but not on, the bed, and Fish considered going in to rescue him. Would this kind of help really be appreciated? Padding upstairs in his bathrobe and slippers, Fish paused in front of Liam's bedroom door, then decided to go back downstairs into the office.

Lighting a cigarette and gazing briefly at the empty whiskey bottle, Fish turned on the computer and thought about whether he was in the mood for sex. There were too many teenagers on-line now, and their idea of foreplay was to ask, again and again, if anyone wanted to talk dirty. Fish longed for someone inventive and witty and well-read who could circle around the subject, tantalizing him with literary allusions, provoking him with double, triple, even quadruple entendres.

Instead, he was likely to get some horny nineteen-year-old who would describe in endless detail the underwear she was wearing.

Sighing, Fish logged on as IClaudius and scrolled through the chat-room titles. The married room, as always, was full, as were the various dungeons and hot tubs.

Someone cleared his throat, and Fish, startled, looked up to see Martin Thorne, looking surprisingly bedraggled in loose linen pants and a rumpled green T-shirt.

"Hoped you might be up, Fish. I don't suppose you have a drop of whiskey handy?"

"Whiskey's gone," said Fish. "I have vodka, though."

Martin considered this. There were dark circles under his eyes. "No gin?"

Fish felt deeply saddened to admit there was none.

Martin eased himself onto the stool with tired grace. "I'd take orange juice with the vodka, if it's not too much trouble."

"Not at all." Fish took the carton of juice from the small office fridge and fixed them both screwdrivers. "Want to talk about it?"

"Just feeling my age tonight. Or rather, this morning. Your friend nearly drowned me."

Fish sighed. "Probably trying to out-tough you. He'll have a burst of comprehension at the age of sixty, if he lives that long."

Martin toasted the sentiment. "What about you? Insomnia acting up again?"

Fish sighed "I just said that last time to make the situation sound better. Truth is, some nights I have to get up and pee six times. And I can only fall back asleep four times."

Martin sipped his drink and looked directly at Fish, his deeply blue eyes oddly compassionate. "Sure it's not another kind of problem? Liam hasn't exactly been faithful, you know."

Fish nearly spat out his drink on Martin's chest. "Christ, no. We're not—He goes with women, just women, and so do I. Or so I did. I don't really do much of anything anymore, except on-line." Fish tapped the computer.

"I say—I do apologize, old man. I just assumed you two living together here were—that is—I do apologize." Martin's face seemed flushed beneath his dark tan. Fish had never seen him so discomfited.

"I'm not offended, really. It's just that I see Liam—well, more as a son, really." Fish stubbed out his cigarette and lit another to busy his hands. "That's why I'd appreciate your not telling him about the little venture we've been discussing."

Martin tapped his fingers on the countertop. "Why ever not?

Even if you were Liam's father, he's grown up enough to stand on his own."

"That's the problem. The business can't stand on its own without me, and no offense, Martin, but he thinks you're the enemy."

Martin laughed. "So when are you planning on telling him? When Fish's Late Night Café has its opening gala?"

Fish laughed politely but didn't reply. He had it in his mind that Liam was due for some kind of change, some growth, and that if it were at all possible, he would let Liam be the one to move on first.

If Fish left the dive shop now, then Liam would be forced to become one of Martin's employees. And Fish couldn't do that to the boy, however much he longed to take Martin up on his offer of opening his own bar for the resort. He could just see it now: concocting manhattans and blue martinis, serving those bacon-wrapped liver things nobody made anymore, making four-cheese fondues. Overseeing all night-poker games while a pale miasma of smoke and jazz insinuated itself into people's clothes.

"You know, Fish," Martin said, standing up to leave, "you do have to make a decision. Sooner or later, Liam is going to find out about us."

"Christ, Martin," Fish said, "you make it sound like I've been running around with you on the side."

Martin only smiled before emerging into the weak beginnings of daybreak.

9

It was the hardest call of Lydia's life. For a long moment, she just stood underneath the large overhead fan in the wet heat of the main hotel lobby, contemplating the beige 1940s-style rotary phone that was partially concealed by a potted palm. Was this a deliberate design concept, like the rattan chairs and wicker birdcages, or couldn't the resort afford in-room phones and air-conditioning?

Lydia dialed the operator and read out the long sequence of her calling card, and then waited, wishing with each heavy thud of her heart for a private phone in her cabin. The phone clicked and then rang.

Somewhere on the other end, Lydia thought, a young girl is calmly going about her business, and then she will pick up the receiver and enter a tunnel of grief.

You'd never know I had training dealing with people in the throes of violent emotion, thought Lydia. Which was why she'd dropped out of graduate school—there were certain careers that required a certain baseline level of natural ability. Lydia's fingers twisted in the phone chord, and she thought of puncturing Kira's blithe imperviousness with the worst possible news. "She's a happy person," Abe had said of his sister. Why had that quality, uncomplicated by too much reflection, made Lydia feel so old by comparison? Even as a teenager, Lydia wondered, had she ever been that sure, that self-centered, that unfazed by anyone else's opinion?

And yet Lydia liked the girl. She'd cut flattering layers into Kira's thick, silky brunette hair for free. She'd helped the younger woman choose her first tailored suit for a job interview. Why, Lydia had even sold her father on the glittery Scientique line of cosmetics that Kira represented. Still, at times, Lydia found herself less than perfectly comfortable in the younger woman's presence. One night when they had been having a Turkish dinner with Abe at Kira's apartment, Abe's sister had jumped up on a table to perform an impromptu belly dance, sweatpants rolled down over her perfectly flat stomach. It had seemed to Lydia that there was something more seductive than playful in the girl's manner. Then there was the Saturday when Abe was on that business trip and Kira had come over and cheered her up with champagne and vodka.

"So tell me. Why do you have a little bit of an accent when your brother doesn't?" Lydia had inquired drunkenly.

Kira's eyes shuttered. "I do not have an accent."

"I thought—just a faint sort of touch of something sometimes . . ."

"Maybe I'm just one of those people who pick up accents. Sign of a weak personality, they say." And it was really just a hint, a flavor of foreignness, possibly something put on to seem exotic.

"You don't seem weak to me, Kira."

"No?" But the bleak look on the vivacious younger woman's features had hinted at unknown minefields of old resentment and sorrow.

And now Lydia was about to tread right in the middle of that dangerous ground.

"Hello."

"Kira, this is Lydia. Listen, I have—"

"You have reached the number—"

"Oh, no." What message could she leave Abe's sister on an answering machine?

"—of Kira Bohemius and Scientique cosmetics." Listening closely, it struck Lydia once again that she heard the elusive thread of a Russian accent woven into Kira's speech. "I'm sorry I can't come to the phone now, but please leave a message."

"Kira, this is Lydia. Listen, I need you to call me as soon as possible, because . . ." Lydia floundered, tearing at a fingernail. "Because it's important."

"Hello? Lydia? It's me, I'm speaking to you in person now. What news do you have?" Abe, unlike Kira, had always spoken perfectly idiomatic English.

"Oh, Kira, you're there."

"Yeah, sorry, I was just checking my stock. I think your father's shop ordered all my cleansing cream. What's going on, you and my brother have some news to tell me?"

"Oh, Kira . . ." Lydia choked, not knowing what to say. Abe's engagement ring, too tight on her heat-swollen knuckle, had begun to feel like an instrument of torture.

"What is it? Something has happened?" Pause. "Something bad?"

"Abe . . . we were on a dive and . . . Kira, they're still looking but it's been sixteen hours and I don't know if . . ."

Kira's scream rang in Lydia's ears for moments afterward. Then, in a rough, sobbing voice, Kira said, "When will they know? When will they know where Abe is?"

"I'm not sure. They said—I think if they don't find him tonight . . ."

"Then he will be declared dead?"

Lydia was taken aback. "I don't know, Kira. I just know that the odds of finding him go way, way down." She paused, wishing she could touch Abe's sister, wishing she could offer some firmer comfort. "Oh, Kira, I'm so sorry. I don't know how to do this."

"Abe, my brother. My big brother." Loud sobbing ensued.

"I'm so sorry. I'm so sorry." And she was. Lydia felt responsible.

"What do I do, what do I do now?"

"Kira, there's nothing any of us can do now, we just—"

"No, I mean, what do I do now? Fly over there or just wait?"

Lydia realized she didn't know. It all depended on whether or not they located the body, she supposed, but she didn't want to say that aloud. "I guess I'll have to find out," she said.

"Call me as soon as you do," Kira said.

§

The second phone call began more easily, but ended harder.

"Dad?"

"Who is it?"

"Daddy, it's me." Silence. "Your daughter." More silence. "Dad, it's Lydia! Can't you hear me?"

From an ocean away, Lydia heard her father give a long sigh. "Lydia, I'm not sure that I can talk to you right now."

"What's wrong, Daddy, are you okay? Is Mom?" Her father always wanted to talk to her, usually to tell her what she must do, and what she must not. "What's happened? Daddy?"

A hotel staff person gave Lydia a curious glance as he walked by pushing a rack of suitcases, and Lydia lowered her voice. "Actually, Dad, I should tell you something before you say anything else. I—"

"Lydia, I can barely bring myself to listen to the sound of your voice right now. I think you'd better get off before I say something both of us will regret. After all, you are and will always be my daughter." Victor Gold did not, Lydia noted, sound happy about this fact. It was finally penetrating Lydia's befuddled conscious-ness that her demanding, perfectionist, but nevertheless loving father was speaking as if she had just committed some horrible crime.

"Daddy? I don't understand what you're saying. I called because Abe's had . . ."

The phone went dead in Lydia's hand.

On the third try, Lydia's mother picked up. She sounded nervously cheery, as if a hijacker was holding a gun to her head and demanding that she speak naturally. "Hello, darling," she said. "Having a nice time?"

"I was," Lydia began, "but then——"

"Good, good. Listen, sweetie, don't worry about Daddy."

The perfect inappropriateness of this confused Lydia for a moment. After a moment, she said, "What?"

"He's gotten some bad news today . . ." There was a roar of rage from the background.

"Mom. I need to tell you something." Lydia's voice sounded small to her own ears. "Abe's died. He's drowned, they think he's dead." Lydia began to cry. "Oh, Mom, they say he must be dead because they looked all night and we were diving and he went on his own and then he just——his tank——and there was a ring in his bag, in his suitcase I mean. He was going to ask me to marry him."

There was a very long silence on the other end.

"Mom?" More silence. "Are you still there?"

"Oh, God, darling, I just don't know how to respond to this right now. He's——you said he's dead? Oh, honey, honey. I just——don't know what to say right now. Let me——I'll tell your father, I don't know if that makes things better or worse. But try not to worry. You know how Daddy is. He still loves you, you know he does. He gets mad, he gets mad at everybody. He'll come around."

Lydia, who had been slightly more concerned about the disap-

82   § *Alisa Kwitney*

pearance of her boyfriend than she had been about her father's anger, opened her mouth to respond, yet only managed to utter an odd croaking sound.

"Now, there is one thing, though, one thing that your father wants me to ask . . ."

There was a muted sound, as if Lydia's mother had cupped her hand over the receiver. Despite this, the angry bark of commands issued forth from the phone, and Lydia held it away from her ear.

"What was that?" she asked when there was silence again.

"I want to know if you goddamn gave Abe Bohemius a blank check to the salon bank account," demanded a voice so unlike Lydia's father's that for a moment, Lydia did not know who had taken the phone.

"No," said Lydia, and then remembered writing a check for Abe to invest and Abe saying something about not knowing what the interest or tax or something would be and could she just leave that part for him to fill out after he crunched a few numbers. But that had been from her own personal checking account. "I wrote a check for him to invest in mutual funds but it wasn't the business account, it was—"

Lydia had to hold the phone away from her ear.

"What I don't understand is how somebody could study psychol-ogy for two years and still be so unbelievably stupid about people.' Her father took a breath. "But maybe what I'm really mad about my own stupidity. After you got so damned depressed, you sta bouncing all your checks, so you asked if we could link your ac to ours. And then when we all went out to dinner, I wa enough to talk to your hairy little boyfriend about the impr your mother and I wanted to make to the business. S exactly when we'd have a nice large sum sitting there duck. That little error in my judgment just cost your mother and myself our entire business."

This time, when Lydia heard the dial tone, she made no attempt to call back. An hour later, still crying, she dialed the numbers with trembling fingers, and heard her mother say, "Lydia, I just want to assure you . . ." But the assurance never came. The phone went dead one final time, and Lydia stared at the receiver, aware again of the background murmur of hotel lobby noise as she wondered what she had done to lose a fiancé and her parents in fewer than eight hours.

§

Rodney Gold, whose feelings toward his older sister were an uncomfortable mixture of ancient affection and embarrassed concern, thought for a moment before telling his secretary to punch Lydia through.

"Lydia, hello. Now, hold on a moment. Yes, I can pretty well imagine what Dad said. Just try to catch your breath. There. No, I want you to calm down before I explain." Rodney glanced at the picture on his desk of his new wife. Jenna's amused blue eyes seemed to say, Aha, caught you. She had posed for the picture half-hugging herself, with her left hand on her right shoulder, so he could see the large, square-cut diamond he had given her. Her smile let you see she was in on the joke. Some photographer had asked her to pose that way, but she was too clever to simper sentimentally into the camera lens, advertising commerce as emotion.

Lydia would just have beamed ecstatically, in love with love, flashing that ring like a beacon of hope. Which is why poor old Lyd would probably never get her diamond. Men wanted girls who valued their freedom, they didn't go shopping for the neediest mutt in the pound.

For as long as Rodney could remember, he had felt that he was the wiser, more experienced one. Well, all right, back when she was five and he was three, she'd been like a god to him, all calm and loving when their mom got insane over a little Magic Marker on the wall or their father howled that he was going to start throwing toys out their twentieth-story window if they weren't cleaned up off the floor *now*.

And when he'd started kindergarten, it was Lydia who'd made sure no one bothered her little brother on the school bus to their private day school. Such a plump little mama hen, even back then, the kind of girl who already had little bubbies on her chest, while her classmates were all legs and headbands.

Rodney, who was small and sharp-tongued for his age, was a different sort of child entirely. His favorite fairy-tale hero was the opportunistic Puss in Boots. He had a Jewish-comedian shtick down so well that even his Sunday school teachers laughed when he was rude.

Now, listening to a thirty-one-year-old woman sob brokenly about a situation that was, after all, only her own fault, Rodney suppressed a shudder of irritation.

"Lydia," he said, "calm down. Let me begin by making sure I understand this—Abe's dead in a diving accident?"

Lydia sobbed that he was.

"Sorry about that. All right. Let me begin by asking you how much is in your joint checking—just that? No recent big deposits, say, from that fund Abe got you into?"

Rodney listened. "Damn. Damn. All right." He turned his chair, looked out at a big chunk of Fifty-second street and Broadway, and gazed at the skyline. Here and there, people scurried across the avenue. "This is the situation, Lyd. Three million is missing from the salon account." Rodney tapped his gold pen, waiting out the anticipated gasp. "Yes. Yes. Everything Mom and Dad have been saving for the past nine years toward their retirement.

"What do you mean, how? With a check. That's all it takes, Lyd. God, don't you ever pay attention when Dad talks about the company's finances? The business has a sweep account, which means it's basically a checking account that earns interest. But you can write checks on it, with an authorized signature. And since your personal checking account was linked, your lovely boyfriend was able to write himself a tidy little check for three million dollars.

"And, frankly speaking, Abe's the only one who could have known there would even be three mil in the business account, because he's the one who convinced Dad to get an early distribution on his retirement funds and roll the money over into capital improvements on the salon." Rodney's voice was shaking with anger now, and he tried to control it. It was just that he was going to be the one picking up this mess, he just knew it, and this was not what he wanted to think about, not now with a new wife and a new apartment and everything happening so fast at Dunham International.

"Lydia. Lydia. Lydia, will you just—just shut up and listen for a minute? What I'm trying to say is, I know you don't have much of a head for finances, and we're all well aware of what a lousy judge of character you are, but how dumb can you be, to hand a guy a blank check for your father's business?

"Yeah, well, I am sorry he's dead, because that means that now his brainless kitten of a sister gets the money. No, Lyd, unless you're married, it doesn't count. So unless Dad does something pretty radical, he's out on the street at sixty-five."

Rodney glanced at his wife's picture again, and thought how much he wanted to just go home and hold her, because there was something raw and bad in the back of his throat, a taste that reminded him of drugs and misbehavior.

"Lydia, you're not thinking this through. What good's it going to do to come back today? I'm trying to tell you, sis. They've moved your stuff out." Rodney resisted telling his sister she was a shmuck to have been living at home at her age, no matter how low she'd felt after screwing Jenna's brother. Well, this would teach her a lesson— no job, no home, and no one to bail her out this time.

Looking one last time at Jenna's amused eyes, Rodney worked up the courage to say, "Look, Lyd, I know this sounds kind of harsh, but I can't put you up here. We've only got one bedroom." Rodney knew that was the right thing to say. Jenna would despise having an indefinite houseguest, especially his sister, whom she held in particular contempt. Besides, it would do Lydia good to stand on her own two feet for a change.

"Just think things over before you make a move, Lyd. I'll talk to you in a day or so, to see how you're doing. Okay? Love you, Sis. Really." Rodney hung up the phone, and decided he needed to wash his mouth out with something. That aftertaste was really something foul. Maybe he was getting sick.

§

Lydia hung up the phone, a strange, numb blankness where her thoughts ought to be. The buzz of people in the hotel lobby going about their holiday business seemed at once very close and very far off, like the hum of a television in another room.

Abe had embezzled her parents' money.

No. Impossible. Even she could not have made so massive an error in judgment. Lydia stared at the ring on her hand. In the sunlight, the sapphire glittered like a diamond. How much would a stone like that cost—five, six thousand? Abe was well off. "Here," he'd tell a cabdriver, "keep the change." He always had plenty of cash. He never even had to use plastic. Why would he need . . .

He wouldn't need to steal her father's money. As a professional investor, he had access to other people's accounts. He had references, some of whom he'd insisted she contact ("I want you to check me out," he'd said). She'd called and two men and one woman had all vouched for Abe, saying they'd made great profits from the mutual funds that he had managed for them. And finally, she herself had made money—a thousand dollars from a five-hundred-dollar investment. Naturally, she'd rolled it over into another stock. But she'd held the check in her hand, so she knew it had existed.

Three million—no. A surge of panic rushed through her. It was impossible. Abe's sister did business with the salon. Scientique was their main makeup supplier now. He couldn't have—and besides, he had been the most utterly honest person Lydia had ever met. He'd told her about his struggles with dyslexia. He'd admitted to her about being short all through his early childhood. Things she never would have known had he not informed her. He had made himself vulnerable to her. No man had ever done that before.

In fact, she remembered laughing to herself that Abe, with his vaguely designer-simian-criminal air, had turned out to be the most dependable boyfriend of all. So dependable she hadn't hesitated to hand him a blank check. "Fill it in when you calculate the taxes due," she'd said. She'd thought he was doing her a favor, investing her money. She hadn't asked too many questions. All she'd said was to go conservative, not too many high-tech stocks. That was all she knew about the market. She had been relieved that he'd done all the legwork for her.

But surely most investors didn't follow every rise and fall on Wall Street? There was always some element of trust involved. And how could she be sure now that there might not have been some strange deal that Abe could explain, that might even still pay off, if only Abe were alive to manage it?

There had been an engagement ring in Abe's bag. He had been about to propose. How could he have stolen her parents' money? There was a misunderstanding. There was some huge miscommunication, and wasn't it just like her father to rush to judgment and lay the blame at someone else's feet? At her feet. You didn't act like that when you loved someone. You gave someone a chance. You listened. You didn't just excommunicate them.

Despite herself, Lydia had begun to cry loudly enough that some of the children racing around the potted palms in the lobby stared at her. Their parents, probably all New Yorkers, were used to ignoring outbursts of madness and violence, and only glanced up to ascertain that, yes, the busty blonde was the one making that sick gulping sound. Lydia's hands were shaking as she smoothed her wet cheeks and walked outside, where she allowed herself to cry a bit louder, picking a path at random through the unlit tiki torches.

In a way, though, it really didn't hurt that much, what her father had done. It was all she expected from him, really. But Rodney— that was a different story—"I can't put you up." As if she would have asked! But to hear that tone in his voice. It was one thing for their mother to treat Lydia with the special concern one reserves for the defective. It was another for Rodney to speak to her as if he had grown up in some way she had not.

But now she had nowhere to live. Which was her own fault, really, she knew it had been a mistake to live at home at her age, but it had seemed so practical. So temporary. So comforting.

Oh, God, Abe, she thought, what did you do?

Lydia looked up and saw the vulture angling its wings to make another pass over the dining hall. Upset and grief churned in her stomach and Lydia thought that this was worse than last time. Last time she'd raced home; now she was alone in a strange place, and there was nowhere to run.

10

Abe Bohemius was feeling exceptionally cheerful. There was something liberating about being dead. Should he take a new name? he wondered as he began lathering his head with shaving cream. Allan Brown. Victor Brooks. Alfredo Balducci. Or maybe something completely new, like Stratos Philharmonic. No, wait, there was a guy back in Brooklyn named Stratos Philharmonic.

Abe held up the razor and grimaced. It was fine for the budding baldies to go for broke with the cue-ball look, but it was a lot harder to part with a good, thick, healthy head of hair. Good-bye hair, see you again soon. At least he *would* see it again. He didn't have one of those noble, high foreheads about to turn into receding hairlines like that smug Irish dive-boat sonofabitch.

Had the handsome captain felt a moment's pleasure when he'd discovered Abe wasn't returning from his solo dive? If so, he was probably too much of a stand-up asshole to admit it. Abe knew the type from his days in the army—easygoing on the surface, but deeply, guiltily, tiresomely responsible underneath. Regardless of his personal feelings of like or dislike, MacNally would've steamed on back to port, comforted poor Lydia, then gone on to help search for the missing body, which was a good thing. Had the do-right captain decided to just ditch the missing person and continue taking the group on their scheduled dive, he might have bumped into Abe, making his way underwater to the other side of the island. Say what you like about the army—and Abe usually did, cursing the day he'd chosen to defy his father in order to be all he could be—at least they taught you useful things, like how to navigate by compass.

Abe took one last look at his reflection in the mirror, and then began to shave off the expensive Wall Street haircut Lydia had given him back in New York. Crying shame—if there was one thing she knew, it was hair.

For a moment, Abe wondered how poor Lydia was doing. Lord, that girl possessed a nice pair of tits. And the way she had thrown herself at him their last night together—kissing him every which way, up, down, and sideways—it was almost as if she'd known this was good-bye.

It almost made him feel a little guilty.

Not that he had done anything so very terrible to her. Daddy would bail her out when she discovered her investments had not exactly played out. Considering the wealth that family had—gilt and full-length mirrors on the walls of the salon, marble floors, velvet draperies, the place was a friggin' palace—it wasn't as if they couldn't stand to take a little hit. That was, after all, the *familya*'s first rule: Don't take from them as can't afford it. And as pretty as Lydia was, now that she'd dyed her hair blond and started wearing those little body-hugging numbers, she'd find a new guy by late spring. No harm done, really.

All she'd needed was self-confidence, and he'd given her that, in spades. And the "death" of her true love would grow her up a bit. His Kira was ten years younger but light years ahead in savvy and experience. There were moments when he felt as if Kira knew more than *he* did.

Glancing at his watch, Abe calculated another four hours before his plane took off. He wanted to call Kira but she had made him promise to wait till he reached Miami. His stomach growled, and he cursed the little shit Thomas who'd brought him a brick of tasteless cheese and a stale loaf of bread when he'd first arrived late Wednesday afternoon. This was late Thursday morning, and Abe wanted some eggs and bacon. The kid had done fine stashing the spare regulator and tank in the wreck, but for five hundred dollars, which was a friggin' fortune here on Epiphany, you would expect better service afterward. Like maybe a truck instead of a crappy moped ride to the other side of the island, and a little more than a lousy stale sandwich for dinner. The motel room couldn't be faulted, as Abe had requested as rundown a place as possible.

Shaving off another stripe from his scalp, Abe wondered who'd been the last sucker to inhabit this room—probably some drunk local nailing his best friend's wife. No tourist would ever consider sleeping in this dark cupboard on that limp piece of foam nailed to an old door. No, this was strictly for down-and-outers, which was why Abe felt sure that no one from the resort would stroll by and spot him here. Not even the most intrepid tourist seeking local flavor would choose the bar downstairs for his lunch, and the only other attraction on this block would be the recompression chamber, which mainly served the local fishermen who didn't have dive computers to calculate their dives. Abe's stomach growled again and he wondered if he should chance going downstairs to get a bite of something hot.

His brother, Stefan, would say, Go ahead, treat every moment as if it is gold, that is the Rom way.

Kira would say no. Kira would say, Play it safe, don't gamble anything now. She was an awfully conservative little con girl, his Kira, but considering the life she'd led in Russia, it wasn't surprising.

Yet what use was living life if you didn't take a chance or two? Which was why his little surprise for her would be all the more satisfying. Oh, she would yell at him for a moment. She would probably hit him and say that it was foolhardy and reckless and why hadn't he stashed the money in a Swiss bank account? But accounts leave paper trails, and besides, there was something in him that wanted to do it this way, put the ring on her finger, all three million dollars' worth, and say to her, Now you don't have to go out with those disgusting old men. This is enough to pay back those gangsters and more. We can afford to do what we like. Travel. Open that men's-spa thing. Get married in style.

Best of all, this con was something his mother could brag about. Like many converts, the former Barbara Miller was especially devout after her marriage to his father. She had spent years writing the history of the Gypsies in eastern Europe, and encouraging her children to buck the system.

Abe's father, a Toyota salesman who kept limited contact with his relatives in the old country, humored his wife, but had suggested to both his sons that they might consider the advantages of going to college. He'd been born in a museum-quality painted caravan just outside Prague, and didn't remember one romantic thing about his childhood.

But given their mother's vision of a wild, mystical, antiestablishment tribe of wanderers, and their father's terse remarks about having villagers throw rocks at him when he tried to go to school, Abe and his brother formed their own idea of their Rom heritage.

Abe knew that his joining the army had just about broken his mother's heart. His supposed death would be a kind of rebirth: Look, Mom, I didn't just break the rules, I rewrote them.

It made such a good story. The three-million-dollar ring. They could even make a movie out of it, with John Travolta playing yours truly. How could his mother complain about her new daughter-in-law after that?

And he would explain how it was his stroke of genius to pick a stone no one would guess cost that much. No boring, run-of-the-mill white diamond for Kira. A white diamond worth that sum would have to have been the size of a bird's egg, anyway. Besides, to a gypsy, white was for mourning. This was better. Rarer. A blue diamond, flawless and as deeply blue as a sapphire, but with a diamond's hard, reflective brilliance.

This one was fifteen carats of precision-cut perfection, but what really made it worth the big bucks was the stone's history. It had once belonged to Catherine the Great, the one they said did it with a horse. According to the salesguy, this was not just bullshit, either. There was a famous painting of her back in Russia in which she was wearing the ring.

But no average Joe would look at the thing and know how much it was worth, which made it the perfect way to hide three mil. Abe wondered if he should take the ring out and check that it was okay. He hadn't had a spare moment today, had barely managed to cram the ring box into his dive bag while Lydia went for what was surely the quickest fucking pee he'd ever heard. It was like she hadn't wanted to let him out of her sight, which was bizarre. Maybe she did have some kind of sixth sense, like they say dogs do when their owners are set to pull up stakes and ditch them.

For a moment, Abe felt a stab of self-doubt. Should he have asked his mother to throw the cards, to ensure that his plan would work? Should he have consulted his father before embarking on this project? No, this was better. He would show them once and for all that he was a grasshopper, not an ant—one of the Rom, not one of the *gadji*. He would show them what he could do, without their help. He would win their respect when he explained the whole sweetheart scam, how he had set this rich young woman on the path to beauty and confidence, surely sufficient payment for some money her father would never miss.

He would show them that he had taken care to kill off his identity as Abe Bohemius so that the girl would never learn that she had been conned at all—a perfect touch, that. In a sense, he had laid down his life for her. His mother, a great romantic, would be especially pleased.

Abe's stomach rumbled wetly. Where was that shit-for-brains kid? Off buying up the island with his newfound wealth, probably. Well, maybe it would be okay to go downstairs once he'd shaved his head. With the dark glasses, he'd be pretty much unrecognizable. Maybe the grim-faced hotel staff could manage some fried fish and french fries. That would help pass the time until ten o'clock, when Abe Bohemius would have been missing twenty-four hours.

At which point, Allan Brown would get on a plane for Miami and start a new life.

Finally, for the first time since his mother and father had told him that he just didn't have what it took to be in the family business, Abe felt at peace with himself. So what if Stefan was the most skillful computer hacker on the East Coast, and Rosalia had started her own psychic hotline? What Abe had just pulled off was going to blow all their accomplishments away.

Whistling under his breath, Abe pulled the peacock-blue ring box out of his dive bag and flipped it open.

What he saw plunged his stomach into his bowels.

11

In his youth, Fish had believed that intimacy was achieved by the unburdening of secrets. You told the lady in question about how your mother forced you to wear white britches and long blond curls until you were six, you described how, in the army, a stray cat had adopted you and become your special mascot until she dropped a litter of kittens and some cruel bastard decided to dispose of them.

These stories, he'd believed, conveyed your sense of self to the other party, and she, in turn, unburdened herself to you. The traumatic bloodstain on her skirt at the high school prom, the solo bus ride to Florida with only a handbag and the promise of a secretarial job from a guy her mother used to know.

Now Fish saw these revelations for what they really were, the rituals of the religion of romance. He figured it was nice to reminisce about the past, but it wasn't as if it were the key to the great mystery. There was no key. There was no great mystery. People bumped along and sometimes they bumped into each other.

So it was to his great surprise that he found himself sitting at his computer at all hours of the day and night, typing out his life story to some unknown quantity who called herself Messalina, and described herself as "slender, handsome, well preserved, clever, critical, probably arrogant, sexual, discriminating; and beneath a tough and leathery surface, surprisingly romantic."

She was his soul mate.

She flirted with the kind of intelligence that courtiers had used in the polished courts of England and France. She was as blunt as a sailor, and as perceptive as a psychiatrist without resorting to any of that profession's jargon.

She was also mysterious, his Messalina. She cagily refused to reveal certain facts about herself. It did not seem mere coyness. Fish had a funny feeling that this lady had a secret.

So distracted was he by his on-screen love affair that Fish did not immediately notice how sick Liam was. On Thursday, Liam seemed hungover and had gone back to bed. But twenty-four hours had passed since then and there was still no sign of him. Was it arthritis, brought on early from all the diving Liam had done? Was it the flu? Liam steadfastly refused to see a doctor.

Perhaps he was still upset about finding the tax and business records. Yesterday Liam had discovered that Out of the Blue Diving required an influx of some thirty thousand dollars within the next six months if it was to survive.

"Jesus, Fish," Liam had said, his face looking aged and drawn, "when were you going to tell me about this? Can't I trust you at all?"

Fish, thinking guiltily of Martin and the prospect of his own bar and all-night poker games, said nothing. But that night, unable to sleep, he wrote to Messalina. She was out there somewhere. She met him in the never-never land where there is no accountability and everyone is young.

Fish logged on and felt a thrill of pleasure as Messalina's name appeared on his screen. This time, they didn't mention sex at all.

§

For two days after Abe's disappearance, Lydia sat in her cabin, sleeping and drinking diet soda, unable to read the heavyweight book she'd packed, and uncharmed by the lightweight one. If only there were a television set to ignore. Lydia missed the comfort of flipping through the channels, past all the earnest talking heads. In the absence of easy distractions, she drifted into a state that reminded her of early childhood illnesses, transfixed by the play of light and shadow on the floor, catching fragrances of dust and sap, of some plant or flower's bitter muskiness, evocative of elusive memories. She had no idea what to do next and only emerged from her holiday confinement to sit out on the dining room veranda at sunset, enveloped by the cloying smell of a massive citronella candle. The savagely confident parrots eyed her basket of sliced bread and then flew off to another table, where someone was being served fried clams. Lydia allowed herself one glass of white wine and then put an orange in her pocket for dessert, figuring people would come for her if they needed her.

It was late on Friday, the second day after Abe's disappearance, that Lydia learned that Kira had called off the search. She'd tried to reach Abe's sister on the phone, but had only succeeded in leaving three messages on the answering machine. Martin Thorne informed Lydia rather stiffly that Miss Bohemius felt it merely painful to continue searching for a body. Yet it had seemed to Lydia that there might still be a chance, however slim, to find Abe alive. She was so confused by Kira's decision that she began to go over the entire history of her relationship with Kira and Abe.

Lydia had never met any other member of their family, had never met Abe's friends. He had not liked to talk about himself much. When pressed, he would present the facts, but without embellishment. His father was controlling. His mother had died. There was no detail, no color, there were no little scenes distilled and preserved as examples of seasons past. He always turned the conversation around to her likes, dislikes, her past tragedies and triumphs. She had enjoyed the novelty of being so closely attended, and figured that this was one of the proofs of how much he loved her. But now she found herself reconsidering. Wouldn't a man in love want to be known, seen, understood himself?

The natural consequence of too active a mind and too inactive a body is a sleepless night. At two in the morning of what was meant to be Lydia's next-to-last day on the island, she turned on the bedside lamp and remembered Abe's calm, deliberate way of touching her, as if she were a radio he was learning to tune, as if this were a job and he took his responsibilities seriously. She thought about three million dollars, and stared down at the ring on her finger. The blue stone, which she realized now was too large to be anything valuable or real, seemed to wink at her even in the half-light.

At last she forced herself to voice the unspeakable question: What if he hadn't loved her? What if, as Rodney and her father claimed, she had been used, duped and discarded?

And then, belatedly, as dawn broke over the horizon, Lydia realized that if Abe really had been faking it the whole time they'd been lovers, then she should stop taking anything at face value.

§

The blonde came into the dive shop and Fish knew instantly that she was the one, even though she was not what he had expected. For one thing, she was much prettier—softer, more worn looking, with wide, dark, red-rimmed eyes. Hopeful, but not trusting. Fish had the sense that this lush, lived-in female was not as naive as Liam figured. Fish was really beginning to despair of the Irishman's ability to read character.

"May I help you?"

"Is Captain MacNally around?"

Captain MacNally. So he had nailed her. Nobody was that formal on the island unless they had something to hide.

"He's feeling a bit under the weather."

"Oh, gosh, I'm sorry. Has he been out searching for Abe? I'm the missing person's . . . girlfriend."

Fish hesitated. "Actually, he's been feeling sick for the past couple of days."

"Sick? How sick?"

Damned if he knew. The usually stoic Liam had seemed in terrible pain, but it was always hard to tell when healthy young men got sick. Some of them were babies about it precisely because they were so unused to their bodies betraying them with weakness. "It's probably just a little bug."

"If I could just talk to him for a moment—"

"I don't think that's wise."

The blonde considered this. "I'm not afraid of catching the flu."

Fish wondered if Liam had, in fact, nailed this pretty kumquat, and if so, what his attitude toward her might be. Going over the financials with Fish last night, Liam had admitted that every joint in his body still ached, even though he hadn't gone diving or had a drink in forty-eight hours.

Fish glanced down at the blonde's pretty, tight, pink terry-cloth sundress. His own mood had been seriously lightened by the deliciously witty Messalina, with whom he had been enjoying fast-paced flash sessions in the naughty lit chat room. Having recently enjoyed his first amorous encounters in quite a few years, Fish felt sensitized to the signs of lovemaking. There were no love bites on this woman's soft, lightly tanned neck. Strange, Liam was usually into necks. For a moment, Fish spared a thought as to what Messalina might really look like; then he discarded the subject as beneath him. She'd read

James Joyce and she knew how to pun about being strict and firm; any physical meeting would surely prove a disappointment, if not a legal conundrum, as it had last time. Besides, Blondie here was a perfect example of why to avoid real up-close and personal physical contact during sex—if you were there in the bed at night to get laid, you'd be there in the morning getting the brush-off.

Except this time it seemed to be Fish having to do the dirty work. If Liam hadn't been so sick, Fish would have gladly killed him.

"Look, I don't know how well you know Liam, but he's not exactly a great patient. This is the first time I've seen him this sick, and I don't think he'd appreciate someone stopping by unless he knew them pretty well." Fish watched. No blush. But she couldn't quite meet his eyes for the full moment.

"This is important."

"Should I give him a message?"

The look she gave him was a rather more careful assessment than Fish was used to receiving from young women these days. Or from anyone, really. At a certain age, he'd discovered, you ceased to be seen as either a potential love interest or a threat. And then you just ceased to be seen.

She seemed to make a decision. "He said something to me a couple of nights ago. Something about trying to help people, it being kind of a character flaw with him."

"That's true enough." And more than Liam usually revealed. Fish looked at her, measuring her in turn. "Why?"

"He also said—he said he'd recovered missing persons. In New York." The soft brown eyes were welling with tears, changing their color to something approaching green.

"That's true."

"But he didn't find Abe." Tears falling now.

"Yeah, I know. But they're still out there, searching."

"But not Liam. He worked for the police, right? That makes him more than qualified, right?" No answer. "He's the most expert, isn't he?"

Fish nodded. "Well, I guess he has a bit more active experience searching—"

"Because I need, really need, to locate Abe."

Fish frowned. "I understand," he said slowly, "the need for closure—"

"No, no, it's more than that, it's—"

"But I don't think Liam will be up to this kind of thing today."

"I just need to talk to him . . ."

Fish sighed. "Look, he's sleeping now. I'll tell him you wanted to talk to him when he wakes up, but I don't think you should pin too much on this thing with Liam. Though I'm sure he's very concerned for you." Damn, Fish thought. Women were always expecting men to be brave. How could you explain that things are no easier just because you pee standing up; disgusting, soul-numbing work was just as damaging to the male of the species. As was too much nitrogen in your bloodstream, exacerbated by a surfeit of alcohol immediately after.

"Look, my boyfriend's dead, and my father thinks he embezzled three million dollars of his money. Liam was a cop, and he said he would try to help me. So please stop treating me as if I'm some stupid duckling imprinted on a member of the wrong species."

"I see." Fish tried to remember what one did in this sort of situation, and failed utterly. Before, he had only ever faced teary, irate women at the moment of leaving, when you weren't expected to reason or comfort them, unless maybe to sleep with them one last time.

And this one had a real fighting look in her eye.

"So why don't I go get Liam?" he suggested.

§

Liam thought his head might explode. He also thought this might be a kindness. Blinking back tears, he tried to take inventory of the damage. Sharp pain in the head. Roil of unsteady stomach. Clammy hands and numb feet. Knees and elbows that felt like someone had been boiling them for glue. Liam rolled himself up to a sitting position and moaned. For some reason, he was on the floor.

"Liam?"

"Ung-oaah."

"Liam, I'm coming in."

Liam turned his head, which made the white knife in his brain twist to the left. "Fugoff, Fish," he whispered hoarsely.

"Listen, I know you may be feeling a little rough, but . . ."

Liam retched.

"Jesus, man, you're in a sorry state." Fish dabbed at his face with a cool, wet cloth, and helped him up onto the bed. "Here, take this."

Liam stared at a glass of something fizzy and foul. "Do I have to?"

"Your head feel like you've got mad-cow disease?"

Liam nodded, sending shards of pain flying through his forehead.

"Then you have to."

Liam drank it down and the two men sat, waiting for the pain to subside. "Need a shower," he said.

"I'll run it."

Liam looked at him through bloodshot eyes. "You're being awfully nice. Worried about me?"

"Worried about your blonde. She's out there, waiting for you to make an appearance."

"The hell you say—ouch."

"Try not to shout." Fish stood up. "Here, put the damp cloth on your head and I'll get your shower going."

"You gonna soap me, too, Fish?" Liam sounded as sour as his stomach felt.

Fish gave his younger partner a suspiciously genial smile. "I have a better idea."

§

Two minutes of hot water pounding on his shoulders and back, and Liam was just beginning to feel human again. Just as he was sluicing his eyes clear of soap, however, he heard something that made his heart lurch into his throat.

"Fish said you might require assistance."

Through the flimsy nylon curtain, Liam saw the blonde, looking pale and wan in the harsh morning light. She was holding a cup of coffee. Aw, Christ. What was he supposed to say to her? What *had* they done the other night, anyway? All he had retained was a vague impression of damp limbs and sharp teeth and an aching erection. That and the feeling that he might have done something wrong.

"What's the matter? Not used to women on dry land?"

"I'm not exactly dry." Liam turned off the water and held his hand out for the coffee. The blonde managed to pass it to him without taking any more of an eyeful than she had to. Turning around, she said, "I want what you offered two days ago."

That sounded promising. She had a nice back, Liam noted—long and straight and supple in that little beach towel of a dress she was wearing. Somehow he'd missed that before. All that topload hadn't spoiled her posture; she moved like a dancer. "Right now that feels like a long time ago. Can you be specific?"

"You said if you were the right kind of person, and someone needs help, you try to help that person out. I need your help, to find my—to locate Abe Bohemius."

Liam didn't recall saying any such thing, but that didn't mean much. In his present state, he could barely remember his mother's first name. "Ah, right, with you in a minute. Hand me that towel, will you?" She threw it at him without looking, making Liam smile despite the low-level tom-toms still pounding in his frontal lobe.

This time, she did turn around, and Liam realized that without makeup, you could see traces of the very grown-up little girl she'd once been. She still retained that childlike look of alert watchfulness, as if she were still at the stage of watching closely and learning. There was a lot going on there, when you got beyond the unlikely moonbeam shade of her hair. And the tits.

"They're real," the blonde commented mildly. "Mind if I ask you a question about Wednesday night?"

"I, uh, don't exactly . . ."

"You thought I was busy drowning myself. It took me a little while to think things through, but now I'm curious. Why the hell were you playing footsie with me in the ocean instead of back out searching for Abe?"

Liam stepped, wet and irritated, out of the shower and into the narrow confines of his bathroom. Holding the towel in place with one hand, he let himself loom over her. Then, looking down, he saw the mauve shadows beneath her eyes and remembered, with a shock, that she was in mourning. "Look, I understand you're upset. But I pushed my limits that night—pushed someone else's as well, I'm ashamed to say."

"Pushed your drinking limit, I would say. Why aren't you out there this morning? Or yesterday?"

Liam, who felt that complaining about being ill was somehow unmasculine, even if you really were unwell, choked back the first reply that came to mind: Because I am fucking sick as a dog. Instead, he said, "Because about half a dozen other guys in better shape than I am right now are taking their turn."

"That's bull. You're the expert. Nobody else here would have your kind of experience. Why the heck aren't you out there? Because you decided to go out on a bender two nights ago? Or is that a regular occurrence?"

Liam stared at her, a slow burn of indignation waking him up fully for the first time in days. "I hate to be blunt, but if your man's alive, the choppers or boats will locate him, not the divers. My expertise is in locating corpses." Liam drew a deep breath. Tears were running down the girl's face. Lydia. Her name was Lydia. "Look, Lydia, I'm sorry about—"

"The hell with you and the hell with sorry. I've just been disowned by my father, I have no job, I have no place to live, and I need to figure out what Abe would have done with the three million dollars before he died."

"Whoa, back up." Liam searched for a cigarette, found one, and then searched for a match. "What's this about three mil?"

"My father thinks Abe made off with it. Abe suggested that my father roll some money that was coming due into checking so he could use it for capital improvements on our salon. But then I wrote Abe a blank check on my account, and the two were linked."

Liam, who was having trouble lighting the match, stopped and stared. "You wrote someone a blank check?"

Lydia tucked her hair behind one ear. "It's called 'trust.' "

Liam lit the cigarette. "That's one word for it." Exhaling smoke, Liam began to feel a little better. "So Abey goes down the drink a few days after you write him a blank check for Daddy's business?"

Lydia nodded. Her hair swung forward like a bright curtain, hiding her expression.

"Shite, that's some story. I suppose it's occurred to you that Abe might not be quite as dead as presumed—and not quite as missing as he'd like us to believe?"

Lydia's head shot up at that. Liam watched the play of expressions cross her face. Then her features crumpled and she began to cry.

"Oh, God, it's worse when you say it out loud."

ॐ

"There, there, now." Liam looked at his cigarette with momentary regret, then tossed it in an old coffee cup before enfolding the sobbing woman completely in his arms. He patted her awkwardly, as if she were somebody else's child. "It'll all turn out right."

Lydia tossed her hair back. "You must be joking! We're talking about Abe walking out on me with all my parents' money in his pocket. It is absolutely not going to be all right unless we do something to make it right."

"So we'll make it right."

Lydia spun out of his embrace. "I need to find a goddamn body, MacNally. Sometimes, it actually does matter whether or not you find the corpse."

"I'm not saying it doesn't matter—"

"That's exactly what you did say. Now I am sorry if your work did not agree with you, but this is no time to get religious about your career choices."

Liam felt a knot of anger replacing the bright flicker of sensual awareness. "First off, you don't go lecturing me about my choices. Second, it sounds to me like you're wanting to search for a person, not a corpse. Have you even checked the airport? Did you think to look on the other side of the island?"

"The other—"

"Because if your man is hiding out, that's the place to do it."

Lydia drew in a deep breath. "That's what we need to do, then."

"Do you mind if I put my pants on first?"

"Yes. I'm booked to go home on a six o'clock flight the day after tomorrow. I mind everything that wastes any more time." She folded her arms under her breasts and regarded him with a coolness that Liam found more than a little unnerving.

Liam turned to go into his bedroom. "Are you always this hostile first thing in the morning?"

His uninvited guest followed him, casting a sardonic eye on the clutter—the half-empty bowl of melted corn flakes in milk sitting on top of a pile of poetry books, the half loaf of white bread spilling out onto the scattered piles of business records, the dirty underwear—woops—tucked as a place keeper into a dusty old paperback copy of *To Have and Have Not*.

"Jesus, look at this mess. What are you, thirty? Thirty-one?"

"Thirty-five."

"You live like a teenager."

"Christ, woman, hold your tongue. I'm the good guy, remember? The one who tried to save your life?"

"And an innovative technique it was, groping me to safety. Except, as I recall, the main danger was from you." She had followed him all the way into his room and was now standing, arms still crossed, far from the tangled chaos of the bed. Liam hoped the room wasn't too odoriferous. Luckily, Fish appeared to have cleaned up the vomit and opened the window. Liam had brushed his teeth, but had a brief, inappropriate concern about his breath.

"Don't seem to recall your getting up and running anywhere screaming, sweetheart. And you *were not* in any danger from me. Sorry to burst your bubble, Blondie, but you're not my type."

"So I came on to you, did I?" Her eyes were darkly furious. She, of course, smelled wonderful, all clean, unperfumed woman.

"What was this, then?" Liam pointed to the place, high on his shoulder, where her teethmarks were still visible.

"Maybe it was self-defense."

"No woman has ever—you lying little—you little—" Liam was speechless with anger, and, behind the anger, fear.

"Bitch? Whore? Slut? Tramp?" Something about the sight of her, calmly regarding him as she offered to fill in the gaps in his vocabularly, sent the hot blood rushing through Liam's veins. With his own pulse pounding in his ears, Liam grabbed her by her shoulders, for what purpose he could not imagine. Surely not to shake her. He had never laid a finger on a woman in his life.

"Get your hands off me. Now." Five feet two inches of pure defiance, she took one disdainful look down at his hands and then flicked her contemptuous gaze back to his face.

"No problem," he said, holding his palms up and backing away.

"It sure looked like a problem to me."

"Hey, I don't need to force women into my bed."

"Not when there's an ocean so close by."

It was the sarcastic half smile on that sexy, innocent mouth of hers that did it. The next thing Liam knew, he had her up against the wall and he was kissing her, not even thinking about what he was about but just grinding his mouth into hers, and then he pulled back and looked at her, and there was something so profoundly, gently, bottomlessly sad in her dark-amber eyes that Liam found himself wanting to reach out to her somehow. Cupping the silky contours of her cheek and jaw in his callused hand, he moved the pad of his thumb against the fullness of her lower lip, gazing into her eyes, questioning her wordlessly before bending his head again to press his mouth against hers, angling her chin with his hands, stroking his long fingers down the quickening pulse in her neck.

"I. . . ." Her mouth, opened to speak, gasped instead as he entered her with his tongue, moving his hands to the back of her head, tangling his fists in her silky hair. She was so deliciously compact that his hands seemed to learn her in an instant, roving down her lovely spine, past her hips, until he was cupping that incredible pear-shaped ass of hers, her little terry-cloth dress riding up, but even that wasn't enough so he tugged her white bikini panties until they covered no more than a thong would, baring almost all of her bottom to his touch. And then even that wasn't enough, so Liam lifted Lydia up until she was riding the lean muscle of his thigh, her back jammed up against the wall.

He stilled for the briefest of moments as her hands moved to catch at his hair, perhaps to pull him away, but no, she was not yanking his head away, she was holding him there against her mouth, he was seeking, learning the rhythm of her kiss, the rhythm of her passion, and then Liam reared back to bury his head in the fragrant hollow of Lydia's neck and he felt her gasp as his towel slipped and he knew she was feeling the throbbing length of him against her, because he could feel the curve of her belly hard up against him, and a bolt of electric desire shocked him into motion.

His hands supporting her under her buttocks, he moved her a little against him, and she gasped, her hands pulling a little at his hair, and the slight sting of pain was nothing, nothing at all compared to the feeling of her mound pushing against him.

There was nothing between them below the waist but a scrap of white cotton rucked up so he could look down and see the dark-blond curls on either side of her panties as he moved her just a little up just a little down oh jesus sliding against him. Liam slid his hands back between her thighs and his fingertips came away slick with her moisture. Liam looked up to see that Lydia was watching, too, and then her brown eyes lifted to meet his gray in startled recognition of what was happening between them. She looked like a doe caught in the headlights. He wondered what he looked like to her.

Holding her gaze, Liam lifted Lydia again, moving closer into her this time, sliding past the entrance thinly shielded by her panties. His eyes shut as he gave himself over to the ferocity of the sensation. Something, some muscle deep inside him, convulsed sharply with pleasure, maybe his heart.

Oh, sweet lord, he was so close to inside her, and why should it feel this intense when all he was doing was dry-humping her like some schoolboy, this was like being sixteen again, this was better than being sixteen, this was like being in love with someone you didn't even know yet.

And while he was thinking, he was thrusting against her, the steady build of pressure in his testicles blending with the painful pleasure in his scalp as she pulled at his hair. I'm going to come like this, Liam realized, thrusting steadily now, grinding against the damp musk of her, a mindless drumbeat in his head and his loins, the promise of imminent release tingling at the base of his erection and ah hell they were both going to come like this, he was going to take her there because she had to be as close as he was, her head was whipping back and forth, back and forth, almost as if she were saying no, no . . . and nails were raking sharply down his back and—

Jesus, what was he doing, what was he doing, was she willing or was she—Christ, he had her pinned, she was shaking her head no and scratching at him to get free, was it—

He was no better than his father.

Thrusting her away, Liam snarled, "Get out of here, now!" Lydia stumbled into the hallway as he turned on his heel and marched back into his bedroom, slamming the door shut behind him.

§

It was the most incredible kiss of her life. Shaking, limp with unspent passion, Lydia stared at the door to Liam's bedroom and tried to understand what had just happened.

He had kissed her to the very brink of orgasm.

He had taken her where no man had ever taken her before.

Without even taking off her clothes. Without even making love to her.

And then he had just slammed off in a fury and told her to get lost. Pushing her hair out of her sweaty face with trembling hands, Lydia replayed their conversation in her mind.

Admittedly, she had been a bit out of line, blaming him for not being out on a boat searching for Abe. If the man was sick, he was sick. It had been more the laid-back, easygoing beauty of the man, so self-sufficient and impervious, that had made her direct her frustration and anger his way.

She hadn't really expected to get to him. He didn't seem the type to react to a few misplaced insults. Ah, but she'd reckoned without his feelings of culpability, that was his Achilles' heel. The man had a lot of self-blame going on, and woe be unto anyone who added their voice to the silent chorus already echoing in his head.

And then Lydia felt a flash of anger burst into full-fledged consciousness. He had used her to prove his point! That whole passionate encounter, the most knee-trembling, heart-pounding, mind-rending sexual experience of her entire life, had been a sordid little demonstration of masculine prowess to soothe masculine ego—proof positive that she was the one yearning for him.

Well, fuck him!

But oh, she kind of wished she had, with that long, leanly ridged torso pressed up against her, the broad, flat planes of his chest and shoulders so beautiful that she had wanted to trace every working muscle. But that wasn't the best part, the best part had been the way he kissed her, with hunger and passion, so unlike the tentative, respectful kisses Abe had given and no, she wasn't going to compare them, or even think about the way Liam had moved against her, so violently tender that—

She had been so close. So close she had felt herself closing in on it, brighter and sharper than any pleasure she had found on her own, this was a pleasure that had threatened to swamp her whole body and soul, the great man-woman mystery finally about to be revealed to Ms. Lydia Gold.

And he had just been proving a point—that he was the studly master, and she was a little slut panting after his brand of sexual healing.

With a snarl, Lydia kicked his door open. Jeans now hugging his long legs, Liam turned to her, still red-faced with anger.

"Lady, don't you know when to just leave a man alone?"

"Oh, believe me, mister, I'm learning. But you just might think about this, Captain MacNally. Will you stick your tongue down Martin Thorne's throat if he asks too many uncomfortable questions?"

Turning on her heel, Lydia was all set to make her dramatic exit when she heard his voice call out.

"Oh, Lydia?"

"Yeah?"

"You might wanna get your knickers out of your crack before you go marching off, darlin'."

Flashing Liam a look of scathing contempt, Lydia marched out his front door. And then, with a tug and a wiggle, she rearranged her underwear before setting off for her own cabin.

Time to take matters into her own hands.

12

Kira Ludmilla Bobkova was the kind of woman men do not understand and other women understand far too well. She possessed an absurdly plump pout of a mouth and a delicate, kittenish prettiness that did not require makeup, and so was a natural to sell it. All colors looked appealing on her porcelain skin, against her darkly shining hair and eyes. She was not tall or photogenic enough to be a model, but had she been a fraction more ruthless, she might have considered becoming the kind of girlfriend rich men use to decorate first their birthday parties, and then their bedrooms.

But such women must convey a purringly sympathetic focus on their men, and Kira always got carried away with telling other people what she thought when she knew she should be silent, smiling and sipping her drink. She wanted a man who was interested in her, who would pay real attention to her needs, and listen respectfully to her ideas. Rich men did not listen to their decorative girlfriends. They paid them compliments and teased them about being too young to remember some old song on the radio.

Abe, whom she'd initially mistaken for rich, didn't require that kind of false applause. He looked at her with a kind of astonished happiness whenever she took her clothes off, and was very polite about the whole business of sex. Someone had taught him to take turns, and he was scrupulously fair. She couldn't figure out where he was from, Italy or Albania she supposed. He said his family back in the old country had been mostly wiped out in the Holocaust, which he called the Devouring, so for a while, she'd thought he might be Jewish.

The night Abe confessed his true, unwealthy identity to her, Kira had not been too thrilled. Her mother had always said gypsies were untrustworthy, but when Abe told her a little Rom history, she saw *they* were actually untrusting—of outsiders. Perhaps it amounted to the same thing. In any case, Russians weren't too trusting of outsiders, either.

And even among those Rom who were engaged in less than legal professions, there turned out to be a kind of honor among thieves. You were not supposed to cheat someone completely—you were meant to give some sort of payment, though not always in the coin the outsider was expecting.

Kira liked the idea. She thought about Pyotr and his gang of thugs and wondered if they had any such ethics.

So she snuggled up next to Abe and told him her big dream. She'd been peddling Scientique cosmetics for a few years, ever since she'd bought a starter kit from a friend, and she felt she'd learned the market. The thing was, everyone thought the same way—wrinkle creams, fancy names for the same old colors, facial masks, goopy substitute soaps. No one had any vision. No one ever considered, say, the market for men's cosmetics.

Now Kira knew cosmetics and she knew men, and she felt she knew with absolute certainty that she could revolutionize the industry with a deluxe gentlemen's spa, with pretty girls to give manicures and pedicures and cut hair and do facials. It would be like those day spas in midtown Manhattan, she explained, only just for men. The girls would all wear cute little uniforms, little short, white tennis-style outfits. There would be a health-food restaurant with cute waitresses. Men would go there to get pampered. It would be the Playboy Club for the new millennium.

Abe had called her brilliant and asked her to marry him and be his business partner.

She'd been truly sorry to turn him down—if it hadn't been for the money she owed Pyotr for helping her leave Kiev and setting her up with a job and an apartment, she would really have loved going into business with Abe. Instead, she was stuck singing at Moscow Nights down in Brighton Beach, and escorting Pyotr's scary friends when they came to New York.

If only that one fellow, Grigor, hadn't taken her to Atlantic City. That one weekend of gambling was what had turned her debt to Pyotr into virtual slavery. She now owed too much to ever be able to refuse Pyotr's requests, whatever they might become.

And then Abe had offered her a way out. He'd checked out one of those midtown day-spa salons that Kira had mentioned, and the most interesting thing had occurred. For every question Abe asked, the owner, a silver-haired man with a barrel chest and a black-on-black suit, had a question of his own. Was Abe looking for a complete corporate relaxation package to relieve the stress of, say, a job on Wall Street? Did he need a haircut? Was this a gift from his wife or girlfriend? When Abe responded in the affirmative to all three queries, the owner's wife came up, blinking her tinted blue contact lenses and grabbing him by her french-manicured hand. She had just the hairdresser for him, their best hairdresser, and, a funny coincidence, their daughter as well.

Abe had gotten the feeling that they had been trying to fix her up for a while.

At first, Kira had been prepared to dislike Lydia, what with her being so rich and all. But, as Abe pointed out, disliking her was just a side effect of guilt, and there was no reason to feel guilty.

"She's unhappy. She's lonely. I'm gonna give her a good experience," Abe had insisted. "I'll build up her self-confidence, and, at the end, I'll just conveniently die so she won't have to walk away feeling rejected."

Not to mention they could take out some life insurance on her.

There would be money, enough to free Kira from her employer, enough to get married and set up a legitimate business. Buoyed by this goal, Kira had thrown herself into playing her part as Abe's sister.

The funny thing was, Lydia was actually the closest thing to a female friend that Kira had had since she was thirteen. Sometimes, when Kira was doing business with Lydia's father and he said something particularly mean-spirited about his daughter, Kira found herself defending the other woman, who really was the other woman. It was all a bit weird when you thought about it.

Now, as it was time to close the show, the prospect of getting rid of Pyotr and his ubiquitous goons was as heady as champagne.

Thinking these happy thoughts, Kira opened her door on the second knock without asking who it was.

It was one of Pyotr's goons.

"I hear you are waiting for a phone call from your boyfriend, Kira," he said. "I have come to keep you company." This was the second goon Pyotr had sent in as many days. The first had been harelipped and surprisingly gentle, and she had gotten rid of him with a garlic sausage and a promise.

This one didn't appear so easily malleable. Hunkering down on the wooden stool by her kitchen counter, the broad, blond goon in the cashmere sweater crossed his arms over his chest and regarded her out of his expressionless pale-blue eyes.

He did not look like a man who could be charmed. "I told Pyotr that as soon as I collected the money, I'd be able to pay him back in full. What use is it hovering over me?" There. That was direct. Perhaps he'd respect that.

"Pyotr is just maybe a little concerned that you are leaving the country and maybe you might forget about paying him back."

"That's ridiculous! Who would take a chance on crossing him? I'd never be able to come back to the United States!"

The blond goon raised his pale eyebrows.

The phone rang, breaking an increasingly uncomfortable silence. Kira was so happy to hear Abe's voice that, for a moment, she did not understand what he was saying.

"What did you say about a ring, Abe? Never mind, tell me that part later. First, let me know when you meet me in Miami." Glancing over at the goon Pyotr had sent, she smiled reflexively, then bent her head to concentrate on what Abe was telling her. Catching her image in the large mirror that reflected back her studio apartment, Kira realized her hair needed a shaping. She wondered who would be cutting it now that Lydia was out of the picture. Not that it mattered; with three million dollars—well, two million after Pyotr took his share—you could have your pick of the best hairdressers in the world.

There was a silence on the other end of the line, and Kira realized Abe was waiting for her to say something. "So sorry, darling, but if you could just repeat that last part aga—" And then her brain suddenly computed what Abe had said. "Did you—did you just say you bought a ring? For the whole, for all the, with the three million dollars?" As the goon stood up, shaking out his Ralph Lauren corduroys, Kira realized she should not have said quite so much. "But that's wonderful, darling," she said into the phone as the goon approached with the rhythmic creak of new leather shoes on old wooden floors.

"Didn't you hear me, Kira?" Abe sounded less frantic, more exasperated. "I said the ring is missing. Lydia must have found it in my suitcase."

"And she thinks you are dead," Kira replied brightly. "In that case, I'll just hop on a plane and see Lydia. I will cry a little, say we could not afford the ring, she will give it back, and we can repay Pyotr."

"That might work—that might actually work. What time can you get here, baby?"

'Sweetheart, I am taking the next plane to Epiphany, okay? I better go pack, okay?"

"You sound a little—You're not alone."

The goon pressed his face close to Kira's and listened.

"Ha ha ha. Now, no more jokes, please. Where should I find you when I arrive?"

"Just look for the seediest motel on the wrong side of the island. But wait, Kira, I need to—"

She hung up on him before he could ask her anything else. The goon looked at her and sighed.

"Kira Ludmilla, now are you planning to leave the United States without a valid passport?"

Kira smiled at him. "I have my Russian passport and resident alien papers. I am legal."

"But maybe they will not let you back in. Maybe you do not plan to come back."

"Of course I am! I've told you! Where else would I go?" Kira turned her back on the goon, only to realize she could see his oversize, designer-clad reflection in the mirror. "You will excuse me, I must hurry now."

"*Slushish, dyetka*. You owe Pyotr Alexandrovitch a million dollars, Kira. Do not think that is a small sum, even for such a businessman as he is."

"First of all, I am nobody's baby. Second of all, I am planning on paying in a lump sum, as I said."

"It might be safer to go on giving some money every month, little one."

Kira glanced up at the goon and forced herself to smile. "Then you and Pyotr would keep visiting me until I am a very, very old woman. No, I think it better if I go to Abe and get the money. I will call you from the island."

The goon smiled back with all his newly white teeth. "There is no need for that, Kira. I will go with you, to help you finish up your business."

For the first time, Kira visibly lost some of her composure. "But I will see Lydia. If Abe is supposed to be my brother, who will I say that you are?"

The goon reached into his jacket, which was hanging over the back of a chair, and extracted a Cuban cigar. "Do you mind? Thank you. Well, I can be your—your boyfriend, just arrived from Moscow. You will call me Misha. I will call you darling. What do you think?"

Kira watched Misha the goon light up his cigar from her ancient stove.

"I think you are going to screw everything up."

§

For the first time since his wedding seven months earlier, Rodney Gold wasn't feeling so lucky. He had waited until Friday evening to tell his wife about Lydia's predicament, and Jenna, whose rosy complexion tended to turn white whenever she felt strong emotion, had become ghostlike with fury.

"How long have you known?"

"Just a couple of days."

"Why were you keeping this a secret?"

"I wasn't . . . I was just so busy at the office—"

"Your sister's not going to live with us!"

"I already told her that."

"And we aren't loaning your parents our savings!"

"Don't be ridiculous. My parents wouldn't consider . . ." Rodney paused. "Well," he said, "we won't have to lend them our whole savings, but certainly, after all the wedding money they set us up with, we can afford—"

"Don't even think it. My folks footed the whole bill for the wedding, Rodney. Yours gave us a bit of a nest egg. Now it's our security, and we're not dipping into it. That money belongs to our future children. That's money for a really good nanny, for medical bills, for schooling up ahead. And what if we have trouble conceiving? We might need to pay out huge sums for fertility treatments."

"But . . ."

The look Jenna had given him from her electric-blue eyes had silenced Rodney. Yet how could he refuse to help his parents? There was something wild and furious about his new bride that seemed strangely alien to Rodney. His parents had argued loudly, but never with the air of barely restrained fury that Jenna communicated. He had long ago thought he would pick a woman who didn't get angry in any intimidating way—like his sister, who was more inclined to tears than to tantrums. But here he was, married to a woman so fiercely unapproachable that he was scared to broach the subject of money ever again.

She hadn't seemed this way when they were dating. Although now that he thought about it, she had always seemed pretty ticked off about Lydia.

It seemed different, somehow, now that the person she was mad at was him.

Rodney walked away from his new wife and locked himself in the bathroom, where he flipped on the air conditioner and lit himself a cigarette.

"Rodney, are you smoking in there? You know I don't allow that in the apartment."

Rodney ignored her and thought about his sister. Trust Lyd to pick a guy who even *looks* like a con man, all gorilla muscles and Mafia smile. But you had to hand it to the man, he sure picked the perfect exit: off a boat, presumed dead, and three million dollars gone with him. Rodney took another drag of his cigarette and wondered if the sex-kitten sister had any idea of what her brother had done with the cash.

Kira.

There was a pounding on the bathroom door. "Rodney, I can smell you smoking in there. Cut it out, do you hear me? Nicotine affects sperm production. I do not want you to smoke."

Rodney put his hands over his ears and concentrated. If Abe was a con man, then his sister was probably in on the deal.

If she was his sister.

If he really was dead.

Rodney slammed the bathroom door open so quickly that it nearly caught Jenna in the face. "I knew it! Smoking! And you just took my face off with that door!"

"Be quiet, Jenna, I need to call my father. I think I have an idea for how we might be able to get the money back."

13

Lydia's first disappointment on Saturday morning was discovering that no one at the little airport would tell her if Abe had taken a flight off the island. She'd suspected that this information was, strictly speaking, classified, but had figured that her situation warranted bending a few rules. Besides, Epiphany wasn't exactly a major tourist destination. Lydia had called yesterday afternoon only to discover that the airport had closed early. She figured she could be forgiven for thinking that the airline workers here would be a bit less formal.

"It is an FAA regulation, ma'am," said the hard-faced woman with the faint mustache at the sides of her mouth and the "Miss Timms" badge on her left breast. "You would have to ask the police to become involved." Clearly, Miss Timms felt Lydia had no intention of calling the police. She gave Lydia a frigid smile that reminded Lydia of her brother's wife. Lydia explained that she had already spoken with the police once and would be only too happy to do so again. Could she use their phone?

The policeman on the other end of the line was so laconic in his responses that Lydia had to fight down the urge to start shouting. Instead, she found herself growing increasingly sarcastic. Abe had disappeared on Wednesday afternoon. Even if his sister had called off the sea search for his body, surely the island force was not so busy that they had completely closed their investigation into Abe's disappearance? There was a grunted response that seemed to suggest that, yes, this was exactly what had occurred. Striving to suppress her irritation, Lydia attempted persuading the bored cop that there just might be a little more for him to do on this case. Was it possible, given the fact that her fiancé seemed to have absconded with a great deal of her parents' money, to check into the airline's passenger roster?

The police officer paused meaningfully and then said he would look into it, and Lydia understood that he thought she was a ridiculous tourist with no concept of the realities of the situation. She thanked the man, slid her handbag over her shoulder as if she had concluded a business meeting, and walked off, trying to ignore Miss Timms's look of smug triumph.

Then Lydia asked the taxi driver if he could take her to a hotel that was a bit off the beaten path. Somewhere tourists wouldn't usually go. Pleased with her own initiative, Lydia hadn't hesitated to walk into the place, despite the rather graphic hand-painted sign in front depicting a screw working its way into a hole.

Lydia's second and more jarring disappointment was discovering that every single person at the Loose Screw Motel and Bar was staring at her as though she'd just landed from Mars.

She'd thrown a light cotton jacket over the terry-cloth sundress before heading off for the airport, but suddenly Lydia found herself feeling extremely undressed and altogether too blonde for the present company. Even though the sun was shining with full midday strength outside, the bar's shady, windowless interior imparted a purposeless, middle-of-the-night quality to the afternoon. The air had a moist, alcoholic smell, and the four drinkers, all of them male and appearing to be in their late forties or older, had turned to look at Lydia with a blank intensity that fell just short of hostile.

"Hello," Lydia said, and then stopped short, not knowing how to politely inquire if there was a white man staying at the hotel.

The man closest to her, who had the heavy look of a weight lifter gone to fat, looked past her with an amphibious expression of disinterest. His hair waved in greasy ribbons down his neck, an oddly old-fashioned, 1950s look set against his dark-umber raw-silk shirt. The scarred man just behind him lit a cigarette that smelled strangely sweet, then grinned, baring a mouth only half-filled with teeth. His hair shot straight out of his head in an electric tangle that was too matted to be an Afro.

Oh, hell, they were smoking marijuana. That wasn't legal to do in bars here, was it?

Lydia cleared her throat. "I'm sorry to intrude," she said, realizing fear was making her sound like Mary Poppins, "but I'm looking for my . . . for a man named Abe. Abe Bohemius. He's, ah, about my height, a little darker than my complexion, very muscular, curly, dark-brown hair?"

All the men looked past her or through her, except for the very thin man in the back of the room, whose eyes were so bloodshot that he seemed hardly able to see out of them. The fourth man's face was half hidden beneath the brim of his hat, a fedora with a black feather. Without moving his head an inch, he stuck out his hand and accepted the joint from his companion, inhaling for what seemed like half a minute before exhaling a plume of aromatic smoke in Lydia's general direction.

Get out of here now, she thought, but then remembered her father's fury, and Liam's indifferent seduction, and decided to try one last time.

"I'm assuming that none of you has seen him? Or think you might have seen him?"

The largest man, the one with the 1950s marcelled waves and

amphibious eyes, let his gaze settle on Lydia. He smiled, slowly. "Maybe," he said, very slowly.

"You think you've seen him?" Lydia forced herself to move closer to the man. "Was he here in the bar? Or staying at the hotel?"

"Maybe," the man said, even more slowly. "If you want, I could buy you a drink."

"Oh, no, that's very nice, but . . ."

The scarred man with the missing teeth and the burn mark over his right cheek smiled encouragingly. "Baron don't talk to nobody that won't drink with us, miss."

"You tell her, Sizzle."

Lydia thought about it. "Listen," she said carefully, "you can make fun of me. I don't care. You don't have any reason to help me, so I can't blame you. But right now a man who said he loved me is probably running off with all my life savings, and that might even be all right, it's my fault, maybe I deserve it. But he's running off with my parents' money, too, and they don't deserve it. So yes, I'll drink with you, but if you're just stringing me along—just don't. Please."

The fat man called Baron turned his full attention on Lydia for the first time. "You all right, baby girl," he said. "You got attitude. You got attitude, but you know how to give respect." To the bartender, who had just appeared, he said, "Hey, Bibi, give this girl a gin fizz. A gin fizz okay with you, baby?"

Lydia said it was, still trying to assimilate the compliment he'd paid her. Was "attitude" confidence? If so, then hers was as fake as her hair color. Still, what did it matter if both left the correct impression?

The bartender, a woman with a massive shelf of a breast, handed Lydia the drink with sublime indifference.

All the men in the bar, and Bibi the bartender, watched Lydia as she took her drink in one hand. Recalling the bar scenes from a dozen old movies, Lydia tried to throw the drink back in one swallow and wound up choking, slamming the glass down as gin ran out of her nose and down her chin.

Baron raised one eyebrow. "You need a napkin? Bibi, give her a napkin."

Lydia took the cloth from the bartender without looking at her and wiped her face. "Thank you," she said when she had caught her breath.

A hand-rolled cigarette appeared under her nose. "Smoke?"

"No, thank you, I only like to cough my guts up once a day."

The scarred man laughed, revealing gold teeth and empty spaces. "I'll get you a drink then. Hey, Bibi, another drink for the lady."

"No, really, I guess I'd better be going now," Lydia said sliding off her stool.

"Don't be insulting old Sizzle. You don't like my face? The ladies don't seem to like my face."

Lydia looked at the man, saw the belligerence and anger behind the banter. "Why do you think that is?"

"Because it's ugly. Because it's ugly as sin."

"Is that how you feel?" Lydia held his gaze, saw it widen. Saw the moment he let in what she was asking.

"Shit. I don't know. I guess it ain't pretty."

The bartender handed Lydia the new drink. Lydia sipped it more cautiously.

"I don't think it's ugly," Lydia said. "I think it looks like it must have hurt."

Sizzle looked surprised. "Hell, it was that long ago, I barely remember."

Baron leaned forward, his heavy arms spreading against the

counter. "Sizzle got burned in a tent when he was just five. Plastic melted on him."

"Oh, God." Lydia reached out a hand to the man, stopped, then took a deep breath. "I don't know what to say."

Baron smiled. "Seems to me you said plenty. What do you think, Sizzle?"

"I think she's all right, man. She can't drink worth a damn, and she don't smoke, but I think she's all right."

Lydia thought this was the moment to quit while she was ahead. She put down her half-empty glass and took her purse off the bar. "Thanks for the drink, guys."

"Now hold on a moment." Baron slid Lydia a bowl of nuts and cocked his head to one side. "I'm thinkin' you might be kosher here. But before I go telling you something, you got to tell me something." Baron leaned forward. "You dig jazz?"

"Excuse me? Jazz? No, I'm sorry, I don't."

The man's brows came together. "No jazz at all? Louis Armstrong? Duke Ellington?"

"Oh, well, yes. Big band is nice. Does that count? Stuff you can jitterbug to, I like."

"You mean you can jitterbug, girl?"

Lydia smiled, feeling more comfortable. "A little, maybe."

"A little, huh." Baron considered this. "So what's your favorite tune? Not this year's favorite, mind, but your all-time favorite."

Lydia thought about it. "My favorite song? Fast or slow?"

Baron's heavy-lidded gaze widened fractionally with interest. "Say slow."

"Slow, slow—oh, God, probably that old Roxy Music song, 'Avalon,' you know." Lydia hummed it.

"That's jazz."

"No it's not."

"I say it is, and I should know. What's so great about that song, girl?"

Lydia tried to put it into words. "It's just—it feels—" She took a deep breath. This was a test. She knew nothing about music, so she felt fairly sure she was going to fail. "Because, it's . . . well, it's . . ."

"Yes?"

Lydia realized that at some point during this exchange, the man with the bloodshot eyes and his fedora-wearing companion had sidled closer. Bibi the bartender refilled Lydia's glass and Lydia drank it, even though the gin tasted like something she'd use to clean the sink. "Because," she said in a firm voice, "it's the saddest, sexiest song to have nothing to do with sex ever written."

Baron began laughing, a big, liquid, heavy-smoker's chortle, and his friends joined in. "All right, baby girl, all right. Maybe we can do business here. I'm not saying for sure, mind, but maybe we can do some business here. Hey, Redeye," he called out to the man with the bloodshot eyes, "get out your ax. Chicky, you help Sizzle here with his gear."

Lydia forced a smile and wondered what the hell she'd gotten herself into.

§

Before Liam and Fish had even set foot in the dimly lit and smoke-filled interior of the Loose Screw's bar, they commented on the fact that the boys in the band were playing, even though carnival was still two days away.

"And it's your tune, son," said Fish, whistling.

" 'You and me and the bottle makes three tonight,' " sang Liam as he shouldered his way through the swinging doors.

"Hoy, Capitán," shouted Baron, who was one of the few men on the island who disliked Martin as much as Liam did. Something about a disagreement over a noise ordinance, dating back to the early seventies.

The second thing Liam noticed was what must have put Baron in his good mood: a shapely blonde, expertly jitterbugging along with Chicky, stepping in and out of his arms without missing a step. Chicky paid his partner the compliment of tossing his hat onto the bar. Usually the twenty-year-old liked to keep his lid on, as he believed it helped him blend in better with the older men, who had played Harlem back when Harlem was the place to be.

It was only when Chicky flipped his partner up into a virtual handstand, revealing a pair of familiar white bikini underpants, that Liam's eyes adjusted to the gloom and he realized Miss Lindy Hop's true identity.

Liam leaned over the bar and asked Bibi for a Guinness and a Jack Daniel's. He nodded to Baron, who was doing a mean Richie Havens imitation into the bar's ancient standing microphone, while Redeye's fingers licked up and down the strings of his guitar. Chicky's synthesizer was half hidden behind Sizzle's vast steel-drum set. Liam found himself wondering whether he could get Chicky's hands off Lydia's waist and back onto the keyboard.

"That your blonde?" Fish gestured with his shot glass. Liam nodded.

"She's sure made an impression on Baron and the boys," offered Bibi, coming up from behind the bar to take a cigarette from the pack Fish offered. "Maybe she can do a little number with them for carnival."

"I don't think so," said Liam. "Her boyfriend's just disappeared at sea and I think she's supposed to be leaving tomorrow night."

"She was asking Baron about some guy. Seems she thought he might've washed up here."

"Did he?"

Bibi shrugged. "Lord only knows what goes on upstairs. For all I know, we could have a corpse or two up there."

"Remind me to do my drinking elsewhere."

"Hey, look at that." Fish gestured at the dance floor. "I haven't seen that in years. Right through his legs and up the other side."

Liam raised his beer in salute. But the truth was, there was something a little troublesome about watching Lydia getting tangled up with Chicky. "Hey, Baron," he called, "got something a little less ancient? How about a little New Wave eighties something?" That was sure to require the synthesizer, Liam thought.

Lydia, hearing his voice, turned and stared.

Chicky greeted Liam with a wave. "You want some Yaz, Captain? How about 'Only You'?"

"That'd do fine." Liam walked up, still carrying his beer, to where Lydia was standing, fists clenched, just staring at him. She didn't seem to notice when Chicky took his place with the rest of the band.

"What the hell are you doing here, Captain?" Lydia made the title sound vaguely insulting, like something you might call a particularly obnoxious drunk. Liam decided to ignore this.

"Having a drink. Checking out the other side of the island, like I suggested before."

"I thought you were too hungover."

Liam took a last swallow of his beer and rested his glass on a counter. The truth was, his joints still ached and his back felt stiff. Still, he wasn't about to let her know that. "I'm all right. I checked the airport first. Your man Abe hasn't taken any flights."

In the background, the boys launched into the plaintive rhythms of an early eighties song. Baron allowed the hint of a throb to enter his surprisingly mellow tenor. He sang with an older man's subdued fervor about a younger woman's yearning for a touch behind closed doors. Liam held out his arms.

Lydia walked into his formal embrace and allowed Liam to move her slowly around the room. The only sign of her resistance was in the set of her jaw. "I checked the airport, too. They said they could talk only to the police."

Liam spun her into closer contact. "Yeah, well, they told me. I used to be a cop, remember?" He danced her out of a small knot of people, into an empty corner.

"You move well," she offered. He watched her cheeks warm up.

"Yeah, well, not like you. That thing you did with Chicky, that was really something."

"I took some lessons, but to do it right, I think I'd need a little more leg and a lot less chest. I'm not exactly built like a dancer. Now tell me what you think it means, about Abe. Do you think he really did drown?"

There were other voices in the bar, the early evening crowd filling the empty stools and chairs. Liam kept his eyes on Lydia's. "You really sell yourself short, don't you? The way you just said that— 'I'm not built like a dancer.' Don't you like the way you look?"

Lydia ducked her head, letting her hair fall into her eyes. "I look better now than I ever did before. I guess I like it."

Liam smiled. "Good," he said, waiting for her to meet his gaze again. "Because I do."

The music swirled and Liam turned Lydia again, bringing her into him and brushing her full, terry-cloth-covered breasts against the white cotton of his shirt.

"This is silly," Lydia said. "What does this have to do with finding Abe?"

"I'm not the one who started the dancing, am I?" Liam's breath stirred the hair on Lydia's brow.

"I was trying to gain Baron's confidence. Find out if anyone had seen Abe."

"Mmm." Liam breathed in the fragrance of her right where her ear met her neck. Lydia's arms tightened reflexively at his shoulder and waist.

"Oh, God, what are you doing to me?" The moment the words were out, Lydia regretted them.

"I'm not sure," Liam said. He pulled back, still holding her in his arms, his eyes scanning her face. "The fox-trot?"

Lydia snorted with laughter and they resumed dancing. The bar was now packed with appreciative customers, drawn by the unexpected attraction of the band's free gig.

"How do you know how to fox-trot?"

"My grandmother made me go to lessons."

"I find this hard to imagine. How old were you?"

"Fifteen. Sixteen."

Lydia leaned back so she could see Liam's expression. "Sixteen? And you went?"

Liam kept his face turned away. "I owed her a lot. She took me in after I got into some trouble, and besides, I suppose I hoped I'd meet some girls there. I was pretty cadaverous looking."

"Oh." Lydia pressed her face into Liam's chest. It was surrender. Liam had held too many women in his arms to mistake the moment. Although no other woman had yielded to the idea of him, gangly and uncoordinated, shepherding giggling teenage girls around a dance floor. Christ, he had been unpopular. So tall the girls could see just what any inadvertent contact could do to an adolescent male.

Liam leaned his head into hers, spoke into her hair. "I would have given my eyeteeth then to have known that twenty years later, the lessons would pay off." She gave a little shiver, and then tried to hide it.

"So, ah, what do we do next?" The tone of her voice sounded so studiously matter-of-fact that Liam wanted to laugh, or squeeze the delicious indent of her waist. What he did instead was ruin everything. Later on, Liam could never quite figure out why he'd answered her the way he had. Was he mocking himself for his surprisingly powerful attraction to this woman whom he'd dismissed just a day earlier as a sweet, brown-eyed spaniel? Was he trying to seduce her with shock tactics, a ploy that, he knew, worked on some women, but only on the brash, take-no-prisoners kind?

Or perhaps he was just trying to scare her away from him before she had a chance to finish whatever she'd started thawing back there in his bedroom. Before she had a chance to work her way into his heart.

In any event, he couldn't have picked a better way to piss her off.

"What do we do next?" he repeated, in a considering tone of voice. "I don't know. Screw each other's brains out?" Liam knew instantly that he had made a major mistake. He watched her expression slam into some invisible door. She looked like she'd just been punched. By him. "Sorry," he whispered. "Bad joke."

"You're the bad joke." And then she was shouldering her way through the throng and away from him. As she passed the stage, Liam saw Baron put down his microphone and lean over to whisper something in her ear. Lydia nodded, head down, and Baron shot him a look of undisguised contempt.

Then she was gone, out the door so fast Liam couldn't break through the crowd to follow her.

Just inebriated enough to do it, Liam shouted her name, then shouted it again, loud enough to be heard over the music and din in the bar. Loud enough to be heard in the rooms upstairs.

She didn't look back.

14

Tired, hungry, and disheartened by Liam's unflattering assessment of her morals, Lydia rode back to the resort wishing she'd never gone into the Loose Screw. She hadn't learned anything, and, worse, she had the vague feeling that she'd made herself look ridiculous, not only to Liam but also to the men in the band. She probably looked like a cheap blonde, or worse, like a cheap *dyed* blonde. Like a bad fairy, the sun had turned her gold to straw.

Stopping back at the main house to see about a late dinner, Lydia discovered that the kitchen had closed. Half-relieved to avoid another helping of the watery fish stew that seemed to be the chef's mainstay, Lydia thought about heading back into town and looking for a restaurant, only to realize that she'd left her pocketbook somewhere. A cab, perhaps, or the bar. She had no idea who to call. At least her passport and travelers' checks were safe in her room.

Lydia walked through the empty lobby to the small store that sold shell-encrusted souvenirs, T-shirts, and very expensive aspirin. Relieved to find the shop still open, she chose two snack bags of salt-and-vinegar potato chips and a protein-rich candy bar before catching sight of herself in a mirror. Her hair was worse than she'd anticipated. If I go back like this to New York and start looking for a new job, Lydia thought, they'll ask me where I studied color, at the local mortician's college?

She paused to look over the store's limited selection of hair dye, and even though she knew intellectually that the color of the model's hair on the package bore no resemblance to what she would get on her own head, Lydia found herself deliberating. Little-girl blonde again, or something more drama queen, or perhaps the look of a dominant blonde who wielded ice-pick authority even when her underwear was showing? Lydia selected medium-ash blonde and charged it to her room.

§

An hour later, Lydia was sitting naked on a towel in the bathroom, her hair stinking of chemicals and tucked up under a plastic bag, when she heard a kind of rustling thump from the other room, or maybe just outside the other room. The walls here were pretty thin. At first, Lydia thought it was an animal, then, wrapping the towel around herself, she realized it might be a human intruder. The towel was too small to reach all the way around; Lydia had figured she'd just stay undressed to avoid staining any of her clothes.

"Who's there?"

No answer. Lydia glanced around for a weapon, and found a can of hair spray. Which meant she had only one hand to hold the towel closed.

There was another thump, this time clearly from inside the room. Lydia realized she'd left the lights off; maybe the intruder thought she was still out somewhere.

Except she'd said, "Who's there?" so now the intruder would know he'd made a mistake, she was in her room after all.

Heart pounding, Lydia crouched near the door. Either the intruder would go now, or else he'd open the bathroom door. If he opened the door, she'd spray his eyes. His eyes! Lydia flicked off the bathroom light so he wouldn't squint at the transition from dark to light. Hey, she thought, I'm good at this.

The bathroom door opened. Someone said, "Lydia?," and she squeezed the nozzle on the can and sprayed a steady stream of hair spray straight into Liam's chest.

"Are you out of your mind?" In the dark, Liam grabbed her wrists and held them together. Her towel slipped.

"Oh, please, my towel—"

"Christ, woman, you nearly blinded me! A few inches higher, and—What the hell are you doing in here!"

"My hair—I heard some thumps . . ." Mortified, Lydia hoped he wouldn't turn on the light. "Please let me get my towel back!"

Lydia knew the precise moment Liam realized her predicament. His hands, even his breathing, seemed to still. She could make out his face but not his eyes. Then he sniffed. "What's that on your head?"

"My hair—I was just—what the hell are *you* doing here? Let go of my wrists!"

Liam released her wrists. "I came back because you forgot your handbag at the bar. I heard a noise outside and wanted to make sure everything was all right." And he wanted to apologize. But Liam couldn't quite bring himself to say the words.

Lydia wrapped herself in the towel and checked her watch: Damn, she had four minutes left before she had to rinse out her hair dye. Then she realized what he'd said. "So there was an intruder? Other than you?"

"I didn't see anyone. It might have just been an animal." Liam sniffed again. "What is that godawful smell?"

Lydia flushed. "Hair dye. Please, could you go now?"

"You're dying your hair?"

"I'm a hairdresser."

Their eyes having adjusted to the gloom, they just looked at each other, a weighted silence growing between them. Liam became aware of her nakedness; only the chemical odor of dye stood between them.

"You said you were a social worker. I remember."

"Well, I'm a hairdresser now. And I need to wash the dye off."

"I'll wait in the other room."

Lydia rinsed her hair clean. In the artificial light, it appeared darker than she'd anticipated. She left it wet. "Hey," she called to Liam, "could you pass me some clothes?"

There was a moment when Lydia, pained, realized he was going through her suitcase. "Here," he said, wedging the door open. handing through her stained terry-cloth dress.

"Something *clean*," she objected. "And a bra." She didn't want him to see her without a brassiere; what if she looked dumpy, saggy, frumpy?

Not that it mattered, really.

"How's this?" Liam's hand was held palm up, offering a black sports bra and a strappy blue sundress that required a much thinner strap underneath. Lydia sighed and got dressed.

"So, ah, can you hear me in there?"

Lydia said she could.

"What did Baron say to you, back in the bar?"

"Well, for one thing, he suggested I find Thomas and ask *him* a few questions. Abe went diving with him a few days ago." Lydia opened the bathroom door. "I probably should have thought of him right away."

"Yeah, well, you may not get much out of Thomas. He's one to keep his own counsel." Liam stood up. He had been sitting on the edge of her bed. He had turned on only one bedside lamp. The rest of the room remained in shadow. "You look different. Your hair—is it going to stay that dark?"

"No. It's still wet now." Lydia touched her head, unable to tell Liam's thoughts from his expression.

They stood about a foot from each other, next to the bed. Lydia realized Liam knew she wasn't wearing any underwear. He hadn't given her any.

She looked at his eyes and realized he knew that she knew that he knew. Too much knowledge.

Don't do this, she told herself. Have more respect for yourself. Remember the bar. He thinks you're a slut. If you do this, you *are* a slut. Fight it. Prove him wrong.

Liam reached out a hand, stopped just short of touching her. Said, "Lydia." His voice was hoarse.

"I think you need to go now."

She watched him catch his breath, exhale through closed teeth. Still they stood, a foot apart. Her hands began to shake with not touching him. Why? Why was this feeling so intense?

"What if there was an intruder?"

"I don't think there was, Liam."

"But what if?"

"You mean, what if it's Abe? He's got what he wants. Why would he come back?"

Liam took her left hand in his much larger one, examining its short, unvarnished nails. Her ring finger was bare. "Maybe he wants his ring. Where is it, by the way?"

Lydia looked down at her hand, still held in his. "I took it off in the bathroom when I was doing my hair, though I probably didn't need to bother. Given everything that's happened, it's probably a fake."

Liam's thumb moved over her palm in a brief caress. "Or else it wasn't ever meant for you."

The feeling of having been fooled and cheated hit Lydia all over again. The sense that she was to blame for not having seen through his deception.

She was pulled into the padded muscle of Liam's chest. Her cheek was resting over his left, stitched pocket; if she listened hard enough, she thought she would hear his heart. "I'm sorry—shit, Lydia, he isn't worth it. We don't even know if it's true."

Lydia realized she was crying. She raised her head. "It is true. He took the money."

"Ah, well, look at the bright side—he really might be dead."

Despite herself, Lydia laughed, then cried harder. "What a terrible thing to say. And I'm laughing."

"You do what you like. You feel betrayed."

"You say that like you've been there yourself. Somehow I can't imagine anyone conning you like this." She tried to move out of his embrace, but he increased the pressure of his fingertips on her lower back and she remained.

"I wasn't conned. Well, I suppose I might have conned myself. When my dad—after my father left, my mother was never around. I suppose she thought she was doing enough just to be sticking around with her hooligan kid." Liam paused, continuing to trace steady patterns of comfort through the thin cotton of her dress.

"You didn't feel she loved you?"

"Nah, I was arrogant, wasn't I? I thought, I'm the most important thing in her life even if she doesn't act like some conventional mom, baking cookies all day and asking, 'How was your day, dear?' And one day I learned she was still talking to my dad, still seeing him, and not telling me. And I—shit, what am I going on about, this has nothing to do with you." Liam looked down at her, his face astonished, his

hands falling away from her as if he'd just been caught in the com-
mission of a crime.

"Maybe it has something to do with you."

Lydia reached up to touch the hard sides of his jaw, feeling his
momentary hesitation before his hands came around to hold her again.
His fingertips, callused and roughened from outdoor work, were
pressed against her shoulders where her sundress left them bare.

They looked at each other for a long, naked moment, her hands
still framing his face. Liam swallowed once, hard, and then leaned
closer, his clear, gray gaze never wavering from hers. At the last
moment, as his mouth covered hers, Lydia felt the slight hitch of his
breath, and then he cupped his hands over the back of her head and
kissed her with such fierce tenderness that she felt she had broached
some defense in him. And in herself.

Tearing open the front of his shirt, ripping buttons, Lydia ran her
hands over the flat planes of his almost hairless chest, gasping as
Liam bent forward to graze the column of her neck with his teeth,
his lean hips pressing the hard ridge of his arousal against her. If his
arm had not been around her waist, she would have fallen; she
wanted to fall, to slide to the ground and have him on top of her.

Panting, his heart racing, Liam lifted his head. There was something stunned and searching in his face, and then he blew a little huff
of air, straightened a little. His eyes went flat.

"I guess we should slow down before one of us winds up with
skinned knees." His voice was laced with brogue and laughter as he
moved her toward the bed. "If I'd known a bit of classic Irish family
drama was the way to get to you, I would've started back in the old
country, with the time I was seven and couldn't find any food in the
house. Then I could move on to the time my parents vanished
overnight—"

The anger came from out of nowhere. It roiled up inside her at the thought that Liam was using his own childhood pain as part of a canned seduction routine, but it was more than that. It was the insult of all the casual affairs that she'd thought might lead to something more, the awareness that she had held herself too cheap, thinking of herself as a romantic, as open to love, while all the men she'd ever given a chance must have thought something else entirely.

And somehow Liam's embrace was the worst, as it promised more than any of the others.

"What's the matter, Lydia?" Liam leaned forward, pressing his words into her neck like kisses. "Don't you want to hear the pathetic story of my childhoo—"

Lydia shoved Liam away and slapped his cheek so hard his head rocked back. For a long moment, he just looked at her with an inscrutable expression of anger and distance and almost contempt. His hand came up to cradle his cheek, where a white handprint began to turn scarlet.

"Mind if I ask what that was for?" His voice was perfectly even. His eyes glowed with anger.

Lydia's voice was wet with tears. "For not listening when I said no."

"Are you implying I was trying to force you?" Liam laughed harshly. "You didn't exactly need forcing."

"No, you don't force. That's not what you do with your anger. You turn it into seduction."

"That's the most fucked-up thing I ever—I'll have you know I haven't slept with anyone in six months. Not that it's any of your business." Liam grabbed the jacket that he had flung over a chair.

"But how many before that? What about Sheila—wasn't that her name? The woman who killed herself?" The words were out, unplanned, as quick as a second slap. Liam's face drained of color.

"You complete and utter bitch." He didn't slam the door behind him. He pulled it shut, almost gently.

It was only after Lydia went back into the bathroom that she realized just how stupid she'd been to chase him away.

Because the window she'd left open to allow the night breeze to drive away the fumes of the hair dye was raised even higher than she'd left it, and the ring she'd left sitting on the soap dish was conspicuously gone.

Heart pounding, Lydia looked out the window and tried to make out the shadow of her thief, but if he was there he had been swallowed up by all the other shadows. There was no sound but the pretty trills and hoarse shrieks of the island's birds, and there was no one to turn to but herself.

15

An hour later, navigating his way past the northern side of the island in Martin's favorite sailboat, Liam stopped moving for long enough to light himself a cigarette. He was a competent, but not impassioned, sailor, and half-envied men like Martin their love affair with sailing craft.

Liam liked the idea of loving boats: Hemingway had, and Bogart, too. But in reality, he viewed boats as equipment, not as metaphors. He had no great longing to possess one, although he did experience a brief flush of excitement at borrowing Martin's without express permission.

Still, it was lovely to be out at sea without the distraction of motors. There was a clean, economical beauty about sailing. A masculine beauty, to Liam's way of thinking. He breathed in a lungfull of still, starry darkness, thinking that it was the kind of night that was now only possible on a small island, where city lights did not compete with the brilliance of the constellations. Liam recalled watching Carl Sagan on television saying we are the stuff that stars are made of. What were the minerals in blood? Liam wondered. Iron, magnesium? He'd been about fourteen when he'd seen that program; he remembered because it was just before everything went to hell in his life.

Suddenly, Liam felt a premonition that he was saying good-bye to something. He felt that in the years to come, he would look back on this night and think, That was just about the end of that phase of my life. Liam shivered, moved with a kind of nostalgia for things he hadn't yet left behind.

As the waves slapped against the boat's hull, Liam hunkered down so that he could rest his head on its side. He hoped Martin wouldn't mind his borrowing *Blue Boy*; Liam had just been in the mood for fiddling with sails, for being taken somewhere by the wind and current. Forces of nature, Liam thought, I'm surrendering myself.

Exhaling a plume of smoke, Liam brought his thoughts back to Lydia. She was right in one respect, of course—he seduced. It was intentional, but intentional on some subliminal level, if such a thing were possible. Deepen the brogue, slow the speech, hold the gaze, move in. It was second nature to him. It was how he'd made his way through all those career women last year. And the year before that. They flirted, he flirted, he played Irish sailor to their urban princesses. He made love to who they wanted to be; they made love to who they wanted him to be.

Except for Sheila, poor, walking-wounded Sheila, whom he'd realized was too fragile for such games. So he'd chosen to angle for another, hardier fish, and had joked with Sheila that he was afraid that with her, he'd get in over his head, he wasn't ready to fall in love. Ego-saving tripe like that.

And then she'd gone and drowned herself.

Could it really have been a kind of anger, he wondered now, that had made him go after all those dozens of women? He never got angry. Well, he never allowed himself to blow his top, that wasn't quite the same thing. Trying not to turn into his father, turning into a different type of monster instead.

And yet, if it was anger, then anger at what? At whom? Anger at those women, for their self-involved games of island love? Anger at himself, for playing along? Or could it just be pent-up anger, anger that had accumulated in his system over the years, finding an outlet where it could, like steam hissing through random vents?

Liam stubbed his cigarette out under his moccasin and bent his head. He was tired of himself. He wanted a divorce from himself. The big lover who hardly even felt desire anymore.

Except for Lydia. Whom he hadn't really bothered to seduce. Who hadn't flirted with him. His clever, resourceful, brown-eyed girl, brave and unflinching and rather more than she seemed, when you looked beyond the beach-girl hair and curves and voice. He supposed he must've sounded a right smug bastard, going on about how useful his miserable childhood could be at getting her into bed. He'd just been so embarrassed about inadvertently spilling his guts, so he'd tried to make a joke of it. It's what he'd always done with Altagracia, and although his ex had finally gotten disgusted with what she termed his "inappropriate sense of humor," she hadn't whacked him in the head to drive the point home. She'd just left him, rather coolly, saying she didn't have time to wait for Peter Pan to grow up.

In retrospect, he rather liked the idea that Lydia had cared enough to get that mad.

She'd dyed her hair the color of a second cup of tea. It had made her look younger somehow. Sharper, too, as if a camera had suddenly come into focus. A hairdresser, she'd said. He supposed she'd dropped out of social-work school. That seemed a shame. Hairdressers were meant to be good at listening, but she also seemed able to hear what he *didn't* say.

For some reason, Liam found himself imagining her as a nurse, her hands on his head, stroking his hair, taking care of him. A little embarrassed by himself, Liam lit another cigarette. Ah, what the hell, who would know? She wasn't staying on island long enough for him to taste the real thing. He granted his thoughts permission to turn prurient: the little blue dress, her fingers trailing down his chest, over his abdomen, between his thighs.

Curling up on the hard deck, Liam watched the moon's progress across the sky, smoking cigarette after cigarette, deliberately not touching himself, savoring the hunger even though it would not be satisfied.

It had been a long time since he'd felt an arousal deeper than physical—a hunger for some joining of more than mere flesh.

16

Kira had taken extra care with her eye makeup, hoping to create the effect of maximum innocence. Liner only halfway across the eyelid, so the eyes seemed very wide set and disingenuous, a drop of translucent white eye shadow near the inside corner where it would catch the light and glisten like a tear.

She might as well have drawn on whiskers and a black nose for all the difference it made. Misha sat next to her in the plane, his heavy body folded into the seat, his pale eyes observing everything but reflecting no curiosity. He seemed devoid of romance. Presumably, he was capable of sex and desire, but Kira had the impression that if she offered herself, he would partake of her as if she were a sandwich, and proceed to shoot her afterward if necessary.

"Stop looking at me as if you are about to say something and then turning away. It makes you appear frightened of me." Misha continued studying the duty-free catalog. "If you appear frightened of me, it will attract attention."

"I was just wondering what to do first—contact Abe, or contact Lydia."

Misha put down his magazine and fastened his emotionless blue gaze on her. "Are you asking my advice? I am just here to observe—it's all the same to me whether you go to your boyfriend first or not. As long as you get what you came for, and return to give Pyotr his share."

"If that's the case, then why don't I go to see Abe while you stake out the airport?"

Misha turned away, and for a moment Kira thought, Why, he's jealous. Then he turned back and she felt a surge of cold fear sweep through her stomach. "If you go to see Abe, of course I will go with you. There will be no chance to whisper even one word of information that I do not hear, do you understand? And if you think your pretty face will save you if I catch you cheating, think again. At the age of seventeen, my mother was worried I was running with a bad crowd. She tried to call the police to do something about Pyotr."

Kira looked steadily at Pyotr's goon, and then realized he was more than just a goon. This was a man who had proved his loyalty. He was someone Pyotr trusted enough to send out with an attractive young woman in pursuit of an object of considerable value.

She pretty much knew what Misha was going to say before the words left his mouth.

"My mother doesn't leave her house much anymore." With that, Misha settled back into his chair and summoned the attendant to sell him some cologne and some brandy.

§

Ten rows back, on the other side of the plane, Rodney Gold and his father sat side by side, both dressed in pin-striped, button-down shirts and khaki slacks. A copy of the New York Times was folded, unread, under Rodney's hands. His father's Business Week magazine was tucked into the pocket behind the meal tray.

"I mean, just how do you get to the age of thirty-one and not gain even a hint of common sense?" Victor Gold raked a hand through his short, gray-streaked curls. Half-hidden in the older man's heavily jowled and shadowed face was the ghost of a resemblance to his lean and pleasant-featured son.

"To give her credit, Dad, we didn't know Abe was up to anything. I mean, you were doing business with his sister. Mom was hoping he'd propose soon. It all seemed pretty kosher."

Victor flushed with anger. "There's trust and there's stupid carelessness. You don't go rushing in and signing over blank checks to anyone unless *they are* family. And it's part of a syndrome, anyhow. Taking all those ridiculous poetry classes in college, then not having the least idea how to make a living afterward. Would she listen when I said Yeats, Keats, and Dickinson may be nice, but they're not going to give you a job?"

"She didn't want to go to law school, Dad."

"She didn't know what she wanted. You, you listened. Lydia had to have it her way. 'I'll study hairdressing, Dad, that's a career.' Not for my daughter, after all I spent on private schools and Wesleyland!"

"Wesleyan, Dad."

"It was four years of Disneyland."

Rodney noticed that the drinks cart, which had been serving the passengers sitting closer to business class, had mysteriously disappeared. Could he order a drink this early? You had alcoholic drinks with brunches, he reasoned—mimosas with omelets, Bloody Marys with bagels and lox. A drink would make traveling with his father so much more bearable. Why was it that Lydia broke the rules and he got the lectures?

"And then it was social-work school. 'Now I know what I want, Daddy, I want to help people.' 'First help yourself,' I say. So what does she do? Takes two years off work while I support her and pay for graduate school, and then quits right before graduation!"

Rodney, who had known about this when it was happening and had heard it recited many times since, viewed this narrative as the

Golds' special Passover ritual. As they approached the holiday when most Jews recited the story of the ancient Israelites' exodus from Egypt, Victor Gold recited the story of Lydia's exodus from the Wurzweiler School of Social Work. To anyone.

The flight attendant, a redhead in her early fifties, walked by wheeling a cart. She offered them a tray with a small packet of cheese sandwiches, a sad little apple, and a Hostess Twinkie.

Victor Gold stopped her with a hand on her arm. "You call that lunch?"

"It's a snack, sir."

"But we're not getting to Epiphany until twelve o'clock. Why aren't we being served a lunch?"

"I'm sorry, this flight carries only a snack." The attendant tried to move past him with her cart. Rodney wondered when the drinks would be wheeling by.

"Now listen, ma'am," said Victor Gold, "I understand the airlines are cutting costs now, but really, to offer no more than a snack on a noontime flight . . ."

The flight attendant did not blink an eye. "You may write a letter to the airline, sir, but you really must let me pass."

Why didn't they serve drinks first, then food, like they used to? Rodney wondered, glancing at his watch. He didn't want to sound like his father, but the airline industry really was going to hell. Half past eleven. What was Jenna doing now? Packing her bags to go spend the weekend with her parents on Long Island? Calling up some old Princeton boyfriend and inviting him out to dinner? When he'd left for the airport this morning, she'd turned her face away before his lips could meet hers.

Was there a way to ask his father if he'd ever felt a moment's panic that he might have chosen the wrong life? Victor Gold had always stressed the importance of follow-through: You start a thing, you finish it. When Rodney had entered law school, his father had said, "Just remember, dropping out is not an option; if you do, you'll flip burgers for the rest of your life to repay me."When he'd told his father he was going to propose to Jenna, Victor Gold had said, "Just remember that if it's a mistake, it'll cost you for the rest of your life, and I'm not talking pennies."

Outside the tiny, double-glassed window, the clouds looked like floating islands. Rodney wished for a moment that he was going out to comfort his sister, or to run away from home with her the way they'd planned when they were kids.

Victor Gold slid his tray down as the flight attendant approached with her cart. "So let's go over what we're going to do again. We get there, we go to the police station, we find out whether Abe's been declared dead yet."

Rodney accepted a tray and repeated his request for vodka. "In the States, the police would keep searching for at least three, four days. But this is a small island. The way I figure it, worst-case scenario, Kira's called in, said her brother's dead, they've called off the search and Abe's taken a flight under a different name, probably to Miami."

Rodney watched his father unwrap his cheese sandwich as if he expected a snake to slide out of it. "That's pretty worst case. But if we go directly to the police and explain things, we can probably get some cooperation from the Miami police."

"And there's always a chance that Abe could still be hiding out on the island, Dad."

"What makes you think that?"

"People launder money in the Caribbean. People have rollover checking accounts that deposit their money there overnight. Maybe this is all part of some huge scam. Maybe you and Mom were just the tip of the iceberg." Rodney saw the flight attendant loping swiftly down the aisle and tried, unsuccessfully, to catch her eye. "Maybe Abe's some sort of modern-day pirate king."

"You're out of your mind."

"Dad, you are just always so sure of yourself, aren't you? Well, this time, you might want to listen to me. Because I'm not the one with the three million dollars missing, and this time I'm not the one who made the stupid mistake." Hardly believing that he'd just talked to his father that way, Rodney averted his gaze and stared at his tray.

"Pirate king. This is about Jenna, isn't it? You're off here looking for some kind of adventure to escape your marriage, aren't you? Well, don't tell me about it. If another one of my children is in some kind of trouble, I just don't want to know it."

Rodney turned to the window and refused to speak to his father until after they'd landed.

§

Things were beginning to look up. Biting into the fried-egg sandwich he'd ordered from downstairs, Abe admired the brilliant blue diamond, back where it belonged—in the palm of his hand. He'd had a nervous moment there, thinking that hard-ass captain was going to catch him snooping around Lydia's cabin, but then Mister Faith and Begorrah had gotten all hot and heavy with Lydia, and he'd spotted the ring where he never would have imagined he'd see it, on the bathroom counter, out in plain sight.

Clearly, God was smiling on him today.

The only problem now was whoever was in the room when he'd spoken with Kira. He knew her too well to mistake that note in her voice—one of Pyotr's men had been watching her, threatening her, even. It didn't take a rocket scientist to figure out that she probably wouldn't be arriving in Epiphany by herself.

Running a hand over the unfamiliar smoothness of his head, Abe considered his options. Option one was to hand over the ring to the heavy, and never see a cent of the money again. Pyotr would give him some inflated claim for what Kira owed, and some deflated claim for what the stone was worth, and Abe would have to grin and take it or be shot like a dog.

Option two had him hiding the ring here in the room and claiming to the thug that Lydia still had it. That would send the heavy out looking for Lydia, though, and it wouldn't take him long to discover she'd lost it sometime Saturday night.

Abe grabbed a Styrofoam cup of brackish, lukewarm liquid that bore only a faint resemblance to coffee, sipped it, winced, and then put it down. Outside his window, storm clouds were beginning to gather. Pretty soon it would be pouring down rain. At least the divers would be happy—it doesn't rain underwater.

Watching the palm trees begin to sway in the wind, Abe got an idea. Pulling open the plastic bag he'd been using as a suitcase, Abe extracted his face mask and snorkel. The vest and regulator he'd worn for his last dive were hanging in the tiny closet, and the remaining air tank was propped up on the floor. How many psi had the gauge read when he'd finished the dive? He was pretty sure that he'd come out of the water with half a tank.

Abe removed his compass from the desk drawer and studied it, looking out the window again, trying to judge the distance. If he swam to the wreck site from this side of the island, it wasn't really very far, a quarter of a mile, maybe less. He could put the ring in his small dive bag and secure it in a hole in the engine room in under fifteen minutes, but could he get back here before Kira and her guard arrived?

In the sky, a large black bird began to circle the dock, and Abe made his decision.

17

For a moment, Thomas considered advising the woman against it one last time. After all, she was hardly an experienced diver, and Martin and his crew had been out searching for more than thirty-six hours. What did she hope to accomplish?

"Just take me where you took him," she'd said in her soft, deliberate voice, looking right in his eyes. And for a crazy minute, Thomas had felt this compulsion to do just that—gun the boat's motor, head 'round to the northern side of the island, tie off in back of the Loose Screw Motel and Bar. Baron and Chicky wouldn't blame him. The boys had been giving him dirty looks ever since they'd discovered the lady knew four variations of the lindy hop and two of the West Coast swing.

Still, a man took that much trouble to die, you knew you were letting yourself in for trouble if you brought him back to life. So Thomas kept his mouth shut.

The woman turned to him, the wind blowing her hair over her face. The sky was a low, gray blanket of clouds, and each gust seemed to fling more moisture back at them.

"Is it okay to dive in the rain?"

"Yeah, the only hard part is getting out when the sea gets choppy. But this is going to blow over soon. We'll be fine."

The wind tangled her hair again. She pushed it away from her eyes, a gesture that reminded Thomas of things models did in photographs. "Your hair looks nice," he said.

His passenger looked at him distractedly, as if she couldn't quite understand what he was saying. "Is this the first place you took Abe?"

Thomas nodded yes, then watched her turn her gaze to the horizon.

"Did he seem happy to you? Excited? Or was he nervous? Did he strike you as someone with a lot on his mind?"

Thomas swallowed and realized for the first time that not telling the whole truth meant committing himself to a series of small lies. It wasn't easy to lie to a woman when she had that look in her eyes, as if she already knew what you weren't telling. Maybe, Thomas allowed, he should have taken Baron's advice and refused to take her out at all.

But he'd already borrowed Sizzle's boat and they were already out on the water, so what good would it do to talk her out of it now? Besides, the sun was sparkling on the waves and there was cold soda in the cooler, courtesy of the blond woman's American dollars. What the hell, Thomas figured, nobody could get hurt on that wreck, it was so shallow an experienced diver could explore it with just a mask and a snorkel.

Besides, she was right. Everyone had been so busy checking out the deep caves and coral walls that no one had bothered to look around the *Sea Witch*. And it was the right place to look, although she wouldn't find her boyfriend's body there.

Bloody hell, but that hairy-backed man had been infuriating. Calling him "son" in that patronizing tone. Demanding to know why he hadn't stashed the tank more deeply in the hold of the wreck. Complaining about the moped. Complaining about the food at the Loose Screw Motel and Bar. Perhaps, Thomas thought, looking at the blond woman's plump little derriere as she pulled on her fins, he really should just lead her straight to the Ape Man.

But however irritating the hairy man had been, he'd ponied up the five hundred dollars, so Thomas supposed he owed the gorilla a modicum of loyalty.

The question remained: What did he owe the hairy man's woman? He stood to make another hundred by taking her for a private tour of the pirate wreck, which was really Martin's old liveaboard sailing yacht, damaged in the hurricane season of '96. Of course, the *Sea Witch* looked nothing like a real pirate schooner, but most of the tourists didn't know the difference.

Particularly, Thomas thought with pride, after the improvements he had supplied: the gilded carving of a busty mermaid affixed to the prow, the handsomely looped and whorled engraving of the name *Sea Witch* on the starboard side, and an old-fashioned steering wheel, the size of a tall man, authentically weathered and worn. Thomas had recently added the finishing touch of a hook, the kind pirates used when they lost their limbs. He'd placed it just inside a door in the engine room, near the trunk he'd fixed up to look like a treasure chest. If you reached for the fake gold coins in the chest and then looked up, it appeared as if someone might be standing on the other side. Now that was something he would have loved to show the prop guys in Los Angeles. The photographs in his portfolio hardly did it justice.

Not that Ape Man's woman would be interested in pirate lore. She said she didn't know precisely what she was looking for, but she'd know when she found it. In Thomas's experience, this was what women always said, and more often than not, they were right.

"Thomas, can you check over my gear now?"

Thomas inspected her voluptuous form from mask to fins. She

looked fine, fantastic even. She had attached everything perfectly, her air was turned on, and she had slicked her hair back out of the way, into a ponytail.

Too bad her knuckles were white where she clutched the boat's rail.

"Lady, are you sure you want to do this? I mean, you haven't really done any search and recovery before, have you?"

"The hard part is getting in, right? Unless you have a feeling that there's a better place to look for Abe?"

Thomas shook his head. "This is as good a place to begin as any," he said, thinking that maybe Ape Man had left an air tank, that maybe she'd find a clue.

There was absolutely no reason to feel guilty.

Besides, her hundred combined with Ape Man's five would mean plane fare to L.A., plus a bit extra, which meant he would get to enjoy a blow-out carnival before setting off to conquer Hollywood. Thomas knew Martin Thorne would be disappointed. Thomas had always felt the older British man was grooming him as his heir, probably because Thomas had no father, and, given Martin's orientation, Martin wasn't likely to be having any sons.

"Are you all ready to go?" The woman smiled, a grimace of fear.

"Righty-ho." Thomas, who had been diving since he was ten, didn't bother to check his own equipment. "Don't worry," he told the woman, "I'll just take the lead and you follow."

"Okay."

"You're absolutely sure, now?"

"Just jump!"

Thomas fell backward into the ocean and waited until he heard her answering splash. They began to pull on the tabs of their vests, releasing air so they could sink down. As Thomas cleared the building pressure in his ears by pinching the nose of his face mask and gently blowing out, he pointed to the woman so she would remember to do the same. She did everything too quickly, with the sharp, jerky movements of the nervous beginner. Still, she was staying with it. Thomas had to give her that.

When he saw her face at twenty feet, though, he thought, Better keep this short. The woman was having trouble clearing her ears, and twinges of pain were probably adding to her nerves. She kept disappearing behind a cloud of bubbles every time she took a frantic breath.

Shallow dive or not, if she kept breathing like that, she'd probably work her way through that tank in no time.

As Thomas paused at the large hole in the *Sea Witch*'s starboard side, waiting for the woman to catch up, he glanced at his dive watch and thought, Thirty minutes. He'd give her till ten o'clock to snoop around the wreck, and have her back up and dry in time for root beer and sandwiches.

A hundred dollars for thirty minutes, plus another hour's boat time all told. Thomas almost grinned the regulator out of his mouth.

§

There was less air in his tank than he'd remembered, and at seventy feet, the engine room was deeper, but Abe was almost done, so it didn't matter. But just as Abe shoved the little dive bag into a depression in a panel, the sharply malicious little face of a moray eel popped out, startling him.

In slow motion, he watched the ring drop out of the bag and fall through the water. Leaning down to retrieve it, Abe forgot that a cabinet door had swung open in the current and he hit his head on the way back up. There was only a faint sting in the back of his scalp, but then a ribbon of darker blue began to ripple through the water and Abe touched his fingers to his shaved head and realized he was bleeding.

Shit. Got to move fast now.

Ring in hand, Abe was turning to make his way up out of the engine room when he felt something bump his arm. Rattled, he turned to see from the corner of his eye the large form of an ugly gray fish, thought, Shark, and dropped the ring again.

The fish, which Abe belatedly recognized as a large grouper, regarded him with its big mouth agape, like an old man, then turned and swam away with surprising speed. Everything else seemed to happen in slow motion: Abe's head, swiveling back from the fish, his hand, moving to catch the falling ring, the ring, sinking somewhere onto the floor. It landed near a big treasure chest that Thomas had told him was filled with plastic coins. Would there be no end to his misfortunes?

A dark mist swam in front of Abe's eyes and he suddenly realized that he might not have time to locate the blue diamond. No, he thought, I've lost the ring and I did it all for nothing and Kira's going to arrive at the airport at any moment. As he thought this, his fingers closed over the ring. Abe formed a fist and thought, Now all I have to do is get the hell out of here.

Feeling a bit light-headed, Abe pulled at his spare regulator again and sucked in a big lungful of air, then pulled harder and sucked in nothing. Abe glanced at his gauge—he was out of air.

As the pressure built in his chest, Abe struggled to turn around and swim up out of the engine room. His right hand felt leaden. He still held the ring in his left fist and couldn't quite seem to coordinate his movements. The water around him was darkened by his blood.

Behind Abe's eyes, he saw flashes of light alternate with dark. Shit, he thought, I'm in real trouble here. His lungs ached with the impulse to breathe, but there was nothing to breathe but water.

And then Abe thought, Kira, and then he thought, Mother. And then he thought nothing at all, his fingers clenched firmly around the tsarina's ring in a cadaveric spasm.

§

This was an absolutely terrible thing to be doing, Liam thought, as he woke up on deck to a subtly charged atmosphere that seemed to press in on his sinuses. Storm coming, and he didn't need a barometer to tell him that he shouldn't be out on a boat right now. The only water he was up to facing was in a glass. Every time the sailboat rocked even slightly, Liam felt his stomach go up with it. He looked up at the sky, where smoky-gray clouds concealed all but the faintest rosy streak of dawn, and realized the rocking was only going to get worse. It was about to really piss down rain in a moment.

He hadn't drunk that much last night. Why was he feeling so hung-over again? Sitting up and wincing as the sun hit his eyes, Liam thought about Lydia—in her cabin, in the ocean, propped against the wall in his bedroom.

Christ, she made him so angry, and so turned on. Maybe he was turning into his father after all: "It's not my fault, son, she goads me into it." But he hadn't hurt Lydia. He wouldn't hurt her.

Of course not, an inner voice mocked. You also haven't known her very long. Think your dad started knocking your mother around on their honeymoon? That came later, with the worries and the bills.

Why should this one small woman rouse the beast in him when he'd faced down some total bitches with perfect equanimity?

Maybe it was her aim. Last night, and this morning, Liam had noticed that every single one of her barbs had found its mark. She was an acute observer, no less so than Fish. And like Fish, you didn't get the feeling of meanness off her, even when she was cutting you down to size. You just got the feeling that, behind that blond-bombshell exterior, there was someone who recognized you too well to lie to you. Someone who could be a friend. Or more.

Liam pulled off his sweat-dampened shirt, noticing a slight rash on his forearms. I'm completely falling apart, he thought. I've got a splitting head, my joints ache, and when I'm with the wench, I don't know whether I want to shake her toothless or kiss her mindless. A good reason to keep away from the woman. Nurse fantasies were all well and good, but clearly he needed to do some mental housekeeping before he found himself in close proximity to her again.

The point was moot, anyhow. The lady had said she was heading back to New York at six o'clock on Sunday, and unless he'd lost a day somewhere, this was Sunday.

Liam thought about pulling anchor and heading back but felt too tired. He fell asleep again under the clouded sky, his head pillowed on a life jacket. He woke again more than an hour later when the marine radio blared to life.

"Mayday, Mayday."

Liam flipped to channel sixteen. "This is the *Blue Boy*. Who are you and where are you located?"

"Oh, Jesus, Liam, is that you? This is Thomas."

"Thomas, what's the matter?"

Thomas's voice hadn't sounded this young four years ago, when Liam had first met him. "The woman—her leg's caught—she's down there alone. I'm anchored right over the wreck. Shit, I've got to get back to her."

Liam felt his heart slam into his chest like a tennis ball. He didn't need to ask who the woman was—there was a horror of certainty in him. "How long?"

"Oh, man, maybe fifteen minutes down time, but there's—the dead guy is there with her—and she's only got—she's got maybe five hundred psi left, but the way she's breathing—"

"Shit. Shit. Leave some spare gear out on deck and get the fuck down there!' Liam turned the throttle on and glanced at his watch. The wreck was only ten minutes away in a dive boat. Liam wasn't familiar enough with sailboats to know how long it would take him to trim the sails and ride there through the threatening storm. The sky overhead reminded him of a deepening bruise.

Liam prayed the winds would favor him.

ℰ

In a strange way, Lydia was not as frightened now as when she'd first gotten caught, even though there was a whole lot more to be afraid of.

She was even getting used to the sight of Abe.

It was better, however, not to look at him.

At first, when she'd gotten down into the wreck, the notion that she couldn't just shoot straight up to the surface had scared her witless. Her air had kept flowing out in a torrent of little bubbles. Thomas kept writing notes on her little pad— "R U OKAY? TRY 2 BREATHE SLOW." Finally, she had quieted herself down.

And then she'd heard something, a kind of thunk. She'd turned around and seen that the passage she was in sloped down. It was darker there. Suddenly, Lydia had thought, *It's there, whatever Abe hid, it's in there.* She'd swum down, clunking her tank against something a few times before emerging into a small room where the water felt colder.

She'd turned around, just checking to make sure that Thomas had figured out where she was, and then something had brushed by her. It was a bald man, and she gasped because the man's mouth was wide open in seventy feet of water and his eyes staring sightlessly were Abe's eyes, and Lydia had thought Deadbaldman, all in the space of about two seconds. And then, without a thought, she'd surged up, to swim back the way she'd come; but in her panic she'd kicked too low and stirred up some sediment, and then she found she'd gotten her spare regulator caught on a hook. What was a pirate's hook doing jutting out of the doorway like some kind of ill-conceived Halloween prank?

Turning, she'd looked at the deadbaldman, and at his dark Abe-like eyes, and realized that this was, after all, Abe, and Abe was, after all, dead. There was a wide gash on one side of his scalp, but the water had washed away all traces of blood. His face looked ghostlike. She had been so certain that Abe was still alive. How long had he been like this? How long would she be down here like this? Thomas would find her in a moment. It was just going to feel longer because she was frightened out of her mind.

Lydia had forced herself to slow down her breathing, wishing she were anywhere but here, in the wreck of a pretend pirate ship with the real corpse of her phony ex-boyfriend.

All the wrong things were lies, she'd thought, and then Thomas's head and shoulders had emerged from the passageway and she'd felt tears of relief well up. He looked at Abe and the hook and then at her. He seemed stunned, frozen by the grisly tableau. Please free me, Lydia had thought. Don't freak out, Thomas, don't fall apart.

As Thomas had begun to tug at the trapped hose, Lydia realized that she was more tangled than she would have thought possible. How could the spare regulator hose have gotten wound so tightly?

Moments had passed, and still Thomas couldn't seem to get her free. Please God, she'd prayed, I'll never sleep with anyone again, I'll give up on romance, just get me out of here alive.

Exhortations of bubbles had risen up with every tug that Thomas made, but all he seemed able to do was scrape her foot back and forth behind the chest. Lydia couldn't tell if what he was doing had been helping or not. She had assumed it had, until she saw the white panic in his eyes.

She'd gestured for him to try again, but he seemed to be crying behind his mask. Grabbing her little slate, he'd scribbled a note: "DO NOT PANIC. BREATHE SLOW. I GET HELP."

And then he'd left her. Alone with Abe.

Lydia kept her eyes on the floor, trying not to look at that horrible, lifeless head that moved with the current, ever so slightly, as if swaying to some otherworldly music. Then she glanced at her watch. Four minutes. Oh, God, please come back soon. Abe's grotesque head bobbed again, as if in agreement.

It occurred to Lydia that she and Abe might wind up together after all.

18

The smell of the tropics was never quite what you expected, thought Rodney as he stepped out of the airport. There was always a disturbingly organic odor to remind you of all the microorganisms and fungi growing and thriving in the moist, womblike heat. Right now, that smell was particularly intense, and there was a bruised gray cast to the clouds rolling in from the east.

"Rain's coming," he told his father tersely.

"Did you bring an umbrella, Rodney?"

"No, Dad. Did you?"

"See any cabs?"

"Not yet."

"Damn." Victor Gold squinted at the darkening sky and then at the quickly emptying parking lot. All the other passengers seemed to be getting into tour busses, except for two skinny men who were opening the door to a battered Ford pickup. Then Rodney watched as a burly guy in a linen suit and a leggy woman emerged from the airport. From twenty feet away it was hard to tell, but they also seemed to be trying to find a cab. Rodney decided to walk over and ask them if they could join forces when he recognized the woman. After three paces, he stopped short.

"Dad!" He pointed at the brunette, who hadn't yet spotted him. "That's Kira. Abe's sister." He knew her by posture alone. She had the habit of standing slightly on her toes, like a princess craning for a look at the white knight riding to her rescue. Jenna, his angry new bride, had double-jointed knees that went back when she locked them. She looked braced enough to withstand tornadoes.

Suddenly, all four of them were looking at each other across the tarmac. Kira's bee-stung lips fell open in surprise. The linen-suited boyfriend, or whatever he was, recovered first. He grabbed Kira by the elbow and propelled her over to the pickup, where he seemed to say something convincing to the two skinny islanders. In a moment, the pickup took off, with Kira and the designer-suited stranger in the back.

"Did you see that?" Rodney's father shook with rage. "That little bitch. I gave her my business! I taught her how to expand her company! I trusted that slut!"

Rodney turned to his father, his jaw dropping. In that moment, he understood something. It was like suddenly being able to speak a foreign language, the language of deceit. "Dad?"

Victor Gold turned to his son, face dripping with sweat and emotion. Too much emotion. The sky flashed white, then went darker than before. "What?"

"You didn't sleep with her, did you, Dad?"

A rapid double clap of thunder sounded somewhere high to their left. Victor's eyes flicked away, but only for a second. "Don't be stupid, son. You know how I feel about your mother." The first few drops of rain fell on Rodney's face. His father shifted the grip on his small overnight case and gestured to the waiting bus. "I guess we'd better go see if that thing will take us. Coming, Rodney?"

Rodney stared at his father as the rain gathered force.

"I said, 'Coming, Rodney?' "

Rodney's hair had begun to drip water into his eyes, forcing him to blink. His father gave a disgusted snort and turned toward the bus.

Yes, Dad, Rodney thought, I do know how you feel about

Mother. You treat her like a child. And then Rodney thought of all the years he had let his father dictate morality to him, of his father's overwhelming certainty, so like his wife's. Would Jenna take a lover with the same calm complacency? *Now, Rodney, don't be stupid. You know how I feel about you.*

Rodney stood, pelted by water, his clothes glued to his body, as his father shouted something from the other side of the parking lot and then climbed up into the tour bus. Victor Gold's angry face appeared in the rear window, his mouth forming words Rodney could not hear but easily imagined: Stop being such an idiot, son, and get into the bus. Don't you presume to sit in judgment on me, Rodney. Wait until you grow up a bit first.

Rodney remained in place as his father's image receded with the departing bus. Victor Gold would be very, very mad at him. For the first time, Rodney thought about how Lydia must be feeling. He wanted to talk with his big sister. He wanted to tell her about Kira, which would only make her feel worse, but still.

Rodney ran back into the airport to call for a taxi.

19

Underwater, Abe's lifeless face seemed somehow fishlike. Lydia kept thinking how alien he seemed, this man who had been inside her. She had thought to marry him, have his children. But he had led a secret life that had led them both here, to this drowning place.

She wanted to ask him who he really was. She wanted to ask what, if anything, she had meant to him. It didn't seem fair to die with that mystery hanging over her head.

She wished she'd gotten her degree. She wished she'd saved someone, done something useful with her life.

Only 150 psi in her tank. How long did she have now? Lydia wished she'd made love to Liam last night. She wished Liam were with her now. She thought of the film *The English Patient,* when the heroine is lying in the cave, unable to walk, trapped in the middle of the desert.

Lydia wondered if somewhere, Liam were trying to get to her, the hero of the movie.

The hell with this. She was *not* going to die waiting. She was going to die trying.

Lydia pulled at her trapped hose again, thinking, They call it an octopus. I'm going to die in an octopus accident. She repositioned herself and her arm brushed Abe's corpse. She made herself ignore it. She managed to get one hand behind a bulkhead and pulled again, biting down to keep from wrenching the regulator out of her mouth.

Okay, she thought, maybe I'm coming at this all wrong. Maybe it's more like getting an earring out of your hair—more untangle, less tug.

Removing her dive gloves, Lydia felt along the contours of the knot and then pulled on a center section until she felt two of her nails tear down to the quick.

And then she was free. Swimming awkwardly, with only one fin, Lydia began to make her way up the passageway. She had just emerged from the hull of the ship and could make out the blessed sight of the water's surface some sixty feet overhead when she saw a pair of familiar pale-gray eyes. Liam. She barely had time to register the fact that there was no regulator in his mouth, no face mask, when she gasped in a breath of air that was not followed by another. Liam reached down to her with one arm, staring into her eyes, and then she felt him swimming up toward the light, pulling her with him as she kicked and tried to breathe out, out, not in. And then the light grew brighter and brighter and then went black.

20

The strange thing, thought Liam, was not the pain of nitrogen trapped in his bloodstream. He'd already figured out that he had the bends; he'd probably had them for days. The strange thing was how right it had felt to risk his life for absolutely no rational reason.

Liam had jumped from the sailboat onto the deck of Thomas's vessel without pausing to tie the lighter boat up, only to discover that Thomas hadn't laid out a spare regulator or tank of air for him. Thomas was nowhere in sight. He must have gone back down. Liam wasted a moment checking beneath the benches, but Thomas's boat was not outfitted for commercial diving. Lydia's going to die, he'd thought, and there's nothing I can do about it.

Liam had just stood there a moment, barefoot and bare chested, looking down at the choppy water as it tossed the unmanned sailboat up and down, moving it farther and farther out to sea.

And then he'd dived in.

The pressure was not as bad as he'd feared, moving so fast. And the fact that it was hopeless, that he could hardly help her if she was trapped at seventy feet, did not seem to matter. There was a dangerous grief waiting for him when he stopped moving, so he didn't stop. For a moment, when he saw her flying up out of the depths, toward him, Liam was too shocked to react. A heartbeat later, he had recovered enough to grasp her by the wrists, kicking his numb legs against the weight of the sea. He hadn't seen Thomas, who had been descending rapidly but not as rapidly as a free diver plunging through the water. But as they broke the surface of the water and Lydia collapsed in his arms, Thomas was there, taking her from him just as the pain knifed through his head and back.

Liam managed to climb up the ladder and onto the deck before collapsing.

Thomas looked up, his hands still busy unfastening Lydia's bright-orange buoyancy-control vest. "Jesus, Liam, you okay?"

"Just—see—to her." The words came out in little pants, and Liam half-rolled onto his back, trying to catch his breath. There didn't seem to be enough air around to fill his lungs. The rain was falling in steady sheets, and flickers of lightning illuminated the heavy grayness overhead.

"Oh, man, I think she's dead," Thomas said, and somehow Liam found the strength to drag himself up beside her. It took him two attempts to form the words. "Oxygen. Give her—get her—to the chamber." She had blacked out. It had to be a gas embolism. Lydia might have held her breath on the way up and allowed some air to expand too rapidly, bursting through the membranes of her lungs. The bubble had probably been pumped to her heart, then up to her brain. It was as if she'd had a stroke. Lydia still had a chance, though, a slim one. If Thomas had a first-aid kit with pure oxygen. If Thomas could get her to the hyperbaric chamber in time. If God was feeling kind today.

Turning to shield his eyes from the heavy downpour, Liam fought back his own panic. His left leg was numb. He felt as if someone had been trying to pry apart his joints with a crowbar. Liam wanted to tell Thomas he needed oxygen, too, but there didn't seem to be two masks in the kit Thomas was opening.

Was she dead? Liam tried to see if her chest was moving. She was dead because he'd gotten angry with her, because she'd thought he wouldn't help her anymore.

Because she was brave. Because she was reckless.

"Thomas, can't you fucking hurry?" Lydia's poor face was unprotected from the rain, and Liam wanted to shield her, but was finding it harder to move than before. He couldn't feel his legs all the way up to his waist. That meant there was a bubble lodged in his spine somewhere. Thomas was fiddling with the first-aid kit, and Liam longed to snatch it from him. Every moment her brain went without oxygen compromised her recovery.

"I've got it, Liam, hold on." Thomas fixed the mask over her nose and mouth, and Liam felt his heart thudding with unallayed anxiety. Was it enough? Had they gotten to her soon enough?

"There you go, sweetheart, there you go," he whispered. "That'll help you. That'll keep you till we get to the chamber."

Why should he feel this way about Lydia? He hadn't really gotten to know her. All he had discovered was that she looked and spoke like a glass of Hollywood champagne but she went down like the best Irish whiskey. All he knew was that she was soothing and clever and sarcastic and sad, and something about her spirit bumped up against something in his when he kissed her.

Lying on the deck, her hair tangled around her head, she looked half dead already. Her mouth was slack. She did not look merely asleep. From somewhere behind and above him, Thomas called out, "Don't worry, Liam, we'll be at the chamber in minutes. Minutes." There was a familiar smell of diesel and salt. The boat hummed under Liam's back as it gathered speed.

Reaching out his hand as far as it could reach, Liam's fingers came close enough to skim Lydia's cold cheek.

"Hang on there, now," he whispered. "Hang on." And then, very softly, Liam recited the words to all the poems he knew, Leda buckling from the swan, ocean kingdoms laid out beneath the waves. Dead lovers and fairy queens, as lovely and merciless as love itself.

Words to magic away the fear, while the rain tapped out its indifferent counterpoint.

§

Lydia opened her eyes and received the blurred impression that she was inside an iron lung. She felt complete confusion. The last thing she remembered was being in her cabin, thinking she should get up, this was her last day on the island.

Now her eyes couldn't seem to focus, she was in what appeared to be some sort of ten-by-five-foot metal tube, lying on a single bed, pressed up against a man's warm body. A light shone in from outside two large round pressure-sealed doors at either end.

She was naked underneath a heavy wool blanket.

"Hello?" The word came out a little slurred. She turned her head and found herself gazing into Liam's palely compassionate eyes. Things were more distinct close up. Lydia wondered if she needed glasses.

"Hello." Liam continued looking at her, but Lydia could not read his expression. He seemed to be smiling at her, but it was with a sad, pained sort of kindness. He looked like Humphrey Bogart at the end of *Casablanca*. Somehow, this convinced Lydia that they had just done something fairly intimate.

"What—what happened?"

"You nearly died in the wreck, next to your ex-boyfriend."

Lydia drew her breath in sharply as she flashed on the image of Abe, bloodlessly nodding in the water. "Oh, God." She closed her eyes a moment, and the memories returned in reverse order: Liam diving down without a mask, Abe's pallid corpse, her spare hose getting caught on a hook, diving down with Thomas, standing on the deck of the boat as the storm clouds gathered. Intimate enough, but it was the brush with death, not sex, that had forged this feeling of bondedness. Lydia opened her eyes again and found Liam watching her, the same tender sorrow in his eyes. A furrow of concentration had formed between his brows.

"Liam? Where are we?"

"In a hyperbaric chamber on the north side of the island, getting recompressed. You had an air embolism. You've been unconscious for about two hours, but we got you on oxygen right away."

"My vision is all blurred. It's hard to talk."

Liam pushed a strand of tawny-gold hair away from her eyes. "We haven't been in that long. You'll be all right."

Lydia swallowed. Forming words took an extra effort. She felt as if she'd just woken from anesthesia. "But aren't there effects, after-effects—my instructor back in New York said—"

"Shh. You're lucky. Some people are."

Lydia swallowed, found her voice. "I wish I felt lucky. Oh, God. Is Abe still down there? Has he been dead since Wednesday?"

Liam was silent for a moment. "How did he look?"

"Bald. Dead. Horrible."

Liam stroked her hair. "Horror-movie horrible? Swollen? Bits missing?"

"I don't know. I don't know."

"Shh, that's all right."

Lydia kept her face down. "No bits missing."

"Then he wasn't there long. Fish are . . . not great respecters of human dignity."

"Oh! That's disgusting." Liam gathered her into his arms and Lydia inhaled the scent of him. "I just had this macabre thought. I think Abe might have been alive last night. After you left, I went back into the bathroom, and my engagement ring was gone."

Liam whistled. "Could have been someone else, but . . ."

"But do island thieves usually open closed windows when the guests are still in their cabins?"

Liam's face was very close to hers as he spoke. She pretended not to notice. "Lydia, if he stole the ring back, it means the thing was probably pretty valuable."

"I was thinking the same thing. Which means it wasn't meant for me." Her voice was steady.

"The more fool he. But if he had the ring back, why dive down to the wreck again, assuming that's what he was doing?"

They both considered for less than a moment.

"But why would he need to hide it there?"

"Well . . . you might hide things because you're afraid someone will happen upon them by accident. But you hide things extremely well when you think someone will go looking for them. I would say this falls into the latter category, wouldn't you? Abe was hiding the pretty ring because someone was going to see him. Someone who knew about the ring, so not just any hiding place would do."

"Kira."

"Who?"

"His sister. Maybe not his sister." Lydia thought about it. "Definitely not his sister."

Cuddled together, Liam and Lydia considered the case of the corpse in the wreck.

"So what we're saying is, the fake pirate ship probably has a real treasure now."

Lydia half sat up. "A treasure embezzled from my family's money, don't forget."

"Don't fret, love. All we need to do is dive back down. Or rather, get someone else to dive—we may well be fish food ourselves if we go back in."

Lydia took this in. "Will you be able to do scuba again?"

"Don't know yet."

"Because of what you did for me? Diving down without an air tank?"

Liam shrugged. "It was a combination of things."

"But you free-dove down to sixty feet. What were you intending to do, try to disentangle me as well? If I hadn't been swimming up toward the surface, you could have drowned yourself."

"You're making it sound as if I had a plan. I have no idea what I might have done. We're both lucky we didn't black out at the surface."

"You risked your life for me."

Liam broke his gaze away from hers, then looked back; there was something fiercer in his eyes than she had ever seen before. He didn't answer her.

Lydia rested her head back against his chest, trying to marshal her thoughts. Finally, after a long moment, she said, "And you're here taking care of me."

"I am doing that, yes."

Lydia drew up onto her elbows on the narrow bunk. "What aren't you telling me, Liam?"

"I'm in a bit of pain. I can't feel my left leg."

"Oh, God, Liam, are you—you're going to be okay, aren't you?"

"People recover at different rates. I think I've had the bends since Wednesday."

"You've had the bends for four days? How is that possible?"

"I'm an idjit, is how it's possible. Thought I was hungover, didn't I?"

"Oh, Liam." She curled up into him, head on his chest, and he placed his hand on her hair like a benediction. "Is this hurting you?"

"Put your head down, you." They lay like that for a while, breathing softly, thinking. The chamber reminded her of a submarine. It contained a small stool and the narrow cot they were lying on. There was one porthole window at chest level and two larger pressure-sealed doors at either end.

After a moment, Liam turned to speak into her ear. Lydia felt his soft, clean breath against her skin, but could not make out the words.

"What did you say?"

His chest rumbled with laughter. "You weren't meant to hear. I thought you were asleep."

"I am asleep. It's safe. Tell me."

"I said"—Liam's finger tapped playfully over her back, as if he were a doctor, testing her lungs—"that," he tapped again, then smoothed the touch away with his palm. "I wished I had not been so stupid as to shoot my mouth off in that bar. I wish I had made love to you last night."

His hands on her back were caressing now, but with such unde-manding gentleness that Lydia was not aware of choosing to let it continue. "Are you saying . . . do you think you might be para-lyzed?"

"Not at all. Both legs numb, now that would mean the spinal cord's implicated. One leg—no, I think I'm not so bad off as that."

"So there's nothing to worry about."

"Absolutely not."

There was a brief pause of things unsaid. Then Lydia cleared her throat.

"How long do they say we should be in here?"

"Five hours. At least five. Maybe need some treatments after. Depends how we respond."

"And we've been here what, less than two hours?"

One side of Liam's mouth lifted in a wry smile. "Who're you convincing, lass?"

Lydia put her hand on Liam's chest. Beneath the warm, flat planes of muscle, she could feel the too-rapid rhythm of his heart. The silence stretched between them, awkward and fearful. "So," she said abruptly, "you're wishing we'd had sex?"

Liam's chest rumbled with laughter. His hand closed over hers, pressing her palm down over his heart, beating just a fraction more quickly than a moment before. "Why, Ms. Gold," he said, "are you trying to seduce me?"

Lydia let her hair fall down over her face, obscuring it. "I think it's better we just imagine how earth-shattering it would have been, don't you? Reality's such a disappointment."

"Is the talking easier now? You sound better."

Lydia looked up, surprised. "It is. The far wall's not so blurry, either. How are your joints?"

"Painful enough to ensure that your virtue goes unmolested. Now back to the main subject, if you please. You don't think I could make the earth move for you?"

"Don't be insulted. It's just that I find the early stage, the desire and anticipation, that's usually the best part. You think the feeling's so strong that you can't not go on, so you go on, and suddenly it's like you're eating a steak but you're not hungry anymore."

Liam's hands stilled. "I've felt that, too," he said. "No one's ever put it to me like that. But in a man, they say it's a sign you're shallow—the conquest is all that matters, that kind of shite. I had a woman throw her shoe at me once, and tell me that at least other guys waited to go off her *after* they'd gone to bed with her, not during."

"At least she noticed. I always find myself lying there, thinking, Hello up there, remember me?"

"Why not get on top?"

"On top is worse! Every guy seems to have read some magazine article saying, 'Let her get on top, you get to look at her breasts, she'll be an orgasmatron and you won't even have to work!' But I just sit up there, worrying about looking droopy and, well, not feeling, you know—oh, man, I can't believe we're talking like this." Lydia pretended she didn't notice how her body was pressed against the muscular length of his. One of his hands had slipped down her back and was resting against the small of her spine, where hip and buttock flared into feminine fullness. She felt his sensual awareness of her in the press of his fingertips. Absurdly, impossibly, given their dire medical circumstance, there was arousal between them.

"No, it's all right, please go on. Please. What's wrong with on top for you? It doesn't hit you right, I mean, hit the right spot inside?"

Lydia nodded. "But this makes it sound like I was just talking about the physical side of things, and that's not it. I'm afraid that when sex goes wrong for me it's more like the soul goes out of the thing, and without that, it all feels kind of mechanical." Lydia took a deep breath, knowing her blunt words were dispelling the erotic atmosphere building between them. Wanting to dispel it, before the dangerous enchantment of his hands, his body and mouth so close to hers, took hold.

"So you start and then lose desire halfway through?"

"It's ironic—I think I've slept with way too many guys, but if I've behaved like a slut, it's because I'm a romantic. I may like the guy, I may be attracted, but once we get into bed it all seems to fall apart, and then I know there's really no rescuing it, so I move on."

"Why do you say that? Why call yourself a slut? I've doubtless slept with more women than you have men. Am I a slut?"

Lydia grinned at him. "Probably. A boy slut."

"No, don't just smile. You really put yourself down when you say that word. And you don't deserve it." Liam had raised himself up slightly. His cheeks were flushed.

"Okay. Calm down. I take it back."

"You are not a slut. I don't care how many men you've been with."

"It's not *that* many!"

"How many, then?"

It was Lydia's turn to flush. "How many have you been with?"

"I don't know. Ten. Fifteen maybe."

"Yeah, well. Something similar." She looked up. "Were you careful?"

"I was careful. And tested." Liam smiled, rubbed his knuckles along Lydia's jaw. "Were you careful?"

"Hypochondriacally careful. I'm one of those people who carries little antiseptic wipes with them at all times. Believe me, I'm not going to come in contact with anything that might make me sick."

"So there we are, two slutty, careful people. Are you propositioning me, by any chance?"

Lydia turned her head away. "No. Even if you could—oh, hell, that came out all wrong—"

"Never mind. I know what you meant. Go on."

"I'm tired of the whole game. I want out. I thought Abe was different. I wasn't in love with him, but I felt that he was wild about me. I thought he *valued* me." Lydia gave a gasp of laughter. "Turns out he valued my family's assets."

"Oh, Lydia, you were going to settle. You shouldn't have to do that."

The single lightbulb and the metallic closeness of the chamber had begun to make her feel vaguely claustrophobic. She realized she couldn't get out. Liam reached out and stroked her arm.

"What is it, love?"

"I don't know, it's—I may have been settling, but at least I was finally getting something, don't you see? I'm tired of having high standards and nothing, nothing to show for it. My whole family thinks I'm a loser. I dropped out of grad school because I didn't think I was good enough, and I didn't want to be responsible for making decisions that could cost people's lives. And they just think—everyone just thinks—I'm not smart enough, I'm not—"

"Shh, shh, shh. Here, wipe your face on the blanket."

She gave a half laugh, half sob. "I'll get snot on it."

"With luck, we'll trade other bodily fluids as well." Liam wiped her face with such tenderness that Lydia almost turned her lips into his palm. Then she stopped, comprehending what he had just said. Liam assumed he would have her. Well, why not? She'd just taken the time to tell him she was an easy lay.

"Here now, Lydia. What's that cold look about, then?"

"I'm not going to sleep with you."

Liam stilled. His eyes went flat, as if with fear. His tone, however, was light and liltingly Irish. "Aren't you?"

"No. Not because I'm not attracted—you know I am. Because I don't want to be hurt anymore. I swore to God down there, if he saved my life, I was giving up the whole thing—romance, marriage, children. I just want to be peaceful. I'll read romance novels where the heroine can take outrageous chances and still wind up with the man of her dreams." Lydia sat up, drawing her knees to her chest.

"And what about sex?"

"It's better imagining it."

"And what about love?"

"That's better, too. You know, I've waited thirty-one years to meet a man who'd make love to me with his eyes open, not because he's judging whether he can finish it off yet and not because he's watching my body, but just staying with me. With his eyes open. With his soul in his eyes."

Liam paused, said quietly, "Maybe that's what men want, too. Not to be judged."

"Oh, that's right. Women don't go around comparing men to some unrealistic ideal up on a movie screen."

"Don't they? I suppose women are just fine if the man they're with gets depressed and loses self-confidence and mopes around a bit. Perhaps you don't mind a fellow who has a good cry now and then. Lets his emotions out."

Lydia held Liam's gaze. "I wouldn't mind."

"The hell you wouldn't! And if he loses his temper, what then? Punches out the wall?"

Lydia hesitated, then began to answer.

"There, you see! You would so mind. Women don't want their men to lose control and get sulky or angry and weep all over them. They want you to be James Bond and then they complain when you don't show emotion."

"Not all women are the same."

Liam raised one eyebrow.

"I don't need a man who never loses control of his emotions."

"You do."

"I don't."

"You do."

They looked at each other, taking each other's measure. Liam took a breath. "I shot my father." Deafening silence.

"What?"

Liam seemed very calm stretched out beside her, but she could feel his heart racing under her palm. She could see how carefully he was watching her reaction.

"I said I shot my father." His brogue was very pronounced now, but for the first time, Lydia knew it was not intentional.

"How old were you, Liam?"

"Twelve."

"What was he doing?"

"He was——" Liam turned his head to face the wall. "He was beating on my mother. And, I suppose, she might've been beating on him as well. She was the one bleeding, though. And he was the one with a bottle in his hand." He coughed. "You know, I haven't told this story in twenty-three years, and I had to go and choose the one time and place where you can't have a fucking cigarette."

"It was his gun?"

"Indeed it was. 'The right to bear arms against a sea of troubles and by opposing end them.' "

"I think you've got your Bill of Rights mixed up with your Shakespeare. So you shot him."

"I said, 'Put the bottle down or I'll shoot.' Very Clint Eastwood, or so I thought. My dad said, 'Get the hell out of it, Liam, you have no idea what's going on here.' "

"And you said?" Lydia's voice was barely a whisper.

"I said nothing. That's when the fucking gun went off, didn't it?"

"Did he—he didn't die, did he?"

"I managed to shoot him in the knee, crippling the man for life, for which he did not exactly thank me. But I did not kill him, no."

"Oh, Liam, I'm sorry."

"I'm sorry, too. I could sit here crying for my poor twelve-year-old self, stuck in juvie hall. Not exactly what the heroes in your romance novels would be after doing."

"Oh, you're wrong there." Lydia threw her hair back out of her eyes and sniffed hard. Tears were trickling down her cheeks. "Everybody loves a flawed hero. The tragic past is good, too."

"Glad it works for you. My record's sealed—that's how I made cop—but my dad never bothered to speak to me again. So I try not to fly off the handle, just in case I turn into some kind of raving lunatic. Only thing is, I think feelings are a package deal. You can't exactly seal off one part without getting rid of the whole lot. So I haven't ever exactly been in love before. I've been married, but I haven't been in love."

Lydia, still sitting up and clutching her knees, felt the blanket slip down from her suddenly nerveless fingers. "You said 'before.' You said you hadn't 'ever exactly been in love before.' I heard you."

"The thing is, I'm not precisely sure what it would feel like. Right now it feels a whole fucking lot like I've been punched in the stomach. Christ, you've got magnificent breasts."

Lydia did not pull the blanket up. She watched Liam's face change as he watched her breasts.

"You're not sleeping with me?"

"No." Her voice was a whisper.

"Can I not touch you, there?"

"No." She kept her eyes fixed on his flushed, beautiful, boyish face.

He lifted his pale gaze to hers. "Can I not kiss you then?"

"No."

He sat up, the blanket falling down to his waist, revealing the tanned, sleek muscles of his stomach and chest, the faint shadow of reddish-brown chest hair, his small, flat brown nipples. He pulled his legs wide to straddle her knees between them, and a wince of pain crossed his face.

"Are you all right, Liam?"

"I'm going to touch you."

"No." The thin woolen blanket covered, but did not hide, his growing arousal.

"I'm not going to disappoint you. The feeling won't go away this time. Afterward I'm going to hold you in my arms and you're going to know I want you more, not less. First times are just learning times. I'm going to learn you, Lydia."

"No." But her denial had a yearning sound this time. She had leaned forward, half-hypnotized by her desire for this man. Poised between safety and the knowledge of his desire for her.

"I won't take you on a no, Lydia. I'm only a man, not a mind reader. If you're meaning yes, please, God, say yes. Please. Say. Yes."

"Yes," she said, throwing herself forward into his arms. His hands came up to capture her head, his fingers twining in her hair as he claimed her mouth with a little cry of surprise and pleasure. He moved slightly so that she felt the shape of him hard against her stomach.

"You're not paralyzed," she said on a small huff of laughter. Liam laughed, and pulled her into his embrace, her face against his chest, caressing her hair in long, soft strokes, as if she were a child. It was so tender. She'd never had a man stop and be tender before. But the heat of his desire pulsed within reach, and when she tipped her head back and looked in his eyes, she saw no humor there.

"I'm scared."

A rueful smile broke over his lean and handsome face, and he said, "Me, too." He showed her his hands; they were trembling. "I promise I won't hurt you."

"I'm more worried about hurting you."

"A good point." He stopped and thought. She did not like being on top, and he was not in any shape to pin her on her back and have his way with her.

Lydia, seeing his confusion, wondered if she would appear to be too experienced if she made a suggestion. Instead of saying what she was thinking, she scooted closer to him, so that her legs straddled his and they were nose to nose.

"Why not just kiss me, sailor?"

He complied, and at first she could feel his smile against her mouth. There was nothing between her breasts and his chest, and Liam groaned, twining his hands in her hair, kissing her with raw hunger. His hands came up to cup her jaw, his thumbs pressed against the corners of her mouth. She bent her head to the hollow of his throat and breathed in the good, clean male smell of him. She traced kisses down his chest, to where the muscles ridged on either side of his flat abdomen, and then, when she paused a hairbreadth from where the blanket tented over his groin, not sure whether she was ready for that intimacy, Liam pulled her up.

"Let me look at you. Ah, God." Liam traced her full breasts with the lightest of touches. "You're a sixteen-year-old's fantasy."

"They're not exactly pointing at the ceiling."

"Are you mad? They're fantastic. They're real," Liam said reverently, skimming his fingers along the crease beneath each breast. Then, leaning forward, his hands holding her like precious fruit, he brought her nipple into his mouth, lightly flicking his tongue against her, then pulling with a firm pressure that Lydia could feel all the way down to her womb.

"Oh, God, Liam."

Bringing her breasts together with his hands, Liam moved his mouth back and forth between her nipples, biting her softly with his teeth.

"Lean back." His voice was hoarse. As she granted him access to the rest of her body, Liam traced a path of kisses along the gentle curve of her belly, until he reached the juncture of her thighs. Parting her with unsteady hands, Liam moved his face into her, rubbing himself against her like a cat. "Ah, Lydia, Lydia." He took his first taste of her and Lydia gave a gasp that was almost a cry of pain.

Liam paused to bring up his head and look at her.

"What is it, Lydia?"

"Nothing, it's nothing." But she was crying, a tear leaking back into her hair.

"Lydia?"

"You're just—you're so damn good at this. Too good." What she did not say, what she could not say, was that she knew his type. He was a man who loved women. A man like that could love an older woman with wrinkles on her face and neck, and show her how soft her skin still is, how fine her eyes are. A man like that could take a woman who hates her stomach, her bottom, and make her see herself as lovely through his eyes.

He was giving her a gift. But with his breath warm and startlingly intimate between her legs, it wasn't enough. And yet another part of her thought, It should be, it has to be enough.

"Lydia," he said, still on his knees, "sit up. Look at me."

Lydia swiped at her tears, feeling more vulnerable than when her legs had been parted.

"You say I seduce. I think maybe you're right—most times I was with someone, I spent more time watching her reactions than I did feeling what I'm meant to be feeling in the moment. But I swear to god I'm not meaning to seduce you. I just want to give you plea- sure. You make me feel like a kid again. You make me feel raw with wanting."

"Liam—"

"Shh. Listen. I'm on a roll, opening up here, and if I stop talking, I might lose my nerve. My whole childhood I watched my parents love each other to pieces. I watched them rip themselves inside out with passion and I didn't want to have any part of it. So every woman I've ever been with has said it felt like part of me was miss- ing." Liam sucked in a breath. "But not now. I'm all here, Lydia. With you. Not that I asked to be—it doesn't seem I have a choice in the matter."

"I don't know what to do. I don't trust myself anymore. I don't know what to believe." Lydia was crying again and thought how ugly she must look, how weak and and insecure she must seem.

"Oh, Lydia." For a moment, she saw her own sadness reflected in his eyes, and then he reached out for her, lifting her beneath her arms, bringing her onto his lap, her tear-stained face next to his, her thighs open to the thrust of him. She started to wonder if she might be hurting him, but he silenced her with a finger against her lips, using his other hand to cup her, and then, very lightly, very softly, to stroke her, feathering touches that teased, but did not press. At first she stiffened. All too often, men had hurt her at this point, but Liam's hand made no rough conquests. He stroked with such sure, soft, easy strokes that her thighs began to shake. And all the while, he watched her, wonder lighting his face.

"Let me inside you, Lydia." This time, she felt him press the blunt head of his erection against her entrance, his eyes half-shutting, like a cat's, with the pleasure of it. Lydia gave a sharp little inhalation of air, and as if her gasp had set something free in him, Liam rocked his hips back and penetrated her, and then, just as she was adjusting to the shocking pleasure of having him buried deep inside her, he went utterly still.

"Oh, shit." His brow was furrowed with what looked like incredible pain.

"What is it? Is it your leg? Your back?"

"I didn't—I don't have a condom on."

Lydia didn't pretend to misunderstand him. She had always insisted Abe use protection, and ironically enough, it wasn't because she'd thought he was cheating on her. Diaphragms gave her nothing but trouble and she got headaches from the pill.

But there was Liam, throbbing inside her, and with a little gasp, she found herself saying, "It's all right." She felt mindless with desire, and she was pretty sure it was the wrong time of her cycle, and then Liam began to move, working his way inside her with little thrusts, banishing all rational thoughts from her mind. Their position forced him all the way up against the entrance to her womb. It was a pleasure very close to pain, but somehow Lydia couldn't bring herself to tell him this. He was deep, so very deep inside her. And though he couldn't move very far, each small roation of his hips pressed him against her most sensitive flesh.

"Ah, Christ, Lydia, sweet girl, I'm not going to last like this."

"Don't stop."

"I—ah, need your help."

Lydia moved onto her back and reached up for him. Liam's face contorted for a moment in a spasm of pain.

"Are you sure you can do this, Liam?"

His grin was pure mischief, but there was something anguished behind it. "I'm sure I'm going to try."

With startling suddenness, Liam thrust himself strongly inside her. She could feel the wildness begin to take him over as he surged up inside her again and again, arms braced on either side of her head, no longer cautious or gentle. He was lost in her, his arms suddenly collapsing as he mindlessly kissed her from collarbone to mouth and back again, biting the tender flesh where neck met shoulder as she gripped the muscles moving in his back, tracing her hands lower, against the tensile firmness of his buttocks as the shiver seemed to go through them both at once, too fast, too fast, spreading from the base of the spine up and outward without effort for Lydia as she felt his movements lift her up and up and over the peak of pleasure, and she gripped him inside as he pulsed within her.

Afterward she began to cry, as silently as possible.

"Lydia."

She opened her eyes, but did not turn to face him.

"Please don't. This is the beginning. Just the beginning. I swear to you."

"I'm not crying because I'm sad. I'm—oh, the hell with it. It never happened before."

Liam rolled over onto his back, grunting in pain as he pulled her against his chest. "What didn't? You're telling me you're really a virgin?"

Lydia wiped her face against his chest. "In a manner of speaking, yes."

It took Liam a moment. "You're saying you never came before?"

"Not with anyone else in the room, no."

Liam let out a long whistle. "Well, then."

"Well what?"

His arms tightened around her, and his lips brushed the top of her head. "That's a gift to me, then."

Feeling the lassitude of good sex down to his bones, basking in an aftermath unmarred by regrets, complaints, or hidden dissatisfactions, Liam gathered Lydia into the curve of his body and slept.

21

Martin knew he was in trouble even before the Armani-suited thug pulled the gun.

He'd looked at the Russian man's handsome, expressionless face, his blond eyebrows and blank eyes, and thought, That's a predator. And yet he had smiled at the man, because Martin was the owner of the resort, and because the man's elegant monochromatic suit bespoke wealth and position. He'd also smiled because the expensive camera hanging around the chap's neck and the pretty, pouty-lipped brunette beside him suggested that, thug or not, the man was here on pleasure and not business. Most Caribbean island resorts were booked to capacity at carnival, which would begin tomorrow. Tiny Epiphany, which attracted only die-hard divers, was not so lucky.

Which was why, when the fellow asked to discuss room rates in Martin's office, Martin acceded. People who requested privacy were usually willing to pay handsomely for the privilege.

It was only when the man had asked where Lydia Gold could be found that Martin had his first inkling of danger. There was something too studied in the casual tone of the question, and the sleek girlfriend had something equally blank in her expression. They were both bad actors, thought Martin, and wondered if that meant that whoever had sent them thought they were expendable.

Then Martin said he couldn't give out room information without authorization, and the man smiled and lifted the large black-and-silver camera. In three practiced motions, the man unscrewed the lens cap, slid out a hand grip, and rotated his palm backward, as if he were holding a gun.

Well, Martin thought, perhaps I'm the one who's expendable.

"I think we can make exception, no?"

"I don't suppose it's any good asking you what you want with Miss Gold. She's suffered quite a shock, you know—her boyfriend's just died."

The brunette smiled. "Don't worry, Mr. Thorne, we aren't going to hurt Lydia."

The blond Russian slanted her a look. "Shut up. Take his arm. Other side. I take this one." Walking with his expensive jacket folded over his gun hand, Misha escorted Martin out of his office and into the tropical afternoon, where birds trilled and the heady perfume of fleshy orange flowers filled the rain-cooled air.

All along the path to Lydia's cabin, Martin rehearsed strategies for outwitting his armed escort. It galled him that after a lifetime of taking charge and taking risks—running a business in South Africa, opening the first resort on Epiphany—Martin had no idea how to keep from being pushed around by a pasty-faced hit man in a designer suit.

At the door to Lydia's cabin, Martin raised his voice. "I don't think she's there," he boomed. "You're wasting your time."

"Shut the fuck up," said the goon, elbowing Martin in the stomach. "Unlock it."

Martin fought down the coffee that had risen sourly in the back of his throat, and clattered the keys as if he were nervous, trying to buy time.

"Here," said the brunette, taking the key ring from him, "let me do that. Which one?"

Martin shrugged. "I can't be sure."

The thug elbowed him again, and this time Martin bent double and retched against the flat stepping stones.

"Jeez, Misha, that is so disgusting. Why are you in such a hurry to use your fists?" The brunette slid one key after another into the lock until the door opened.

"I used my elbow, *dyetka*," said Misha to the girlfriend, and the way he said the last word made Martin think it wasn't exactly an endearment. Misha pushed Martin inside the cabin at gunpoint. "After you, my friend. Have a seat on the bed."

Martin moved slowly into the cabin, wondering if the couple intended to shoot him now.

The blond man motioned to his accomplice, indicating the cabin. "Okay, Kira, check."

"What, you think she's hiding under the bed?"

The Russian flushed with irritation. *"Dyelay shto ya skazal!"*

Kira looked at him with undisguised contempt. "You have no charm, Misha. Nobody ever went far in business without charm." Then she bent and looked under the bed.

"Check everywhere, princess." Misha smiled, showing a lot of teeth. "There? Was that charming enough?"

"No," said Martin from the bed, and Misha cuffed him with the butt of the gun.

Kira came out of the bathroom and folded her arms over her chest. "So, what now? There is nobody here."

Misha gestured at Martin with his chin. "You. Mr. BBC. Where else can she be?"

"I'm sure I have no idea."

"Wait," said Kira, when Misha would have started hitting the older man in earnest. Walking over to Martin, she took his weathered hand in his. "Listen, I know what you're thinking. But it's just a ring we want. A ring Lydia was wearing as an engagement ring, even though Abe—my brother—never really got to propose. We are very, very sad about Abe. Lydia is, too, I know this. But the ring cannot belong to her."

"I should think you could discuss this with the island police," said Martin stiffly. His jaw was beginning to bruise.

"Misha is thinking with his fists, and I am sorry. He is—let me be candid with you? Is that the word?"

"Yes."

"Thank you. If I am candid, then I say to you, Misha cannot go to the police. Not for the reasons you think. He is just—he is not good with authority figures. But we do not need guns, we do not need violence. We will just say, Hello, Lydia, we will embrace, cry, and she will give me back the ring. It was my mother's ring, you see." Now, artfully, Kira began to cry.

"You should have tried this ploy first. I might even have fallen for it."

Kira released his hand with a sound of disgust. "Of course we should! Now he ruins everything!"

Martin and Kira both looked at Misha with amused contempt. After a moment, the fair-skinned Russian flushed, then got to his feet. "Enough of this," he said. "If you will not tell me where she is, then we will take a little tour together. You will show me the gardens, the swimming pools, the dive shops, the restaurant."

"I will show everybody my bruise," muttered Martin under his breath, but Misha heard and swore.

"Kira, you have makeup in your purse?"

"Of course."

Misha cupped the British man's discolored jaw in his hand. "So make him a little more beautiful."

&

After his fourth Jack Daniel's, Thomas stopped rushing to the bathroom. He'd been in a frenzy of terror for hours, knowing he'd killed one man with his badly placed prop and almost been the death of one of his best friends and a lovely young woman besides. Now the sour darkness of the bar had fermented his emotions into something quieter and more deeply felt. He had taken a life, albeit a fairly useless one, and in so doing had effectively ruined his own. Hollywood was not going to go for a prop man who left a trail of corpses in his wake.

"You okay, Thomas?" Bibi the bartender knew that it had to be woman trouble. There wasn't much else that could make a man drink this much, this fast, in the small hours of the morning before carnival had even begun.

"I'm screwed, Bibi. I'm screwed." Resting his head on his arms, Thomas inhaled the familiar sour smell of the bar and wished God would smite him. Instead, Baron pounded him on the back with one meaty arm. Thomas knew it was Baron because the hand felt like a slab of steak falling from a great height.

"You tell old Baron what's the matter, little Thomas. Can't be so bad Baron won't know what to do about it."

Thomas lifted his head and looked the heavy man in the eyes. Seated like the potentate of some foreign power, Baron looked powerful and calm and infinitely wise. Baron, whose nonmusical talents were so rarely called upon these days, was known to have once been a man of much influence and ingenuity, back in the black-and-white days of television. Thomas felt a burst of love for the man.

"I got a corpse I need to get rid of, Baron," Thomas whispered.

"Sweet Jesus," said Baron, raising his eyebrows until the yellow-tinged whites of his eyes showed. "You *are* screwed."

§

In college, Rodney remembered his philosophy professor telling him that hell is other people. Rodney had never really understood what the woman meant, and had received a C minus in the course.

Now, standing next to his father outside the reception desk, with no manager in sight, Rodney finally understood. Both he and Victor pretended to be strangers, waiting separately amid the palm-and-bamboo decorations while the overhead fan whirled the hot air around.

"Goddamnit," said Victor, lowering his silver head to check his Rolex. "Why the hell isn't there a manager here to tell us exactly where Lydia is staying?" Victor reached out and grabbed a slender young woman in uniform. "You, miss. Can you tell someone I've been waiting here for forty minutes cooling my heels?"

The young woman, whose little white badge proclaimed her "Elaine," smiled. "I'm so sorry, sir. I'm sure Martin Thorne will be back momentarily. He likes to book guests in himself."

"Look, it's too damn late for him to impress me with individual attention. I just want to find my daughter, and I mean now."

Elaine looked concerned. "I'm not sure what to do in this situation. We don't divulge guests' rooms without authorization. Please hold on a moment, sir."

Victor Gold could not resist flashing his son a look of irritation as the young woman consulted another uniform, this one young and male. There was some worried whispering. Martin wasn't responding to his pager. If he was on a dive, he usually delegated responsibility to Thomas or Cecile, but Cecile had just gone off island to purchase part of her carnival costume and Thomas was nowhere to be found.

Unhappy at being made to wait, Victor turned to Rodney. A trickle of sweat snaked down the older man's brow. He still had not removed his jacket. "Well, that just beats all. Are you going to just stand here and take this? Well, are you? Because I, for one, am going straight to the police."

Rodney looked past his father.

"So you've still got this cockamamie idea that Abe is hiding on the island somewhere and that you're going to do better at finding him than the police will?"

Rodney continued examining a painting of a hibiscus.

"Fine. Go play boy detective. I'm out of here."

After another half hour of waiting in the lobby, Rodney ambled off to the dining room to have a drink. It was almost three o'clock. Maybe the kitchen would serve him an early dinner.

He imagined his father at the police station, raising hell about the lack of cooperation, and Rodney felt as if he had unloaded the weight of the world from his shoulders.

Now if only he could figure out where to find his sister.

22

As Sunday afternoon faded into evening, Liam and Lydia lay, one on each side of the narrow bed, legs slung over the other's arms, in lazy appreciation of their mutual good fortune.

For Liam, it was a revelation. Lydia did not seem to feel any of the stirrings of remorse that, in his experience, usually prompted women to run straight out of bed and into a bath. Instead, she reclined on the bed, exuding a wholesome, unself-conscious carnal confidence. She seemed to be without vanity. There was no postgame commentary on how her breasts were too large or her hips too generous. She didn't seem to care that he could see the tiny lines on her face in the stark overhead light. She so contradicted what he'd first thought about her that he felt he had stumbled into love through sheer dumb luck. He felt a kind of bewildered happiness, as if he'd swum out over some shallows and discovered a hidden cathedral of coral.

"Liam," Lydia said, gently massaging his legs, which were long and tanned and marvelously muscled beneath a light sprinkling of soft, sun-gilded brown hair. "I just want you to know that I am having an absolutely wonderful time."

"I'm having a rather nice time of it myself." Liam pretended to bite her big toe, but then stopped abruptly as she laughed and tried to squirm away.

"Are you trying to have my foot for lunch?"

"I am getting a bit hungry. Shall we ask our friendly paramedic to send out for a couple of sandwiches?"

"Sure. Liam? I'm going to close my eyes for a few minutes."

"You do that." Liam watched her roll up like a big cat, hand tucked under her cheek, and thought how clever she was to give him space the only way possible. He wondered whether Abe had appreciated her at all, or whether, like a Neanderthal listening to Beethoven, he just hadn't had the equipment.

Liam wondered whether he himself had the equipment. Probably not, but at least he was bright enough to recognize her sensitivity. Women's magazines and his ex-wife had taught him that women believed they were liable to scare men off with too much emotion. Lydia was probably playing it safe, turning down the heat. No pressure, no crowding, no constant chatter about how many kiddies she'd like to have. But Lydia was a romantic. Not the lady-in-an-ivory-tower variety, but the kind that went out into the world and got bruised a bit by experience.

Liam went to the pressure-sealed door, spoke through the little intercom, and ordered two ham-and-cheese sandwiches with mayonnaise, and then just stood there, debating what to do next. This was the point where he usually gave serious women what he thought of as "the speech."

He'd tell them that they should know what to expect from him: He was not built for the long haul. He just didn't have the stamina for it. No matter how happy they were together, it was no use dreaming up an ever after. Because real emotion didn't last forever, not at that peak, unless you kept the flame alive the way his parents had, by burning out of control. He didn't want to live each day of his life on the edge of a crisis. He didn't want to bring a child into a rela-

202 ♪ *Alisa Kwitney*

tionship that was a world unto itself. And yet, strangely, paradoxi-cally, he didn't want less, didn't want the arrangement of schedules and bills and responsibilities that most marriages seemed to become over time.

So, Liam would tell the woman that she could have an eternal now with him, time out of time for talks and the silences, a private lexicon of laughter, the tangled pleasures of noontime sheets and midnight picnics and all the myriad, unremarkable moments of shared glances and inadvertent touches that made up romance.

But now, looking at the perfect relaxation of Lydia's body, the delicious, almost painterly curve of spine and hip under the thin gray blanket, Liam couldn't seem to force the words through his lips. It wasn't that he thought this feeling would last, it was just that the thought of saying it out loud felt wrong right then. It would have been sort of like winning the lottery and then trying to immediately calculate the taxes due. Sometimes you just had to make room for happiness.

The paramedic said something unintelligible over the intercom and then passed the sandwiches through the airlock. Liam sensed, rather than saw, the younger man's smirk, and ignored him.

Liam brought the plate over to Lydia, gently touching her shoulder. "Are you hungry?"

She sat up, blinking. "What is it—oh. Ham."

"Oh, great, you are a vegetarian."

"Ham and cheese." She laughed.

"Can you just eat the cheese?"

"It's not that, it's just—ham and cheese and mayo is so—so goy-ish."

Seeing that she wasn't really upset, Liam took a bite of his sand-wich. "What's 'goyish'?"

Lydia took a bite of her sandwich, tentatively, as if sampling a strange and possibly unsavory delicacy. "The opposite of Jewish," she said, bringing her hand up to cover her mouth as she spoke.

"Oh, man, I didn't stop to think—you mean you don't eat ham?"

"With me, it's not religious. It's just—hey, this is good." Lydia began taking larger bites. "It's just a habit, I guess. Mmm. I did grow up eating shrimp in Chinese food all the time, and that's not exactly kosher, so I don't know exactly why we never had ham in our house." Lydia finished her sandwich before Liam had eaten half of his, and then looked a little embarrassed. "I guess I was really hungry. I don't suppose you got us anything to drink?"

"Lydia," he began, and then stopped, befuddled, not knowing how to make the transition from ham sandwiches to the future of their relationship. He didn't want to hurt her or frighten her off. He felt that this woman he barely knew was his best friend. It was like kindergarten—entering the classroom, seeing that one kid, getting that instant feeling of recognition: Oh, you're the one. He felt a fierce physical need to express his affection, as if words belonged to one side of his brain and feelings to the other. Looking at her softly rounded shoulders and arms, the plump swell of her breasts above the blanket, he could imagine the small boy he had once been nestled against her. There was, he could now see, a small constellation of pale freckles dusted across her chest. It was the kind of thing a child would notice, enfolded in her arms. Connect the dots on Mommy's chest. Would Lydia want to breast-feed?

Why the hell was he imagining her with a child?

"Hey."

Liam looked up to find Lydia smiling at him knowingly. "Don't worry, Liam. My father's not going to show up to interrogate you about your prospects."

Liam opened his mouth to utter some charming, witty riposte and found himself stuttering, "I w-w-wasn't . . ."

Lydia threw back her head and laughed. "Oh, I know exactly what your problem is. You think that what you're feeling has a long chain and an anchor attached, but it doesn't. In fact, I'm supposed to leave tonight. Six o'clock."

Liam, who had been caressing the instep of Lydia's right foot, kissed her sole and looked at her from under his eyebrows. "Well, I think you're stuck here for the moment," he said. "But I'm not sure about this. I think you're trying to use me for sex."

"Not a bad plan. At least this way I won't have to worry about getting hurt." Lydia caressed Liam's chest with her foot. "Why didn't I think of this before? I should write a new self-help book. Hey, folks, deliberately choose relationships that won't last and you'll never be duped again."

"Don't do that. Don't make yourself out to be a victim."

"I'm just making a joke, Liam."

"You're making yourself out to be some poor little miss who keeps getting hurt by the big, bad men."

Lydia pulled her foot back from his hands. "Ac-tually," she said in a tight voice, "I was saying that I am not going to be hurt by the big, bad men anymore. You just weren't listening." She gathered the blanket around her breasts, withdrawing.

Liam tugged the ends of the blanket to him, bringing Lydia closer again. "You can't keep yourself safe by pretending to be some cold bitch, Lydia. Because you're the farthest thing from cold. In fact, when I first met you, I rather thought you were like that lady cocker spaniel, you know the one from the Disney cartoon?"

Lydia gaped at him.

"She was all used to soft beds and hot meals, and when people started acting mean to her, she just fell apart. Until the big hero dog came around to save her, of course. But life's not like that, Lydia, you have to learn to fight for your—" Liam, who had not noticed Lydia getting redder and redder in the face, was shocked when she began leveling open-handed smacks at his arms and shoulders. "Hey! Lydia! Stop! I'm not—Lydia!"

Liam grasped her wrists and held them together. "I'm not saying this to hurt you, Lydia. I just meant to—"

"You just meant to say, 'Hey, Lydia, you're one weak, pampered princess, but in case you missed the last thousand times I hinted that I wasn't in this for the long haul, I thought I'd point it out to you again.'"

In one sudden movement, Liam pulled Lydia toward him, grabbing a handful of her hair and kissing her so forcefully that Lydia began to push against his chest. "Stop it, Lydia. Stop it. Can't you feel that this is not some ordinary thing that happens all the time? Do you think this is casual for me? Do you?" Leaning his head forward so that their foreheads touched, Liam cupped the back of her neck in one large hand. "But just because you love a man, just because he loves you, doesn't mean you can trust him completely. Even good men can make mistakes."

Without looking up, Liam felt some of the anger go out of her.

"You're thinking about your father, aren't you?"

"And my mother. I worry—you remind me of her. A little."

"You idiot." Lydia shook her head, and made a sound of perfect exasperation, a little hiss like an engine letting off stream. "Don't worry. I'm not going to let anyone push me around anymore. And as for the rest of it—I'm not someone who enjoys life on an emotional roller coaster. So even if we did, by some wild miracle, wind up together, we wouldn't replay your parents' story."

"Ah, Christ. Lydia." Liam let his arms collapse, and slipped down to rest his head against her breasts. He could hear the speeded-up rhythm of her heartbeat. His own heart was racing so fast he could barely catch his breath. "I've just totally screwed this up, haven't I?" Liam gave a hoarse laugh. "For a moment, I just——I thought somehow you were——"

"Ssh. It's all right. Stop before you say the words 'cocker spaniel' again." Lydia stroked his hair, and Liam chuckled softly, pressing his lips to the valley between her breasts.

After a while, Liam raised his head. "You're so quiet."

"I was thinking about what I could do with your hair." She made a scissors of her fingers, pretending to trim the long sides. He felt her touch from his scalp down to his groin. He wondered if there were men with haircut fetishes, and if he might become one.

"Do that again. You're sure you haven't gone off me, now?"

"No!" She laughed and tugged lightly at his hair. "You're not very perceptive."

"Of course not. I'm just a simple man." Liam closed his teeth gently over one nipple, then slipped lower to rub his stubble-roughened cheek and jaw against the sensitive skin of her inner thighs. As he neared flesh that was still moist from their combined fluids, she tried to cover herself with her hands.

"Liam . . . what are you . . . ?"

Liam blew gently on the moist, dark-blond curls. "I'm a savage, remember?"

"No——Liam, you're not . . ."

But then his mouth was on her, teasing her, his tongue heedlessly flicking over the sensitized flesh. Her stillness revealed her embarassment, her fear of how she might taste and smell. But as he thrust his tongue inside her, holding nothing back, his movements strong and certain with desire, he felt her begin to respond, pressing herself lightly up against him, then beginning the unconscious slow roll of hips that told him she was getting closer. He grasped her more firmly under her bottom, bringing her closer, trying to demonstrate that he accepted her completely, that there was nothing about her that disgusted or repulsed him. He could feel the release in her thigh muscles as she gave herself over to what he was doing. And then he was stunned to feel a slight pulse down at the base of his erection just as she began to shiver under his hands. Shite. That had never happened before. Well, not in the last two decades, at any rate. He was in danger of losing control.

He paused, and she stared at him with unfocused eyes.

"I have to stop a moment."

"Oh."

"Or this'll be over before it's begun."

"Oh! But you—this—I haven't done anything to you." Lydia raised herself on her elbows to look at him. "I haven't—Move over so I can reach you and I'll—"

Liam licked her, a quick movement. "No. Not this time."

"Why are you doing this?"

Liam threw back his head and laughed. "Why do you think?"

Her face made it perfectly clear what she thought, that this was something men did to prepare women for more conventional love-making, not something they enjoyed themselves.

"Ah, Lydia, come over here and give me a present." He buried his head in the musky, tender flesh of her and gripped her hips in his large hands, pulling her clitoris into his mouth and suckling it until, in a blinding flash, he felt the contractions begin, his teeth lightly closing over her as she pulled at his hair, whimpering deep in her throat as if he were hurting her.

She had slipped half off the bed. Looking up at him, Lydia took in the sight of him, tall and tanned and still aroused.

"Stand up," Liam said hoarsely.

"What for?"

"What do you think for? No, come over here, so you can hold on to the wall."

"Liam?"

"Do you trust me, Lydia?" His hands skimmed over her breasts and belly, and then cupped her mound.

"I do."

"Have you never done it like this, then?"

Lydia shook her head no.

"Do you want to have a little gladiator fantasy?" Liam kissed the back of her neck. "Let me take you like this, Lydia. Trust me."

Lydia spread her legs wider and then he was at her entrance. His hands bracketed hers on either side, and she could feel the lean, muscular warmth of him behind her.

"Pretend I'm chained to the wall. Too dangerous to let loose, but that's what you want. You'll have to help me."

"I feel strange, not being able to see you."

He murmured something half-remembered from Latin class, and then nipped the side of her neck.

He heard the deep breath she took before bringing her hand down to guide him inside her.

With his very first thrust, Liam felt as if he had just sunk down to some primeval level of his brain. He knew he wasn't being gentle, but each time he pulled out and felt the tight grip of her muscles around him, slick with moisture from their previous lovemaking, he found himself mindlessly thrusting back harder. And harder. He heard Lydia's low moan and slowed himself. Beneath him, Lydia gave a slow shudder, and Liam gently lifted her hair and kissed the back of her neck. He felt her excitement, a subtle animal message of scent and stance, a basic and wordless communication he'd never felt with any other woman, ever. The knowledge of her desire rippled through him and he gently bit the nape of her neck, which made her cry out and her back arch.

"Shh." She took his hand and muffled her mouth with it, biting him back on the palm, and Liam felt his balls contract with helpless desire. He was driving into her now, harder and faster than he ever remembered taking a woman before, and he pressed his face close to hers, half-frightened by the strength of his own desire.

And then, because even that wasn't deep enough, wasn't close enough, Liam bent his knees and changed the angle of his entry, and now each thrust brought him up against some place deep inside her that made Lydia cry out.

"Am I hurting you?"

"No. No, don't stop, please don't stop!"

Beyond coherent thought, Liam pressed one hand to where they were joined and kept it there, feeling himself sliding in and out of her as the first tremors rocked through her. And, then, with a muffled shout, he joined her, feeling as if he had released a thousand old angers and fears. Feeling as if he'd come undone.

Afterward, dazed, Lydia felt Liam pull her into his arms. "I didn't hurt you, did I?" He stroked away the light trace of tears from her cheeks.

"You scared me."

"Ah, Christ, no, tell me I didn't."

"Not because I thought you'd hurt me. Because I didn't know I could feel that much."

Liam brushed a kiss across her brow. "Ah, Lydia. I love you." Just like that, the words slipped out, unplanned. The words burned across his chest for a moment after he said them. To his surprise, he realized there was a twist of pain in the emotion. He'd felt like this as a kid, holding a newborn kitten in his hands. As if there was so very much that could go wrong, that what he had could so easily be destroyed.

Lydia buried her face in the side of Liam's neck and whispered into his skin.

"What's that you said, love?"

Lydia averted her gaze and then whispered, a bit louder, "I said, where the heck does a girl go to the bathroom in this joint?"

Liam thought about it. "In a chamber pot, I suppose."

"I can't pee in front of you!"

"Well, I sure can."

"We can't let anyone in here! It . . . smells. Of us. Of sex."

Liam touched her lips with his finger. "Don't worry. They just pass it through the airtight lock. Here, I'll do it."

Wrapping the blanket around himself, Liam went to the door and pressed on the intercom buzzer. After a few moments, a small urinal was placed in the air lock and Liam unfastened the latch on their side of the chamber.

"My lady," he said, proffering the kidney-shaped tray.

"I can't."

"Why not?" Liam kneeled beside her on the bed. "We've shared just about everything else." Liam looked at Lydia, and they both stilled, Liam realizing that he wanted this, wanted the strange intimacy and trust it implied. He wanted to enter the uncharted territory of love, where boundaries are breached and taboos broken.

Lydia looked away. "It's different. Gross."

"Pretend you're going to have a baby and I'm the father." A shiver went through Liam as he said this. He felt as if some strange demon had taken control of his mouth.

"I can't." Lydia buried her face in her hands. "Please don't push me on this."

"All right." Liam paused "Want to help me?"

"Help you pee?" Her voice cracked on the last word. "Well—I guess—okay, the truth is, I always kind of wondered what it'd be like."

"To help?"

"To, you know, do it like a man."

They stood up, Lydia behind Liam, her hands holding him in place.

"Nothing's happening," she said after a moment.

"Actually, something is." Liam half-turned.

"Ah—you can't pee like that, can you?"

Liam gave her a quick, rueful smile over his shoulder.

"I'll go sit down on the bed, then."

There was still more silence.

"Did you forget how?"

Liam laughed. "I think it, ah, takes some getting used to. Right now, your presence keeps affecting me. Maybe after we've known each other a bit longer."

"Or when we're truly desperate."

Liam returned to the bed, wrapping Lydia inside the blanket and his embrace. "Can you tell me now, Lydia, what you said before? When I told you I loved you and you hid your face and whispered?"

Lydia looked at Liam, her face very gentle and calm, as if somehow in all that foolish play she'd lost all her fear of embarrassment and pain. "I told you that the way you've made love to me just changed my life," she said. "I told you I love you."

"Ah, Lydia." Liam traced her cheek with his fingertips as if memorizing her features. "I don't have any words left for what I'm feeling."

"So just hold me." Lydia turned into his arms, and for a moment Liam wished she could meld with him, Eve ribbed to Adam in the earliest days of Eden, before desire separated them and then made them come together again.

23

Martin would never forgive himself for involving Fish in all this. At first, his only thought had been to find Liam. The younger man might be an arrogant little bugger, but at least he'd know what to do when presented with a little post–Cold War hostility.

But Liam hadn't been there, and Fish had.

"It would have gone much better for you, little man, if you were not so clever with your mouth," Misha commented as he tied the ropes around Fish's arms.

"Ah, you mean it would have been better not to have commented on Martin's eye makeup and the solicitous way you kept bumping into his back?" Fish smiled his elfin smile. "True, but then Martin would still be all alone with you two. Now, at least he has company."

Martin smiled weakly at his friend, wishing to hell and back that he'd taken the Russian and his girlfriend anywhere but the dive shop. Outside the window, the sun was settling into the darkening clouds. Martin, bound to a chair across from his friend, turned his head back to Fish and wondered how tight his bonds were. Fish's arms looked as if they were being pinched white by the rope. He thought about what he knew of Fish from having discovered his secret chat-room name, and wondered what the other man would say if he made a joke about armchair bondage. Fish, being Fish, would probably just laugh and say that this was why he liked his games played in virtual reality.

But would Fish still laugh if he discovered that some of the things he assumed were false—such as Messalina's protestations that she had never felt this way before—were real? While other things that Fish probably took for granted—like Messalina's being a woman—were completely and utterly false.

Martin turned his attention back to their captors. "Misha," the woman was saying, "this is stupid. Now we have two men tied up and still no idea where is Lydia or the ring. Why didn't you let me handle it?" She kept fiddling with the clasp on one of her bracelets, and Martin understood that beneath her tone of deliberate normalcy she was worried.

"Don't worry," said the Russian with a lift of his pale brows, "we will find out where this woman is. The little man will tell us. Won't you, Jack?"

Fish raised an eyebrow. "The name is Lionel Fish, my boy. And what makes you think I know anything about this Lydia you're looking for?"

Misha extracted a clear snorkel from one of the displays and whipped it down so that it whistled through the air. "He looks like Jack Nicholson, Kira, don't you think? Anyway, Jack, I don't know what you know about Lydia, where she is hide herself. But I know that you will tell to me everything you do know. Is a lie about judging a man's character by how well he stands up to torture. Torture works for everyone—very democratic. Now," Misha smiled slowly, showing too many teeth, "which one of you shall I torture first?"

§

The problem with corpses, Thomas decided, is that they don't cooperate. Abe Bohemius's body, left in the ocean for nearly seventeen hours, had become as stiff and heavy as an enormous, cold slab of goose-pimpled beef. Wrapped inside the two thick, dark, plastic garbage bags, Abe seemed doubly unwieldy, because you couldn't quite tell what part you were handling until you handled it.

"Are we there yet?"

"Five more feet, then there's three steps," said Baron, watching as Thomas's thin legs staggered beneath the dark bulge of the bag. Baron had absolutely refused to have anything to do with actually touching the body, bagged or not.

Thomas tripped on the first step, dropped Abe's feet, and then had to reposition himself to haul the body back into a carrying position. The garbage bags, ripped now, began to slip off, revealing an arm flung forward, the hand still tightly clenched in a fist. "Shit, he's slipping out. Baron, man, can't you just take the feet?"

"Try a fireman's lift. No, I can't take the feet. I'm an old man and I made it this far in life without getting all touchy with some dead guy," the big man said as he opened the door to the resort's main dining room and flicked on the light switch. Outside, the faint glow of dawn had just begun to lighten the sky, and Thomas blinked at the sudden brightness.

"Uh, Baron, you sure no one's going to notice him in there? Like when the cook goes to cook beef Wellington and comes up with two hundred pounds of frozen tourist on toast?"

Baron, ignoring this last remark, opened the door to the kitchen's large walk-in freezer and inspected the metal shelves where poorly wrapped fish and meats were arranged in haphazard piles.

"Damn. Will you look at that, Thomas? Cooked beef, right up next to that raw chicken. You can get food poisoning like that."

"Baron, this isn't going to work."

"What's your idea, smart boy? You going to ask your daddy to hide him under your bed, and tell the neighbors you're cooking some bad-ass fish surprise when they start complaining about the smell?"

The two men looked around the freezer and finally decided to remove a turkey, a side of ribs, and three boxes of fish to accommodate the body.

Pushing together, they managed to insert the Abe's corpse onto a shelf. After three attempts at keeping the recalcitrant hand from falling out and blocking the door, the two men managed to shut the freezer.

In the outer storeroom, Thomas eyed the thawing perishables with concern. "You think somebody's going to notice any of this?"

Baron grunted. "Course they will. Here's a batch of melting meat, someone goes to open up the freezer, and lo and behold, what do they see but a great big black lump in the middle of all this food. Look closer, there's a hand. Now, a hand, someone's going to notice. But this here's the only freezer big enough unless we want to waltz over to the morgue and start explaining."

Thomas wiped the sweat off his brow with his hand, and then, disgusted with himself, wished he hadn't. His hands had been all over the dead man. His own flesh was goose pimpled with cold and repulsion. "Maybe I should have just left him, Baron. The worst that could have happened then was I get arrested for inadvertently causing this guy's death. Now the police might think I killed him on purpose."

Baron clapped a hand on the younger man's narrow shoulder. "Don't you go double-guessing yourself now, son. You did the hard part. Now we just have to wait for the cook and tell him he has two days off to enjoy carnival."

"This is your plan? We leave a corpse in the resort freezer for two days and give the cook a vacation? What about the rest of the staff?

And who's gonna cook?" Thomas sat down on a box and buried his face in his hands, and then wished he hadn't. "And what the hell do I do with the body next? Serve it at a luau? Jesus Christ, Baron, I should never have moved the body."

Baron sighed, as if momentarily overcome by fatigue at the thought of the volatile emotionality of youth. "Listen, young man, when Baron says he's gonna help you, you don't have any call to get yourself in a panic. The boys in the band and I are going to cook and serve, and all we need is to buy ourselves a little time. Say, a few hours' worth."

Thomas lifted his tear-blurred gaze to the heavyset man with something like hope. Baron had lived in New York City, had been in jail. Maybe he really did know what to do with an unwanted corpse. "What happens then, Baron?"

A slow smile spread over Baron's wide mouth. "Why, carnival happens, little Thomas. And all kinds of shit goes down at carnival. Teetotalers get loaded. Nice married people get laid by other nice married people. And a dead tourist can get himself mislaid. No one's gonna blame you if some drunk tourist gets himself drowned during carnival."

Thomas thought of the dead body, at present a lump of dark plastic with an arm hanging out of it. "We just wait till everyone's so drunk they don't notice we're carrying a corpse?"

Baron nodded, rolling his shoulders up and back inside his large, shiny, orange-striped nylon shirt as if readying himself for a fight. "Just wait and see, Doubting Thomas. Just wait and see."

24

"In all the time we've known each other, I don't suppose I've ever asked you who your favorite author is, have I?" Fish, tied to a chair behind a display of masks and snorkels, kept his voice very calm and even. Martin was tied to another chair, and seemed to be bleeding very quietly from the nose, but the Russian had done some things to the soles of his feet and his abdomen that might have left more serious damage. The Russian gangster—Misha, the girl had called him—had left them around midnight, taking his pouty-lipped companion with him. By the look of the sunlight filtering in through the shuttered slats, it would be mid-morning by now. They would be back soon. That much was understood between Fish and Martin, and so neither had mentioned it, nor the torture that was likely to follow. Instead, they had spent the night talking about the past. Nothing too personal, just cultural landmarks. Where they'd been when they heard Kennedy was assassinated. What they'd been doing in the summer of '69. What their definition of sex was, and what they'd say if questioned under oath.

"My favorite author?" Martin looked up, blearily, then tried to pull himself more erect. His attempts to be stoic in the face of Misha's robust, almost cheerful cruelty had moved Fish more than he could say. Out of respect for Martin's British sensibilities, he was pretending not to notice that the other man was in agony. Fish had been pretending for eighteen hours now, since four o'clock on the previous day's afternoon, and dark shadows of fatigue had appeared under his eyes.

"Unless it's too personal." Martin was wearing the shuttered look of a businessman being made an unexpected offer. Maybe the answer was something embarrassing. Looking away from his friend, Fish thought about how long it would be until the pain began, and then quickly tried to think about something else. Sex. Fish conjured the disembodied Messalina, who had cast her net upon the Web and captured his imagination. You couldn't call it love. He didn't know her real name, only her E-mail address. But still, Fish found himself glad that if he was going to be tortured and killed this morning, he had briefly enjoyed the erotic company of a woman who could quote the spicier sections of Robert Graves's novels of ancient Rome and knew the games Messalina had played back in the later, decadent days of that empire.

The feeling of being understood in all his perverse imaginings had made him feel more alive in the past week than he had in the past ten years.

Fish turned back to his battered friend, slightly startled to see an exhausted smile playing over Martin's chapped and split lower lip. "My favorite author. But you already know that he's Robert Graves," the British man said, his tone perfectly impersonal and crisply matter of fact. "Just as you know a lot more about me than you may realize." And then Martin looked up with his bloodshot Prussian-blue eyes.

"You're Messalina. You must think I'm a shmuck. A total shmuck."

"I don't think anything of the sort, Lionel," Martin said, turning his head away. "I'm just hoping you're not too angry with me. Or disappointed. But don't worry, I'm not going to make a pass at you."

"God, I'm thick." Fish thought about Martin's anger with Liam, his conviction that the younger man was cheating on Fish. And Liam was so like Martin, and yet so unalike. Suddenly all the pieces fit, and Fish was flabbergasted that a man would find him attractive. He was surprised, indeed, that anyone who had seen him in person would find him attractive. He looked down at his firm potbelly and spindly legs as if they belonged to someone else.

"I have no idea what to say. You know I'm not gay."

Martin laughed weakly. "Oh, bloody hell."

Fish shook his head. "If I sound like an idiot, it's because I feel like one."

"Don't. I didn't mean for you to know. I suppose I thought you might as well know it now, because . . . well, unfinished business, I suppose. And it's not as if I've done you any favors. I can't believe I led that Russian bastard right to you."

Fish looked up at him, all trace of puckishness gone from his dark eyes. "You're not to blame for that, Martin."

"I should have done something. I should have been able to protect you." Martin smiled at Fish, and something in his face made Fish wonder if Martin thought he was going to die first. Fish thought the opposite was more likely; today was probably his turn to suffer.

"No bullshit heroics, all right? I have absolutely no idea what you think you see in me. I'm fat and old and have a liver that probably looks like a goose's. And though I'm flattered, I'm too damn old to go changing certain habits. So don't go risking your life to save mine."

"I'll bear your objection in mind." At that very moment, Misha and Kira walked in. The Russian man was wearing a white silk shirt, khaki pants, an ascot tied around his throat, and some kind of safari hat, as if he thought he might be auditioning for the role of colonial

Englishman in Africa. The woman was wearing a pale-blue dress and had a look of pinched misery on her face.

"Good morning," Misha said with real warmth. "But what is this? Look at their faces, Kira. I see we have just missed some important conversation. Can you not see it in the way they look at us?"

"Misha, I keep telling you, this is stupid. If you'd only listen to me, we could——"

"Shut up. You do not see. But I do, and I have a very, very good idea." Misha walked up to Fish and, putting his hand on the man's rounded shoulder, smiled over at Martin's bruised expression. "This morning, for a change, we start with this one."

Fish thought about Martin being Messalina, and felt a pang of regret, although if someone had asked him what exactly it was that he regretted, he would have been hard-pressed to answer.

§

Victor Gold stared at his breakfast, and his breakfast stared back at him. He looked over his shoulder for the waiter, and found that the man had scurried off.

"What the hell is this supposed to be?" A slice of stale bread, a pat of suspiciously yellow spread, and a big, walleyed fish were arranged on his plate next to a cup of sour black water that bore not the slightest resemblance to coffee. "What a disaster."

There didn't seem to be any other guests in the dining room. There was one skinny, sunburned redheaded guy and an older couple out on the verandah, where big, savagely beaked parrots seemed intent on eating anything that wasn't actively being lifted into someone's mouth. God only knew where Rodney had gone. After two hours in the police station last evening, fruitlessly trying to convince the laconic captain that his men should search the island for Abe, Victor had come back to find his daughter still missing. No one would even tell him if his son had checked into Neptune's Rest. Victor presumed Rodney was asleep somewhere, nurturing his grievances against his father.

Well, where did Rodney get off, accusing him of sleeping around? It's not as if Rodney had been married some thirty-odd years to the same woman and could compare track records. And, for the record, he hadn't actually done anything with Kira, although the girl had seemed to give the impression she wanted to, badly—up until the moment Victor had tried to take her up on it.

Which made it all the more irritating that she was here, shacked up with some blond Nazi type, the minute after finding out Victor had lost his money. Thanks to her brother, the little *mamzer*. And where in God's blue heaven was Lydia, who should have been back in New York long before now, begging her parents' forgiveness? If she had taken the first flight home, he wouldn't be here now, on a fool's quest with a son who needed a vacation from his wife less than a year after a twenty-thousand-dollar wedding, which, according to Rodney, was no longer the bride's family's sole responsibility.

The thought of all that money spent made Victor feel sick now. Three million dollars gone, a life's savings gone, and the memory of those little tuxedoed waitresses carrying hot appetizers, the image of that hotel restaurant with every surface garlanded in flowers now haunted Victor like the Ghosts of Money Past. What was going to happen to him and Beryl now? What if one of them got sick? Rodney was too selfish to take care of them. And Lydia was too immature. How in the world had he and Beryl wound up with such feckless kids?

Looking down at the desiccated piece of fish on his plate, Victor felt a wave of fresh rage wash over him. To think he'd spent even a dime coming to this place, and they couldn't even serve a decent breakfast. Scraping his chair back from the table, Victor stood up, fish plate in hand. Enough was enough. He was down but he wasn't out yet, not by a long shot. And the day Victor Gold just put up with being shafted was the day it really would all be over.

Victor made his way to the kitchen, carrying his fish breakfast like a standard into battle. As he'd expected, the place was a shambles. Probably no such thing as a health-code violation on this backward little island.

"You there." He addressed the young black man who was painstakingly trying to arrange two plates of scrambled eggs on a platter.

"What—oh, shit, damn it, no!"

Victor watched in disbelief as the waiter lost his balance, tipping the platter wildly to the right and then to the left before losing the battle and dropping all three plates.

"What are you, retarded? Where the hell's the chef?"

"That would be me, sir."

Victor looked up at the obese cook, a walking mountain of a man who had not even bothered to cover his long, marceled waves of hair.

"There a problem, sir?" The cook continued chopping vegetables with a cleaver, but it seemed to Victor that there was something newly menacing in the way he was doing it.

"I'll say there's a goddamn problem. Smell this fish. Disgusting. I wouldn't serve it to a cat. And I ordered eggs as well as smoked trout."

"That's them on the floor, sir." The fat man chopped a carrot, reached for another, and then chopped that one. Victor wrenched his eyes away from the sight. The man had fingers the size of sausages.

"There's nobody out there. How long does it take to make a couple of eggs? And don't you people have a health code? This place is a breeding ground for bacteria, and what's worse—"

The chef, who had been cracking eggs into a skillet, looked up, his dark eyes unreadable. "Yes?"

"Why's he doing that? Standing there in front of the refrigerator like that?"

"Like what, sir?"

"The waiter is standing there in front of that door as if he's guarding it. Or is he just so fascinated by the sight of you frying eggs that he can't do any work till they're cooked?"

"He's just doing his job, sir."

"Oh, really?" Victor approached the young man. "His job is to mind the garbage? And why does he look so terrified?"

"He always looks like that. It's genetic." The fat cook suddenly turned, an amiable smile spread across his vast face. "You know, you look like a New Yorker to me. I happen to have some delicious smoked salmon. Since the waiter is busy over there, if you could just open the fridge over there—"

"He's not busy! He's standing there like a dummy! What are you hiding, anyway?" Victor tried to get past the waiter, and the waiter kept moving to block him, an impromptu dance of stepping first left, then right, then left again. Victor stopped and glared at the teenager, who had begun to sweat. The chef came up behind them, looking less friendly than he had a moment before.

"Now what the hell are you two hiding back here?"

"We're going to jail," the young man wailed.

"Shut up, Thomas."

"What is going on here?"

"Freezer's broken, sir."

"Have you been serving rotten food? Get out of my way!"

"You're not allowed back there. In fact, you're not allowed in the kitchen at all. Health-code violation. So if you'll step this way, sir . . ."

"Oh, well, if it's against the rules, sure." As the chef tried to usher him out of the way, Victor turned and dodged around them, clasping the latch to the refrigerator and pulling hard.

Now both waiter and chef were standing with their backs to the freezer door as Victor pulled at the handle. "We can't let you in, sir. Dangerous levels of bacteria."

"What the hell is this, a kitchen or a medical facility for treating Ebola? Open the goddamn——" Victor yanked at the door, and the two men began pulling on his arm. "Ow! Off my arm! I ought to have you both arrested." Suddenly Victor went very still. "Do you jerks have something illegal in here?"

The chef spoke first. "Absolutely not."

"Out of the question."

"Then open the door and let me——" Both men released the door at the same moment, and Victor reeled backward.

"See, sir?" The fat man pointed swiftly to the interior and then shut the door. "Nothing illegal there."

Victor stared at the man's calm face. "Are you kidding me? I just saw a hand sticking out of that bag. Tell me that was not a hand sticking out of that bag."

Victor opened the door. There was a hand sticking out of the bag.

"I didn't kill him, he was drowned, we're taking him to the police right now," the man called Thomas babbled, flailing his arms around. "We just needed to borrow the big freezer. It's——the one at the morgue is broken. We found him——the guy——the guy the hand belongs to——we found him, that is, not Baron here, but this lady, she lost her fiancé and we went down to the wreck site to look for him; I thought it was a hopeless cause because Liam and Martin searched and all for days but damned if he wasn't there and oh, man, he might have gotten caught on the hook I put there as a pirate decoration but I don't think that's a crime, is it? Involuntary manslaughter?"

The chef looked disgusted. "Thomas, shut up."

Victor pinched the bridge of his nose with his fingers, trying to stave off a pounding headache. "Are you telling me—is that Abe? My daughter's ex-fiancé?"

The two men stared at him. The fat one recovered first. "Is it, Thomas?"

"Well, ah, yes. I believe it is."

Victor stepped forward, braced himself, and then ripped the plastic bag open, revealing the bald, puffy, slightly discolored visage of the man who had stolen Victor's future.

"Dear God. That is him. Why is he kind of blue in the face?"

"More red than blue."

"Damned if I know."

The anxiety hit Victor in a wave. "What have you creeps done with my daughter? Is Lydia all right?" The two men exchanged looks, and Victor grabbed Thomas by his white lapels and lifted him. "I said, is she all right?"

"She's at the chamber, at the other side of the island," Thomas said slowly. "I don't know if she's regained consciousness. Yet."

For a terrible moment, all the anger drained out of Victor, leaving him with the single memory of the three-year-old Lydia at the playground, all that blood, he'd only looked away for a second. Oh, that ancient fear, you forgot how deep it went.

"Take me to her," he said. His voice was no more than a whisper.

25

"I liked you better without clothes."

Lydia smiled. They'd been allowed out of the hyperbaric chamber for half an hour, long enough to go to the hut's small bathroom and then escape outside to smell the fresh air. A resort employee had brought Lydia some clothes, a pair of khaki shorts and a pink tank top that didn't really match. Liam was wearing cut-off shorts and a faded tie-dyed shirt that read "Spring Fling '86."

"So where'd you go to college?"

"I didn't."

"Oh. Sorry! But the shirt—"

"It's not my shirt. It's just something some tourist left."

"Sorry."

"Don't be. I'm not embarrassed. I've been living with my own private English teacher, doing my own personal tutorial for the past few years." Liam leaned back against the palm tree, his hand keeping Lydia close to his side. "I just don't have the diploma to show for it."

Lydia pressed a kiss to the firm chest underneath the borrowed shirt. "I wasn't judging you."

"Sure you were. Don't worry—it's pretty typical behavior. It's part of what people do at this stage—figure out who they've gotten involved with from the available clues."

Lydia leaned back, squinting in the sun, trying to read Liam's expression. "You're annoyed with me, aren't you?"

Liam smiled a bit crookedly. "I just don't like the idea of you weighing me against some preapproved criteria. I should tell you right now, I'm not going to fit into some mold of the perfect boy-friend."

"Oh, hell, and I always wanted a perfect boyfriend to go with my perfect breasts and my perfect house. Will you listen to yourself? I don't exactly have a job description I'm trying to fill."

"And if you did?"

"If I did, after today I think I'd be rewriting it."

That was the right thing to say. Liam brushed the hair from her forehead and kissed her, softly and fervently.

Lydia sighed and settled back against him. Overhead, the sky was deeply blue. At their feet, beyond the lawn and a small stone wall, the chamber stood, hidden by the thatch-roofed hut. "I don't want to go back in, Liam."

"I know what you mean. From here, it looks just like a nice hut. Something on *Gilligan's Island*."

"You had that in Ireland?"

"In New York."

Liam laced his fingers inside hers and Lydia glanced over at him under her eyelashes. He looked happy. It was nice to be out in the rel-atively cool air of morning. It was nice to be together, in the moment.

And then Lydia realized that there was something she hadn't told him. Something that really could anger him. Liam might have spo-ken of love, but it was all too clear to her that he was not the kind of man for settling down. Before he'd entered her unprotected, she'd said "It's all right," and he'd understood her to mean she had taken some form of birth-control precautions. What would he say if she told him that in the heat of the moment, she'd decided it was all right to take a chance?

Because the truth was, something had taken hold of her that was stronger than desire. In his arms, Lydia had felt truly, completely wanted and cherished. She had known that there was no chance of lasting happiness with this man. He was not a gladiator, but he was an adventurer, beautiful and independent and charmingly reckless. She had no illusions about reforming him. This was not a romance novel where a pirate might hang up his cutlass, set up a shipping company, and find all the adventure he ever needed with the woman he'd originally thought was his cabin boy.

The memory of Liam's room, requiring an archeological dig to uncover the various strata of bachelorhood, intruded. Liam would be the kind of man who would never fully understand the concept of cleaning, who would never notice when a bathroom began to smell of mildew. She could imagine herself, irritated, putting on her coat and leaving their apartment so that she could just sit in a diner over coffee and get over the sight of him making breakfast without doing last night's dishes.

They'd make up in bed, with wild puppy abandon.

But that was a pipe dream. This love wasn't built to last. It wasn't the kind of love that was going to lead to gold bands and Victorian houses. It wasn't going to end in blood and sorrow, either. They were the boy and girl in the metal bubble and, oddly enough, it sufficed.

"You're awfully silent." Liam brought her hand to his lips and brushed a kiss on her palm.

Lydia cocked her head to one side, blew a little huff of air through her nose, swallowed hard, and then sighed again. "Liam, do you remember when you said you didn't have a condom and I said it was all right?"

"Yes?"

"Well, I think it was all right. I'm pretty sure. It's the wrong time of the month and all, but the truth is—"

"Aw, man! I don't believe it! You said you were all right!" Liam dropped her hand, the expression of dismay on his face almost comical.

"It's completely the wrong time of month, Liam, and I was just feeling so——so . . ." Lydia trailed off, watching his face. His eyes were closed.

"Jesus, woman, I'm Catholic. Do you know how many babies are conceived at the wrong time of the cycle? I don't mean to overreact, but this is a little too much. There were other things we could have done."

Lydia, silent with misery, sat there and stared at the sharp tropical grass. He had not been carried away as she had been. He would have been content with lesser intimacies. She glanced at her watch, not moving her head. "Liam, I think we need to head back now."

"You head back."

"But——we both need——Liam, wait. Where are you going?"

"I need a little time."

"I'm sorry, Liam. Please don't blow this into some huge deal."

"It is a big deal, Lydia! This is a very basic question of trust. You don't go tricking a guy with something like this."

"I didn't try to trick you!"

"What if you do get pregnant?"

Lydia looked down at the ground again. A troop of ants was marching under the bridge of her leg, their existence more precarious than they suspected. "I don't know."

"Agh." Liam raked his hair back, pointed his chin to the cloudless sky, the picture of misery. "I'm not sure how I feel about marriage, let alone children. Shite. I need to clear my head." Liam walked off, leaving Lydia with the incongruous thought that he'd said he wasn't sure about marriage, not that he was completely opposed to it.

I've really messed up, Lydia thought. She walked blindly toward the chamber. She didn't see the man with the camera until he was right in front of her. After a moment, she recognized Martin Thorne, Fish, and—a small jolt of adrenaline kicked through her system—Kira.

"Good morning, Lydia."

"What are you doing here?" For a moment, Lydia could make no sense of the whole tableau, and then one fact penetrated the fog of her thoughts: The blond man was pointing the lens right at her, as if it were a gun.

§

Why did life always wallop you with more than one thing at a time? Liam, who had not been in love in so long that he had forgotten the strength of its magic, had barely had time to assimilate this heady new emotion in his bloodstream when he was hit with its powerful antidote—the feeling of betrayal.

Lydia had used him. He knew, from her closed, guilty face, that she had not been so mindless with pleasure that the thought of pregnancy had never crossed her mind. Instead, she had weighed the risk and judged it permissible—the inconvenience of an abortion deemed a dim but allowable possibility, perhaps, or worse, the prospect of an infant considered and accepted. His infant, his child, twenty-one years of responsibility, a lifetime of responsibility, a moral and philosophical and emotional responsibility for some little stranger.

Liam paced, his bad leg dragging a bit. He was pro-choice, yet the idea of his child being aborted bothered him. Not so much a lingering Catholic abhorrence as the first faint stirrings of desire for a child, the sense that such things are, to some degree, fated. And yet, how could one trust that the universe, or God, or whatever powers natural or supernatural governed such things, would send you the healthy child you hoped for, unafflicted by disease or deformity? In Liam's experience, the universe was seldom benign. And even if the baby was perfect, a perfect baby is like a stroke victim, unable to walk, talk, sit, feed itself. Years go by before it can carry on a conversation, and at that point, you have to worry that it will toddle off into some villain's arms. A vision of all the lifeless infants he had salvaged assailed him. People did such unspeakable things.

Liam stopped, and suddenly a shaft of sunlight hit the grass in just such a way as to conjure up some remnant of childhood vision, some memory of grass when grass meant freedom and rolling and bounding joy, all those long-ago impulses to run and run and jump as high as you can. When did it change? Liam wondered, and then thought, Was this what Lydia felt, a moment of impulse to jump?

Liam wandered rather than walked back to the chamber, thinking about Lydia and embarking on the kind of relationship that could end up with his genes carpooling with hers.

When he finally looked up and saw the group gathered around the entrance to the hut, Liam's first reaction was irritation. Just his luck to have to deal with Fish and Martin and a bunch of nosy strangers at this rarely awful moment in time. It was only as he drew closer that Liam took in the worried look that had replaced Fish's habitual expression of ironic detachment, and observed the strain that had aged Martin five years. Even before fully settling his gaze on the blond man, Liam understood that here was danger. The way everyone was looking at the nattily dressed stranger, it didn't take a brain surgeon to deduce that the man had a gun. These were the unwanted visitors Abe had been expecting, and they knew that Lydia was the key to getting what they wanted: that fucking ring.

In the moments before the group's attention fully focused on him, Liam had time to recite a silent but fervent litany of curses. Back in New York, he'd taken a few lessons in hand-to-hand combat from a guy who'd taught Navy Seals and rescue jumpers, but a little knowledge can be a dangerous thing. Liam knew that if he tried to disarm the gunman with some brilliant kung-fu move, he could very well wind up causing the bad guy to take out some innocent bystander. Like Lydia. Or Fish.

So it was time to use the one weapon Liam always had in abundance: bullshit.

§

"Goddamn. Thought I had at least a good six hours before you guys arrived."

Lydia stared in disbelief as Liam sauntered up with no trace of a limp, stopping to grin disarmingly at Kira's new boyfriend. If that's what he was. Liam held his hands loosely at his sides, palms up: *You caught me.* He looked so charmingly, affably rueful that you wanted to tousle his floppy hair.

He hadn't so much as glanced in her direction.

"Who the fuck are you?" Uncharmed, Misha pointed the little camera gun in Liam's direction. The Russian seemed irritable and red-faced in his safari suit and hat. Lydia thought he might be getting sunburned.

"I'm the guy that nearly—and that's nearly, so don't shoot me— stole that three-million-dollar sparkler out from under your noses." Lydia blinked hard, startled by the figure. Surely Abe wouldn't have spent all the stolen money on one item? And yet it made sense, too, given Abe's penchant for the grand gesture. But why would Liam want to reveal this to the Russian before the gun was even pointed in his direction?

"Please to explain." Misha seemed curious about Liam's motives, too.

"Well, to begin with, Abe's got the ring." Liam said this with such easy good nature that Misha seemed unsportsmanlike when he back-handed the taller man.

"We already hear that Abe is dead. Don't play games."

"Hey, I'm not. I'm not. Christ, that stings." Liam dabbed at his chin with his shirt.

"You also see Abe's body?" Kira's eyes were dark and tearless. It was impossible to decipher what she might be thinking.

"Nope. Only Lydia and the other diver went all the way into the wreck."

Kira glanced at Lydia. "Lydia says that you and she have been in the decompression chamber."

"Recompression chamber."

"And you are sure she has no ring?"

Lydia thought Kira had not been expecting Abe to be dead. When Lydia had mentioned finding his corpse, the younger woman had gasped before she'd caught herself, remembering that she was supposed to already be in mourning. Which meant Liam had been right: Abe had died recently.

"Lydia says she had the ring, but it was stolen."

"How do you know she does not lie?"

Liam grinned. "I'm afraid she, ah, had no place to hide it, if you know what I mean."

Kira said one word in Russian, and it didn't sound particularly flattering.

"Who the hell are you to judge me, Kira?" Lydia put herself right in front of the younger woman's face, but Kira continued looking stonily ahead. "Seems to me you and your so-called brother both played me for a fool."

Kira turned to face her. "*Suka. Prostitutka!* He is not dead one week and already you spread your legs for another!"

Liam nimbly stepped between the two women, addressing Misha. "Actually, he wasn't even dead that long. I think he went back down underneath to hide the ring."

For a moment, Lydia's blood rushed in her ears, a red tide of rage, and she thought about raking Liam's back with her nails. Then, holding herself still because she was still enough of a social worker to remember not to lose control in the presence of a gun, she noticed the way Liam's friend from the dive shop was watching him. As if he were at a command performance.

Maybe this isn't real, she thought. Maybe it's a ruse. In a novel, in a film, it's always clear when someone's playing a part, you can guess the next plot twist. But real life is real life. Sometimes the hero turns out to be a villain. Lydia looked at Martin Thorne, his face battered, his eyes darkening into bruises. He was watching Liam with the same watchful air.

"You stupid whore," Kira was hissing. "He thought you were a joke. We laughed at you."

Ignore her, ignore her, Lydia told herself. She is a distraction, and you need to make a decision here.

Misha was saying, "We need to dive down and then we get the ring?"

"We dive down fast, before someone else finds him."

"And what's your stake in this, my friend?"

Liam paused. "I'd say half, but you've got the gun. On the other hand, you need me. So how about a simple fee—ten thousand, say?"

Misha laughed. "I'll pay you two hundred."

Liam looked angry. "Go fuck yourself."

"You forget, I have the gun "

"Yeah, and what do you have in it? Five bullets? There's four of us here. You plan on taking us out one by one?" Liam snorted in disgust.

"Even here on Epiphany, people tend to notice when the corpses start to stack up. And today's carnival—you won't find another diver for a good forty-eight hours."

"He's right, Misha," said Martin, and the Russian turned abruptly at the sound of his name.

"Well—all right. A thousand. Do you agree to a thousand?"

Liam was about to nod when Lydia made her decision.

"What are you doing?" She kept her voice soft, a mere whisper. "You can't dive now. You'll kill yourself. It's not worth it, Liam."

Misha narrowed his eyes. "She is worried about you."

Liam shrugged. "It was boring in there. She was a distraction."

He grinned, suddenly cheerful. "And she's a bit of a Jewish mother, if you know what I mean. Don't worry, I won't fail you. Let's get over to the docks and—"

"Lydia!"

Lydia turned, to see her father striding toward her in creased navy trousers, a blazer slung over one arm. She stood as he came up to her, panting, his face florid with exertion. "Thank God you're all right."

"Oh, Daddy, what are you doing here?" Lydia was almost in tears. She saw Misha half-turn, leveling the gun at her belligerent, habitually argumentative father, and she knew without a doubt that there was a good chance he would be the first to get shot.

"I came with your brother to try to find Abe. Rodney had this half-baked idea he was still alive."

"But he was," Lydia said.

"Not anymore. I just saw him in the kitchen up there, of all places. What kind of a madhouse is this place?"

Martin stepped forward. "You saw a corpse in the refrigerator?"

"Oh, God." Kira crumpled, and Liam caught her.

"Well, my Irish friend," Misha said happily, "it seems I won't be needing your services after all."

Liam was bent over, helping Kira to her feet. He did not look up once as Kira turned her face up toward him, her lips moving in explanation or apology.

Lydia turned her back on him and slipped her hand through her father's arm.

Good, Liam thought. It was better for all of them if she believed he had betrayed her. Left him free to improvise a game plan. Left him free to manipulate the players.

Left him feeling oddly cold and tight inside, as if he'd swallowed ice.

26

Unable to locate either his sister or his father, Rodney slumped into the dimmest corner of the Loose Screw Motel and Bar and watched as two men deposited a third in a nearby booth.

"You think he's going to be all right here?" asked the younger man, who, although half the size of his companion, seemed to be the one doing most of the lifting.

"Carnival's starting. No one's going to pay any mind to another drunk in the corner."

"Yeah, but what if someone comes up to him and starts talking?"

"Well, they'll find he's a damn good listener." The bigger man clapped his friend on the shoulder. "Don't worry so much. We'll be back before the heat of the day."

The two men left their companion, and, after a few minutes, Rodney realized that the newcomer did not appear to be fully conscious of his surroundings. It was hard to be sure, though, because the fellow was leaning back on the red vinyl seat, his eyes half-hidden by a glittery mask.

"You okay over there?"

The man didn't answer. Either he was too out of it to move or he was passed out.

"Well, don't worry. I'm not judging you, buddy. Hell, we're on vacation, we're permitted. Right? Right." Rodney turned back to his screwdriver, leaving his insensate bar friend to sleep it off in the sour shadows. He knew he sounded like a boy pretending to be a man. He was almost thirty. When would he feel like a man?

"Thing is, I've been judging far too much. Far too much. Shouldn't judge other people, you know, till you've walked in their shoes."

The masked drunk made a kind of sighing sound. So, Rodney thought, he was awake after all.

"Yeah, because sometimes you think you've got all the answers and then it turns out that you don't even know what the questions were." For so many years, Rodney had been part of a team with his parents, a card-carrying member of the we're-all-sensible-but-Lydia's-a-problem club. He did well in college, while Lydia couldn't settle on a major; he married a lovely young woman from the better side of Long Island, while Lydia dragged home a bearded psychologist who criticized her to everyone at the table, or a sardonic Israeli from Samson Movers who kept speaking in Hebrew into his cell phone, or a dozen other barely passable candidates.

Most of whom ended up dumping her, anyway.

But now, with Lydia in such abject disgrace that Rodney could have coasted for years on the aftershocks, something had changed. Lydia's earthquake had uncovered his own fault line. He was unhappy.

Jenna, whose sharpness, wit, and strictly unsentimental loveliness had seemed a welcome contrast to his helplessly romantic mother and sister, had turned into some kind of parody of herself. She was so driven and humorless and uncompromising, it was as if he had married his father. And if Rodney dared suggest another way of doing things, the themes of children, money, and security were trotted out, a holy trinity of goals, the three that are one.

Rodney wanted to tell Jenna that you cannot guard your happiness too closely. He wanted to tell her that you need to be a little foolish with happiness, a little reckless with love. Rodney wanted to tell Jenna to be a little more like his sister, who loved with hopeful innocence again and again. There were so many reasons to become cynical, so many opportunities for despair. For the first time, Rodney saw Lydia's optimistic enthusiasm for what it really was, a kind of bravery.

"I can't stay with my wife any longer." Rodney turned to the drunk, who seemed unresponsive again. He wondered if the guy was all right. Surely it was too early in the day for the man to have drunk himself into a coma. In the distance, Rodney could hear the babble of excited voices. Soon the bar would begin to fill. If Rodney wanted, he would probably be able to find a woman, to sign the dotted line on his marital dissatisfaction, so to speak.

Standing up, Rodney made his decision. "I can't stay here," he told the drunk. "I'll just end up doing something I have to defend in a therapist's office and then have to pay for in divorce court. I have to try and find my sister."

The man passed gas in a long, loud bleat.

"Oh, yeah? Well, at least you're not dead. I was beginning to wonder." Rodney turned to leave, and the man made another, louder noise.

"Look, buddy, that's pretty disgusting, and if you're trying to— oh, forget it. You're not worth it."

It was the third explosion of body gases that did it. As the sickly odor reached Rodney's nose, he whirled around and grabbed the guy by his arm, which he twisted up behind the man's back. There was an odd, stiff resistance to the man's limbs, but the last time Rodney had done this, he'd been in grade school. Maybe people just got stiffer after the seventh grade. "Okay, asshole, you got anything to say, you say it——"

As the man's head lolled to one side, Rodney processed the information that the man really was dead.

As the sequined mask slid to one side, Rodney assimilated the fact that the dead man was Abe.

Shocked speechless, Rodney let his sister's ex-fiancé slip from his fingers. As the corpse slid down the red vinyl seat, its thawing muscles released by Rodney's actions from rigor mortis, the clenched hand relaxed and the dead man revealed his final secret, which rolled with a metallic click onto the filthy barroom floor.

§

There are men who, when faced with life's betrayals, will react with rage and bluster. And there are men who will react with cold fury. It was bad luck having one in any group of individuals, Liam thought. Having two was just plain disastrous.

And in this case, one of the two had a gun.

Watching as Misha discovered there was no dead body in the freezer was not a pretty sight. The blond man went very red in the face and his eyes seemed to bulge a bit in their sockets. The rest of the group stood there in the storeroom with the patience of cowed animals.

All except for Lydia's father, who shook his head with a disgusted half smile and faced Misha as if they were vying for leadership of this small tribe.

"You imbecile. If you hadn't made us waste all that time interrogating the dive guide about——"

"Shut up."

"You just have no idea what to do now, do you?" Lydia's father was the sort who waved his hands when he spoke. Funny, thought Liam, as Lydia's father spoke at length about money and Abe and policemen and bad planning. He would have thought it would be Martin making a stand, because Martin was also the type you either declared chief or left staked to a tree for something sharp-toothed or poisonous to find. Desert-island politics: one leader per tribe, please.

But Martin was silent, which meant Martin was either smarter than Liam had ever suspected, or more badly hurt than he appeared.

Lydia's father finished his rant.

"You are a brave man," said Misha, coming up, very close. "You are not afraid at all?"

"You don't frighten me." He was an inch or so taller than the Russian, but his skin was slack and age-spotted. Liam felt his muscles knot, but kept himself seated. He could feel Martin's eyes on him, and Fish's, too. He knew that they were wondering why the hell he wasn't doing something.

Lydia was too busy watching her father, but doubtless she was wondering, too. When was the big Irishman going to pull the brilliant move and take down herring breath? A good question. A fine question. And Liam would have given his good leg to know the answer.

The shelves of bread and boxed goods added a strangely perfect setting for a showdown. Liam thought that if this were a movie, you just knew that someone would wind up tipping that mountain of cans. And would get up swinging. One gun, two of them, five of us. Good odds if you didn't mind taking a little chance on getting gut shot, or having a stray bullet take the lady down.

Before joining the search-and-rescue diving squad, Liam had walked a beat just long enough to know that what most action films leave out is the fear. Most cops shoot because they're afraid of getting shot. And more cops die because the bad guy panics than because it's so much fun to pull the trigger and watch the uniform drop.

Too much fear can be a killer. But fear is also what stops you from perpetrating real stupidity. You have to pay attention when the little hairs on the back of your neck stand up. Sometimes, scared is a smart thing to be.

Lydia's father would have made a lousy cop. Or a dead one.

Misha walked slowly around his challenger. "So you are not afraid of me. Are you afraid of gun? No? Maybe is brave. Maybe is stupid."

"Put aside the gun, mister, we'll see what's what."

Misha grinned, then looked at his gun hand as if considering the matter.

"Daddy, please." Lydia put her hand on her father's arm.

"Get out of the way, Lydia."

Liam watched as Martin struggled to his feet. "I can't let you do this." His face was white with pain. Fish was staring up at Martin as if he was about to join the bastard, just great, terrific, why don't we all get fucking shot?

Fish grasped Martin's shoulder, facing the Russian. "I suppose I'm in, too."

This time the Russian laughed, but it was a short laugh. "*Slushish,* Kira! Do you hear? What a brave bunch of boys, yes? Only the big Irish one is smart. Or scared."

Or both, thought Liam.

Kira looked grimly at Misha. "Do not forget why we are here."

"But there is still time for a little fun. I think these boys want to play."

Shite. There was too much testosterone flying around here.

Someone was going to get hit. Liam looked over his shoulder, feigning boredom. "I say shoot the mouthy old man first."

"Liam?"

Liam met Lydia's gaze with a lopsided grin plastered on his face. "If he gets a bullet, the odds improve for the rest of us."

The old man was shaking, his fists clenching and unclenching. "This another of your boyfriends, Lydia?"

Lydia looked at Liam with cold loathing. "This is one of those tropical diseases you keep hearing about, Daddy. The kind you think's been wiped out, but here it is—a little bit out of date, a little bit beside the point, but it can still do some damage, if you're stupid enough to let it."

Misha slapped Lydia on one cheek, hard, and she fell back into her father's arms. A random slap. Or a test for Liam? Misha was about to come to a boil. Liam could feel the man watching him, and schooled himself into passivity.

"You talk too much. Shut up," Misha said, "all of you, I need to think."

Lydia's father stood up. "How dare you hit her, you lousy coward."

Misha backhanded the old man, this time with the butt of the gun. Lydia's father went flying assward, knocking over three shelves as he fell. A bottle broke. There was some blood.

"Daddy!" Lydia's wail echoed in the small, cold room, too loud, too loud. Liam could almost hear the Russian's heart beating. As if summoned, Liam felt his eyes drift to Martin's. Don't do anything, Liam prayed. Yeah, I know, one of us is supposed to be the tough guy, but what do I do that won't get us all shot? That won't get anyone shot?

"The next person to make a sound is dead meats. Now everyone keep quiet while I think." There was something about the Russian's voice that reminded Liam of an old substitute teacher who'd come into the class full of book learning and good intentions, but then the kids had misbehaved.

Well, good, thought Liam. I can use that.

"Look, I'm sorry to be butting in here, but you know what the Irish solution would be?" Liam kept his voice pitched low, lilting, mild and cheerful. He felt every pair of eyes turn and stare at him.

"Fuck do I care what the Irish do?" But Misha did care, Liam could tell. It was just like the substitute teacher—he needed a student who would do what he asked him to, to turn the tide.

"Pick one hostage, tie the rest of them up, and head on over to the local pub."

Misha's eyes narrowed. "You making fun of me?"

"That's where you'll find out what's going on. Everyone's drunk out of their minds there. There can't be that many corpses on the island. Someone's going to let something slip."

"And you want to be hostage? You want to help me?"

"I want in on the money, ideally. At the very least, I want not to get shot. Also, it's a bit cold in here."

Misha threw back his head and laughed, as he was intended to. It was all working perfectly well, and then Lydia spoke up.

"Don't do this, Liam."

Aw, Christ, no. "Look, darlin', I'm sorry to hurt your feelings, but the romance is over. Finished. Kaput. It's every man for himself, and you might as well get used to it."

She listened to him with her head cocked, as if she could hear something different being said on some other, subliminal frequency. "You didn't have to be a part of this. You used to be a cop. You saw right away that there was trouble. I could tell from the way you went still, right before you smiled at him. You could have just walked away, alerted the police."

Well, it was grand that she was so bright and all, and lovely she trusted him, but for Jesus' sake, did she have to talk so damn much?

"Sweetheart, three million dollars' worth of blue gem is a lot to give up just on account of a little trouble."

Liam watched her think about this. "I don't buy it."

"Aw, bloody hell," he said to Misha in real irritation, "who cares what she thinks? There's my offer to discuss."

"He's lying." Lydia's right cheek was still bright red in the shape of the Russian's hand. "He's lying because he thinks it will protect the rest of us. He's trying to be a hero, and if you take him off on his own he'll probably try to overpower you and get shot."

"You stupid cow," Liam said, too angry to think. He'd finally figured a way to do something to get their bacon out of the fire and she was screwing it up.

"Is this true?" Misha raised his eyebrows.

"No, it's not true! I got a leg over the silly wee bitch and now she's trying to make out we have some big romance going. I have no intention of going against a man with a gun. Particularly not for some chesty blonde." He gestured at Kira. "That one's more my type, anyhow."

Misha looked at both of them. "Is she?" The Russian stroked his smooth cheek thoughtfully. "Go kiss her."

"Do what?"

Misha pointed his camera gun at Kira. "Go kiss her. Kira, come here." He uttered a quick slew of Russian words.

The pretty brunette came over, her expression so weary she looked ten years older. Liam looked at her, looked at Misha. "I'm not sure I know the name of this game."

"No, no, not game. Is test. To see who is telling truth. First you kiss Kira, then you kiss Lydia. A kiss can tell a lot, yes? But you must kiss big, like Hollywood. No little touch on cheek for your grandmother."

"Sure thing."

"Misha, no." The brunette let loose with a stream of invective, but Misha answered her tersely, and then she bowed her head and approached Liam.

Kissing a woman who had just lost her lover was not really Liam's cup of tea in the best of times. Right now, it was close to hellish. But Liam gave it his best shot, tangling his hands in her silky, dark hair, caressing her jaw with his thumbs. He angled his head and bent his body into hers, and stiff and unresponsive as she was, he tried to make it look like he was enjoying it. Her mouth tasted metallic, like fear and injury.

Misha's clapping broke the spell. "Very good. Now, the other one."

Lydia waited for him, raising her chin. She looked proud and brave and vulnerable, face bare of makeup and naked with emotion. She had tried to protect him, but Liam knew her trust was a fragile thing.

He intended to break it.

He kissed her without hands, passionlessly, with no contact below the neck. He opened his mouth as little as possible, just enough to taste the salt of her tears. She was trying to hold herself very still, so tense he could feel the fine tremble in her jaw. It was the kind of kiss you give a lover before you say good-bye. Suddenly, with that thought, the kiss deepened, became tender, raw, charged with all the things they had said to each other. With all the things left unsaid. Liam pulled himself back, plastering a little smile on his lips, as if he were sorry he couldn't do better.

Lydia regarded him, eyes dark with pain, and Liam felt his smile slip, knowing he'd miscalculated; this fraught silence was more elo-quent than passion.

Liam was still trying to figure out how to finesse the moment when a shot rang out. There was a scuffle of feet and a shout, and it was over so fast that by the time Liam got his head up, he saw Mar-tin clutching his bleeding left side, just below the shoulder.

"Fish," Martin said, sliding down the wall.

Fish was there in an instant, trying to hold him up, and failing. "I'm here, Martin."

A thin smile appeared on the injured man's lips. "Sorry, old man."

Fish didn't smile back. "What are *you* apologizing for?"

Liam went over to Martin, checked his pulse. The wound was leaking blood, not pumping it; maybe the tough old goat would pull through. Liam pulled off his shirt and wadded it over the wound. "Put your hands here, Fish. Now press, hard. Harder."

Martin kept his head back, not trying to watch what was going on. "Lionel. I'm sorry about fooling you that way. About Messalina." His voice was flat, uninflected.

Fish watched as the fabric slowly turned red. "I don't suppose I mind all that much."

Martin turned. "You don't?"

Fish's gaze flicked up to Martin's, then back to his hands. "Let's just say I don't want to look a gift horse in the mouth, okay? We have a good thing going."

"You mean—are you saying you would consider—carrying on?"

"It depends what you mean by carrying on."

Liam stood up slowly, trying to use the distraction Fish and Mar-tin were providing to think of the right rabbit to pull out of his hat.

Nothing came to mind. Since brain had failed, Liam decided to let mouth have a try. "All right, that's one screwup. Are we going to stick around here until someone else gets shot?"

Misha raised his pale eyebrows and smiled. "So you say we leave now? Maybe is good idea. Or maybe blond girl is right. You are trying to make safe your friends." The last word was laced with arsenic.

"Hey, I'm lookin' out for myself." Liam spread his hands wide, a wry grin on his face. This was good. He wondered what he was going to say next. "A bit of money goes missing, you can drop out of sight, no problem." Letting the humor drop out of his voice, playing it serious now. "But you go shoot up a bunch of hostages, and you, too, can be famous, your face plastered on the daily rag. Your manhunt covered on national television."

There was a moment of silence in the storeroom. Misha kept his eyes locked with Liam's. More confident now, Liam pointed at the floor, where Lydia had joined Fish in trying to make Martin more comfortable.

"Martin's on his way out, the old man's cruising for a bullet—this whole situation is just going straight to hell, and you know it."

Kira, her lush mouth thinned with irritation, turned to Misha. "He is right, Misha. There is no point to staying here now."

Misha responded in Russian, his tone aggressive but not angry.

It was at this moment that Lydia's father decided to make a heroic leap into action. Leaning sideways, the older man attempted to vault over a box, intending to kick the Russian's legs out from under him. Unfortunately, the box was not balanced correctly and Victor Gold landed on his hip. A bullet whizzed by, glass shattered, and Kira screamed.

Cursing Lydia's old man, Liam took a step forward just in time to look straight into the Russian's eyes as the gun was raised and sighted in his direction. Of course, it's me he's worried about, thought Liam, and tensed his muscles in order to throw himself sideways just as Fish let out a shocked gasp of pain that was so loud everyone turned in his direction.

"What is it, Fish?" Liam ignored the gun still cocked and aimed at him.

"Little pain."

"Little chest pain?"

"No—arm." Fish looked pale. He was gasping a little.

Misha gave a snort of disbelief. "You want me to believe this one is dying, too?"

"His lips are turning blue." Lydia's voice was surprisingly calm. "I don't think he's getting enough air."

"This is a joke, yes?" Misha was still pointing the gun at Liam's head.

"Oh, yeah, I'm laughing." Lydia helped settle Fish down beside Martin, who was reaching out a hand to his friend.

"Careful," Lydia said, "that's making your shoulder bleed again."

This is it, thought Liam. Things were falling apart and fast; there wasn't going to be a better chance. In the split second before Misha turned away from the injured men, Liam jabbed his left elbow into the Russian's gut, grabbing the Russian's gun hand with his right hand and twisting so the weapon was pointing back at its owner. Unfortunately, this put Liam back in front of the gangster, in the perfect position to be punched by the other man's strong left.

"You fool! I kill you!"

Liam concentrated on breaking the man's wrist as he took blow after blow to the jaw and throat. Then his opponent jabbed a knee up toward Liam's groin and Liam jerked back, whipping the man's hand around with an audible crack at the elbow, propelling the gadgety gun through the air and into some dusty corner.

Just what his martial-arts instructor had always warned him not to do, because hey, the bad guy usually has a buddy. Out of the corner of his eye, he could see Kira already heading toward the weapon.

Liam delivered a quick roundhouse kick to the Russian's knee and watched him stumble.

"Lydia, the gun! Get the gun!"

Lydia dove for it just as Kira pounced, and the two women wound up rolling on the floor, Lydia grunting with the effort of keeping the smaller woman's nails out of her eyes. The gun was somewhere down there. Liam moved his big body between Misha and the women, wishing to hell that he was faster, wishing he'd been in a few more barroom brawls.

And then Misha was up and fighting, using his shorter, more muscular build to aim punishment at Liam's bare midsection. Good, the man had no idea what he was doing—Liam's stomach was strongly muscled and hard to injure. Liam had the better reach, and as long as they weren't doing too much running around, his gimpy leg wouldn't trip him up too much.

Down on the ground, Lydia had gained the upper hand. She managed to grab the gun, and then Kira bit her on the soft flesh of her upper arm, right near her elbow. Lydia screamed and whipped her arm around, sending the gun flying back behind some boxes.

"You lousy bitch," Lydia screamed, "you're not supposed to bite!"

Then Misha switched tactics and aimed a kick toward Liam's groin. Liam moved to protect himself and got a swift poke in the left eye. After that, Liam couldn't quite catch what happened next with the women. Truth was, Lydia seemed to be doing better than he was. The blond man had started to use his elbows and kept moving in, aiming for Liam's throat, twisting his punches to tear the skin. Liam realized there was a very good chance he was going to lose this fight.

"Stop playing with him, Liam!"

Liam turned to Lydia, distracted, and took another sucker punch to the head.

"Take him out!"

"What do you think I'm trying to do?"

Liam heard a slap and a grunt from where the women were tangling, but couldn't afford to glance over there again. "I think you're trying not to shoot your dad!"

There was a sudden, searing pain in Liam's knee, and he almost stumbled over Martin, on the floor. Misha had just scored a kick to his bad leg. Shit. She was right. He'd been holding back. And now it was too late.

"Sorry, Martin."

"You bloody bastard! Liam, he's grabbed a knife!"

Liam dodged left, the blade sliding along his naked ribs. Then, instead of retreating, he launched himself at Misha, no longer thinking, just letting go; in some crazy way, it was like sports or sex, he just gave his body permission to take over. There was a crack of bone and Misha dropped the knife. There was the satisfyingly meaty sound of his punches connecting. Liam realized he was beating the shorter man back toward the wall.

And then something came crashing down on the Russian's head and the man went down, the back of his head blossoming blood. A lot of blood, even for a head wound. Liam looked up into Lydia's father's brown eyes. For the first time, he could see the resemblance to his daughter. "I was going to take him," Liam said. "But thanks all the same. What'd you hit him with?"

"A can of tomatoes. You're the most completely incompetent fighter I ever saw," said the older man.

"Why don't you just take some Viagra." Liam turned to see how Lydia was doing. His lady had three deep scratches down her cheek and a few bite marks on her arms, but Kira looked like she was going to have a black eye. The two women were still circling each other, so

Liam reached out, grabbed the brunette, and pulled her shirt over her head to pin her arms behind her back.

"What the hell?" Her little breasts heaved in their lace cups.

"Nothing personal, sweetheart, but I'm tying you up in your own clothes." This, at least, he knew how to do. "Somebody go fetch that gun."

Lydia was bent over at the waist, panting.

"You all right, Lyd?"

She dragged the tangle of hair out of her face, glaring up at him holding the brunette in his arms.

"You did great."

She grunted, in agreement or in pain, he wasn't sure which.

Lydia's father came up, holding the gun. "Found it."

"Well, point it at her, not me." Liam handed Kira over and knelt down on the floor where Fish was fighting for breath, his elfin face mottled and puffy.

"How are you doing there?"

"Okay." His sweat held an acrid note of fear.

"We're going to get you to the hospital right away, Fish."

"Martin—Martin needs help more." Fish paused, panted. "Tell her—tell your blonde—"

"The name's Lydia, and I'm here." She turned to Martin, who looked ashen but composed. "You bleeding again?"

"I think it's stopped." Martin looked at Liam. "You did all right there, MacNally."

"Like hell I did. Lydia's old man had the right of it."

"Don't be—" Martin broke off and winced as Lydia lifted the corner of the makeshift bandage, trying to inspect the wound. "Don't be so hard on yourself. I kept worrying you were going to get us all shot."

"So this time I didn't act like a cowboy. Christ, maybe I should have. Look at you. Look at Fish."

Martin closed his eyes tightly, as if in pain, and then opened them to look at Liam with quiet intensity. "Quit feeling sorry for yourself and go get help, Liam."

"I'm going. Fish, you just hold on there. Can you do that for me?"

Fish opened his mouth, trying to say something.

"Save it for when I get back, Fish. Lyd, you take good care of Fish and Martin."

"Where are you going?"

He spared a moment to touch the side of her face where Kira's nails had left bloody scratches. "To get help."

Liam ran, bare chested, out the door, down the stairs, and straight into the parade of drunken revelers.

27

Rodney had been trying to make his way down one street for the past hour and a half, but had been waylaid by bare-breasted women with skin ranging in color from espresso to latte, their gyrating hips encased in sequinned and befeathered skirts, as well as by a few dozen stilt walkers and sweat-soaked fishermen lifting bottles of beer and cheap wine and tumblers of rum-spiked drinks. There was the muskily sweet scent of marijuana in the air. The steel drums were so loud they seemed to be acting as a frenetic pacemaker. Rodney's heart seemed to be tripping around crazily in his chest in syncopated rhythm.

He'd attempted a detour, but in every alley, a couple was up against a wall, writhing to various rhythms of their own devising.

There was no way out. And in his pocket, a blue jewel the size of an eyeball felt as if it were burning into his left palm. Afraid to remove his hand from the ring lest he be pickpocketed, Rodney had only one hand to push against the crowds.

If only he weren't so damned drunk. Rodney felt his foot slip on something sticky, caught himself, then began to slip again. The crowd surged and pushed against him.

I'm going to die, Rodney thought, as he began to sink below knee level, and then he heard someone shouting, Make way, make way, we need an ambulance. Thank God, Rodney thought, and then he realized that no one knew he was down here.

Someone stepped on his right hand and Rodney screamed. It was barely audible over the din of laughter and music. Rodney remembered hearing of people trampled and killed in just this fashion. I should have stayed at home, thought Rodney. A bad marriage isn't such a terrible thing. Just as tears of fright began to spring to his eyes, he heard someone say, "Hey, there's something under my foot."

A large hand hauled him up and Rodney found himself gazing into the very pale eyes of a very tall, slightly bloody, half-naked man.

"Are you all right, man?"

"I think so."

The tall man turned away and began bellowing at the crowd. Finally, blessedly, the throng of people began to part, and Rodney could see the flashing light of a small white ambulette and the distinctive *nee-na* siren he recognized from British films.

"Clear the goddamn way!" The giant who had saved him bent and hoisted Rodney over his shoulders in a fireman's carry. "Over here, damn you! I'm the one who called!"

How did he know I'd need an ambulance? Rodney wondered groggily, and then someone yelled something and threw a bottle that bounced against the ground and then cracked, splintering glass.

And then everything went black.

§

Lydia sat, watching her brother and thinking about how long it had been since she'd seen his face look this young. There were small cuts and abrasions on his cheek, and a few bandages applied by gentle nurses who wore old-fashioned white caps that looked like wings. There was a dark picture of a Madonna on the wall across from the bed. Or maybe it was just the Madonna who was dark. The infant Jesus had been depicted as pale and blue-eyed. Or perhaps the child had just been bathed in some heavenly light. His little fingers curled shrimplike around his mother's neck.

Rodney opened his eyes, blinked, and then said, "Hi."

Lydia smiled and took his hand. "Hi there."

Rodney winced. "Lydia? What the hell—where am I?"

"You're okay. You're in the Sisters of Mercy Hospital." She glanced over her shoulder. "Dad's here, too."

Victor Gold got up from his chair slowly, his thick, silvery hair tangled over his forehead in a way that made him look older than his sixty-five years. "What the hell were you thinking of, son? Drunk at eleven in the morning? Stumbling the wrong way through that crowd of hopped-up natives?"

"Dad." Lydia put her hand on his arm.

"I thought you were out looking for your sister. Instead, I learn you nearly got yourself killed acting like a goddamn teenager. Seems like your mother and I raised two idiot children."

"Dad, would you shut the hell up?" Lydia could feel her brother's surprise, but she knew herself well enough to feel no shock at her own sudden strength. It had always been easier for her to defend Rodney than to speak out for herself.

"What did you say?"

"You heard me. Your son is lying in a hospital bed, you nearly got yourself killed acting fairly macho and stupid, and, frankly, this is supposed to be the moment where you hug the two of us and tell us you love us."

"I won't be told how to feel!"

Lydia smiled at Rodney, who, although pale and bruised against the white sheets, seemed more recognizably her brother than he had in years. There was a huge wooden crucifix hanging over his head and Lydia wondered if she needed permission to remove it. It looked threatening.

"How are you, Lydia?" Rodney's voice was hoarse.

"I'm okay. Thank you for coming to save me. You too, Dad."

Both men managed to look a bit guilty, and Lydia found herself laughing. "Oh, I know you probably came for the money. But, Dad, I know you weren't worried about the cash back in that kitchen store-room. You were worried about me."

"Of course I was worried about you! You're a walking disaster!"

Lydia hugged him, and for a moment, her father was stiff and unyielding, but then he brought one awkward hand up to pat her back, as if she were a game-show contestant who had gotten too friendly.

"I am so sorry about the money, Daddy," she said, and he patted her again, just as clumsily.

"I guess we'll manage," he said, clearing his throat.

"Well, at least I found Lydia's engagement ring. That ought to be worth a few thousand, anyway."

Both Lydia and her father turned to look at Rodney.

"Hey, what are you staring at? I know it's only a drop in the bucket compared to the three mil, but at least—"

"You found the ring? Are you sure?" Victor Gold moved closer to his son. "Where is it?"

Rodney furrowed his brow. "It was in my pocket when that tall guy hauled me out of the crowd . . ."

Lydia turned and picked up Rodney's stained white jeans, folded on a chair. With her father and brother watching her closely, she shook the pants, carefully patting both pockets before turning them inside out.

There was a strange look on her father's face, a slack grimace, as if he'd just been to the dentist and the Novocaine was wearing off. Her brother simply looked baffled.

"Sorry, guys. I knew that was too good to be true. It's not there now."

"I guess it must have fallen out." Rodney did not sound as upset as her father looked, Lydia thought, but then, he didn't know the whole story. Or that the ring was the whole story.

The three Golds stood in silence, all looking at Rodney's pair of stained white jeans. "Check again," Rodney suggested.

There was a knock on the door, and Liam stuck his head in. "Am I intruding?'

"No. Come on in."

Liam came in, his hair still damp from a shower, wearing a clean denim shirt and jeans over the battered pointy toes of a pair of old cowboy boots. It was the first time Lydia had seen him in anything but bare feet or sandals. He seemed toweringly tall, handsome, a stranger. She knew she looked pale and worn. There were scratches on her face, and she was wearing loose, unflattering seersucker overalls, her travel clothing, the only things she had left that were still clean.

"How is your brother?"

"Just bruised. What about Fish?"

"He's okay. For now." Liam raked his hair back, glancing sideways at Lydia's father. "He's going to have to quit smoking, though, and drinking, too. I have the feeling Martin's going to be helping him clean up his act."

"Martin's all right, too?"

"Yeah, it was just his shoulder, which is what I thought when I saw it—"

"Excuse me. But what is he doing in here?"

"Dad." Rodney raised himself up on the bed. "That's the guy. He saved my life."

"He treated your sister like a whore. And he's probably stolen the ring."

Lydia and Liam both turned to regard Victor Gold, who suddenly looked so tired in his wrinkled suit, a halo of white stubble on his jaw, that he commanded a certain compassion.

"Listen," Liam began, "I want you to know that I'm sorry for whatever I said that gave you the impression your daughter meant nothing to me. I was just trying to lull Misha into a sense that he could trust me."

"You don't fool me. You're good looking and you're slick and you probably never say anything that can be held against you in a court of law, but at bottom you're the type of guy who's out for no one but himself. Now, you may have your own good reasons for being what you are, but I don't care to hear them. You're no good for my daughter, and my daughter deserves someone good. She's been through too goddamn much to have her heart broken by another lousy con man."

"I'm not a con man, sir," Liam said with quiet intensity.

"Prove it."

Liam reached into his pocket, producing Abe's ring. The light from the window played over the brilliant facets of the blue gem. "Here you go, then. This fell out of your son's pocket when I picked him up. I believe it belongs to your daughter."

"Actually, it belongs to me, as it was probably bought with my money. And that still doesn't prove anything to me other than the fact that you're not as blatant a thief as that other one."

"With all due respect, sir, I don't need to prove anything to you." Liam's face was now taut with anger even though he was still smiling. "Lydia's opinion is really the only one that counts. And I'll do my explaining to her alone."

Lydia watched her father turn to her, his eyes sunk more deeply into his skull, his skin somehow looser, more shadowed than she had ever seen it before. He looked like an old man, her formidable father. He looked tired and tender and as if he had just come to the end of a very long road. There was a red crease on his left cheek, where he'd rested his head against the back of the chair.

"Lydia," her father said, "for once in your life, show a little self-respect. Tell this man to just go home and leave our family alone."

Lydia looked at the man who had come closer to her than any other living being, who had touched her so intimately that she had felt the pleasure down to her soul. He looked proud and affronted and so desperately young, despite the size and breadth of him, despite the lines fanning out from the corners of his stormy gray eyes. Lydia suddenly knew that there would come a day when he would stand before her like this, wounded and rebellious, demanding that she expect no proof from him, that she accept him on his own terms or none at all. It was the part of him that had never grown up. He had shot his own father and never been forgiven and now he wanted some kind of Holy Grail of unconditional love to cure him. Except, there was no such thing, thought Lydia, thinking of the picture of the Madonna and child on the opposite wall. Even mothers despair of their screaming newborns and need a moment's relief. Even priests need signs, need talismans and relics to sustain them.

"Are you coming outside with me, Lydia?" He stood, weak left leg bent, like one of two choices in a Renaissance painting: the lover or the father.

"Oh, Liam," she said, feeling older than she ever had before, feeling like the oldest person in the room. "You don't have to explain anything to me. I knew what you were doing in there—don't you remember, I'm the one who called your bluff?"

"You're not angry?"

"There wouldn't be much point in being angry. You were trying to save my life again. I'd be a fool to be hurt by anything you said while you were acting a part."

Liam watched her closely. "You're breaking up with me, aren't you?"

Lydia thought of all the things she could say, but they all amounted to admitting that she was leaving him because if she didn't, if she hung on, she knew he would wind up leaving her. And that was too much honesty. "I have to get back and get on with my life, Liam. There's a seat available on tonight's flight back to New York." She watched his face change as she walked up to him, resting her hand on his lean, tanned cheek. God, but he was beautiful. The pain bracketing his mouth with deep lines only made him seem all the more handsome, a hint of suffering that he could nurture for a while with his poetry and his midnight swims. She thought of how he'd reacted to her telling him about not using birth control, and knew, even though he'd had every right to be upset, that this was not a man who would be ready for children until he was old and gray and well past his time of adventuring.

"Is that all this comes down to, Lydia?"

"What else do you want from me? Liam, you are who you are, and I love you for it, but you're not going to turn into the kind of man who wants a steady job, a steady woman, a family to come home to. You've left New York, but I have a life back there."

"Do you?"

Lydia was silent for a moment. "I will," she said. "I'll make sure of that."

"You could stay here."

"On a permanent vacation?"

"As a hairdresser. You could open your own shop, something here at the resort. We could see what happens between us. What have you got to lose?"

Lydia's father cleared his throat. "Don't do it, Lydia. You'll find yourself stuck here in six months' time while he's out gallivanting with some new girl. Come back home."

"Leave her alone, Dad." Rodney shook his bandaged head. "Don't let anyone decide things for you, Lydia."

"Don't worry, Rodney. I won't." Standing on her tiptoes, Lydia kissed Liam on the corner of his mouth. In his ear, she whispered, "I'll take a morning-after pill. Don't worry about—complications."

Liam gripped her hand, his eyes unreadable. "I'm not asking you to do that."

"I'm doing it for myself. I need to figure out what to do with my own life, and I think, for the moment, I need to put love and marriage and babies to the side." She tried to kiss him again, but Liam stopped her, his hand on her wrist.

"Why are you doing this?"

"Because it's time for me to be on my own for a while."

At her admission, something relaxed in Liam's face, and for the first time since he'd entered the room, Lydia saw the man who'd collapsed in her arms. "But, Lydia, this doesn't have to end this second. We could see each other long distance at first, and then, who knows—"

The lights of the hospital room brightened and distorted, and Lydia felt her mouth begin to tremble. "No, Liam. No."

Liam turned to leave, stopped, turned back. "The doctors checked you out? You're safe to fly out of here?"

She nodded. "What about you? Are you okay?"

Liam inclined his head, a jerky sort of nod, almost a bow. It made him seem Irish in a different way. It made him seem old fashioned. Then he walked out the door, his boots clicking on the floor.

It was funny, but even as she watched him leave, bruised and aching with the knowledge that she would never see him again, Lydia knew that what she felt was nothing compared to the pain she would have suffered had she stayed long enough for him to say the words.

It shouldn't have mattered, but it did. She was glad she'd been the one to break things off.

§

All the long taxi ride to the airport, their car periodically stalled among throngs of flirtatious, screamingly costumed women and their dancingly exuberant men, Lydia waited for the moment when Liam would come, hurtling himself through the beer- and rum-soaked parade, to wrap her in his arms and reveal that he had been changed, transformed by love.

There was a moment when someone pounded on the hood of the old Ford, and Lydia pressed the heel of her hand to her heart, inhaling deeply, trying to prepare for some unforseen danger, the madness of crowds, but it was only Baron, gloriously fat in a pink satin jacket, his face wreathed in smiles. Thomas, beside him, looked drawn and haunted, unmasked, but he, too, smiled at her, happy, no doubt, to be sending her off in something other than a hearse. As the taxi took off again, Lydia heard Baron's surprisingly light tenor calling after her, "*Para bailar la bamba, se necesita, una poca de gracia.*" It took a moment, but then the steel drums followed him, and as the crowd parted to allow them through, Lydia heard the familiar folk song with its rousing, lilting rhythm follow her down the dusty roads of Epiphany. To dance the bamba takes a little bit of grace. A little bit of grace, and a little something else. But what the hell else did it take? Lydia felt all out of grace.

"What was that chef doing, singing to you?" Her father's voice was full of outrage. His spirits were returning at the prospect of returning home, contrite children in tow. "That was the guy who was hiding Abe's body. What are they on this island, cannibals?"

Lydia and Rodney grinned at each other, and the humor of the moment carried Lydia through baggage claim and up into the airplane.

But in the quiet of her seat, as other passengers bustled about stowing their bags, Lydia felt the stabbing pain of loss. Here was the grief she had not been able to feel earlier in the week, the almost physical sensation of trying to hold your body around some impossible injury. Liam wasn't coming after her. There was no final reprieve. He was hurt and mad and probably, way deep down where he didn't have to examine it too closely, relieved. And yet, as the captain announced a five-minute delay so that the Styrofoam meals could be delivered, Lydia found herself waiting again.

"Lydia?"

"I'm fine, Rodney." Their father had agreed to sit alone, giving up his seat so that brother and sister could be alone together for the first time in years. Lydia remembered how they had comforted each other all those years ago during their parents' arguments. Their parents didn't fight like that anymore. She and Rodney were, like all siblings, fellow exiles from a country that no longer existed.

"What are you thinking, Sis?"

Lydia looked out the window and smiled. "That in real life, flights are delayed, and from time to time, canceled, but not for love."

Rodney squeezed her arm. "It's going to be all right."

"I know."

"I'm going to leave Jenna."

Lydia turned from the window and stared at her brother. "You're joking. What happened?"

"A little mess intruded on our perfect life, and I didn't like the way she reacted."

Lydia winced. "Guess I was the mess."

"And thank God for you." For a while, the siblings just sat side by side. At takeoff, as Epiphany dwindled into a green spot in a blue sea, Rodney held his palm out for his sister's hand. And just before landing, he asked her if she'd consider looking for an apartment to share with him.

"It had better be cheap," Lydia said. "I plan on going to back to school part-time." Rodney raised one eyebrow. "Oh, I think I deserve to go back. I've just learned I don't have such bad judgment after all, and I think I did pretty well in the line of fire."

"Dad's not going to pay, you know."

"I'm willing to work my way through school."

"Yeah, well, if I wind up paying more rent, I get to choose the bedroom first."

Lydia looked at her younger brother, the one who always seemed to get the better end of the deal, and smiled. "I'll think about it." Then she turned toward the window again and watched as the toy city of New York grew larger and larger until they touched ground and it was real.

28

Liam stood outside the Chrysalis Salon and Day Spa, cold and underdressed for the gray March day in his thin wool coat, longing for the cigarettes he'd quit smoking. He'd known for the entire month since Lydia had left the island that he would eventually be standing here, but he had delayed as long as possible. He'd waited until the absence of anyone—of Lydia—touching him had begun to make him feel disembodied. He'd waited until he was sure that whatever the hell was going on between Fish and Martin wouldn't wind up sending either man into an early grave.

He'd waited to feel some sign of readiness in himself, to feel the certainty that his rebel spirit wouldn't rise up and want to shoot all the authority figures that came his way. He had to be sure that he was all right in himself before thinking of taking the next step. It wouldn't be fair to go to her any other way.

And then Baron had come to sit next to him in the Loose Screw bar, looking like a hipster juju man in his dashiki and dark shades. "Man, you still hanging around here? I thought you saw that blond girl and that's all she wrote, you'd get your Irish ass back to New York and go get froze looking for corpsicles."

After a beer or two, Liam had said something about making sure, and he might have rambled on about kids and fathers and not wanting to be like his old man, looking a child in the eye and saying, You have to understand why I am the way I am, because children shouldn't have to understand anything about their parents' childhoods. There shouldn't be excuses and explanations and lapses of judgment. Or there shouldn't be children brought into the deal.

Baron had removed his sunglasses, to look at him with something between irony and amazement. "Liam, you all messed up about this. If folks waited till they was one hundred percent ready to move on from the past, till they was totally over what their folks done to them, well, the human race wouldn't need much real estate, 'cause there'd be about three people left on earth, Gandhi and the Reverend Martin Luther King Junior and maybe Miss Ella."

Then Baron had clapped Liam on the back and pressed a cassette into his hand, saying, "Just in case the lady needs a little extra convincing. I know how you love that jazzy eighties shit."

Before Liam had left the bar, he'd bumped into Thomas, still looking unnaturally thin and intense, muttering something about prop men and downtime and flights to L.A. According to Baron, the police were all puffed up at having two international criminals in their custody, and were busy trying to impress the NYPD by continuing their investigation of how one deceased Abe Bohemius had wound up gallivanting through the resort kitchen before showing up in the bar wearing a dive suit and half a mask, especially as the coroner had ruled death by drowning, with no alcohol in the dead man's bloodstream.

There had been a fair amount of beer on the corpse's hair, though this was thought to be a carnival misadventure rather than a contributing factor to the cause of death.

Liam had not really known what to say. Such things were stranger on Epiphany than they were back in Manhattan. Well, to be honest, this would have been a bit out of the ordinary, even in Manhattan.

But Thomas seemed to have come out all right. Jittering with nervous energy, the young man had spun some tale about unclaimed bodies and rights and cadavers bequeathed to medical science often winding up sold for use in horror films. He had a plan, he kept repeating. He had a plan.

"Thomas," Liam had said, "what are you on about?" But he hadn't really wanted to know. If a set of convincingly antique-looking bones wound up as part of an authentic pirate exhibit, Liam didn't want to go looking for fillings.

Selling the business to Neptune's Rest had been surprisingly painless. It had reminded him of how he'd felt when he and Altagracia had gotten divorced; he hadn't realized how much he'd wanted out till he was standing on the other side. All in all, you couldn't say it smelled like success, but it didn't completely stink of failure, either. And Martin didn't feel so much like the enemy now that Fish was Martin's partner, whatever the hell that meant to a man who was having trouble walking and had to keep nitroglycerin on hand. Liam had even felt a moment's affection for the man when he'd said, "Going to find your Miss Gold? Good. She seemed up to the task of handling you."

Fish had been rather less kind. Sulky and snappish, his old mentor had made some catty remarks about how Liam was still searching for a parent, this time for a mother figure. Liam had wanted to say, Look, all you ever wanted was for me to see clearly, and to make conscious choices. I'm doing that now. But Fish was still locked in his role as critic, and, ironically, it was Martin who had made it easier, saying, "Go and find out. It's also all right to be wrong once in a while."

His last day on the island, sitting on the beach at dawn, Liam had felt a presentiment. He'd just signed his name for the sixth time on some interminable contract, and the warm breeze smelled of salt and water and the slightly cloying sweetness of too many different kinds of competing flowers. Dense, low clouds sailed overhead like a ghost armada, a baby crab scuttled near Liam's left big toe, and there wasn't another living soul out yet to spoil his view. And suddenly Liam had known that in three years he would come back to a very different place. Epiphany was changing. Carnival this year had been twice the size of last year. The flights during winter season were beginning to fill up.

Barring acts of God or nature, such as a really bad hurricane or an earthquake, Epiphany's tourist trade would grow. And the vast, colorful archipelago of coral reefs would begin to choke and die from all the clumsy, amateur divers who bobbed up and down and landed in a flurry of spastic motion in the middle of those living aquatic cities like so many frantic chickens trying to come to roost.

If the huge cruise ships decided to drop by, then the great palace hotels might rise up, along with slick arcades of shops filled with pretty coral earrings filched by fishermen from the dwindling reef and endangered tortoiseshell and duty-free perfumes.

Liam wondered why people went all the way to the Caribbean to buy perfume and considered it a bargain.

His only consolation would be that he, too, would have changed. And now Liam thought, The only thing standing between me and my future is that glass door. With that enormous brass doorknob.

§

"It'll look natural? Like it did when I was a child playing out in the sun?"

"That's why I'm using two shades, one a little darker than the other. Trust me, you'll be Toddler-on-Miami-Beach blond."

"Wonderful. Of course, if I could get away with it, I'd go for something like what you're doing these days, Lydia. Is that platinum?"

"Not quite."

"Well, I like it. And the choppy new cut, too. But you won't do anything like that to me, right? Just trim the ends."

"No razoring, I promise." Lydia wrapped a section of Miriam Hirsch's hair in foil and took out her bleach brush to paint the next highlight.

"So how is psychology school, Lydia? Your mother says you're going back."

"Social-work school. I won't begin until June, when the summer session starts."

"Excuse me." Lydia looked up at the sharp-featured receptionist, who was wearing the salon's uniform of black turtleneck and slacks.

"What is it, Jade?"

"There's this guy here to see you. Says he's a month late for his appointment, but hopes you'll see him anyway."

Oh, she saw him instantly. He looked tan and strange in an old wool army coat, his jeans too dark and stiff and new, his hair too long and sun-streaked for a city still in the grip of its long winter.

"Tell him he'll have to wait."

Lydia refused to look up again through the forty minutes of her client's Gorgon tangle of foil highlights. And still he waited, sitting straight backed in a gilt chair as her father glared at him from a back office and her mother came out twice, purportedly to check the schedule book, sneaking glances at him. Lydia wondered what he thought of the very plump, very blond Mrs. Gold, with her dramatically plucked eyebrows and noose of gold chains hanging down her yellow silk blouse. Does he think that's what I'll look like in twenty years?

An hour after Liam had walked through the doors, Lydia offered him a cup of coffee. "Will you talk to me, Lydia?"

"I have another client in ten minutes."

"When are you free?"

"At eight."

"I'll stay." He waited for two more hours, and then, as the other haircutters began to file out, Lydia walked over to him.

"I'm sorry, Liam. I didn't think it would take me quite so long."

"That should be my line, shouldn't it? You've changed your hair."

"I decided to make a stronger statement."

"It suits you."

Lydia couldn't help but smile at that. "Why did you come here now?"

His hand came up, large and warm, to close over her wrist. "A bit of unfinished business."

"Lydia." They both turned, startled, to face Lydia's father. Victor Gold stared past his daughter's island lover as if he had never seen him before. "We're closing up here."

"Leave the keys. I'll lock up for the night."

For a moment, her father looked as if he wanted to argue, but something stopped him. He went away to confer with his wife. After a long moment, they shrugged into their matching camel-hair coats and left the salon.

"Well." Liam laughed, uncomfortable.

"Well."

"Are you going to cut my hair?"

"I think so. But first, I'd better wash it."

As she led Liam over to put on a cloth drape and settled him into the chair beside the black marble sink; Lydia had a feeling that there was some purpose behind this formal dance. She washed his hair slowly, glad of the excuse to touch him. As her fingers massaged his scalp, he closed his eyes.

"That feels like—do you do this for everybody?"

"No. Usually Cilla, the shampoo girl, does it for me."

"Does it always feel like this?"

Lydia smiled. "Like what?"

"Like being taken care of."

Lydia toweled Liam's hair dry and then guided him back to her booth. Outside, the sky grew darker and the lights came on in some of the windows of the broad white-brick apartment buildings, illuminating odd glimpses of dinner tables, arguments, television sets. Other people's lives. She kept the chair facing the outside window.

"How do you want me to cut it?"

"I don't know. A mohawk?"

Lydia ran her fingers through his hair, measuring, considering. "Did you ever have one?"

"When I was sixteen." She worked on him in silence, feeling him change under her hands, growing more aware of her, warming to her, still uncomfortable, trapped in a transformation not of his imagining. She went deep, and gave him a tousled short cut that revealed the faint silver threads tracing through the dark-reddish blond.

"How do I look?" Lydia turned him around to face the mirror. "Jesus, what'd you do? Folks'll think I joined the army." He ran his fingers through his hair, his eyebrows lifted in astonishment.

"You look wonderful, as you well know."

"I look old! You've aged me!"

"I'm beginning to take offense at this."

"Bloody hell! I want my money back!"

"You haven't paid!"

He stilled, his face growing serious. "You're right," he said slowly, "I haven't."

"Liam?"

But he was already reaching into his pocket and removing a gold claddagh ring, two hands holding a heart.

"Why are you doing this?" She didn't extend her hand to touch it.

"It was my mother's. I was going to give it to you a month ago, but you, ah, gave me the boot. And I suppose my pride was hurt. And—well, I had some thinking to do. Here," he gestured at her, "take it."

Lydia shook her head. "I don't understand."

"It's not an engagement ring. It's a ring for friendship. And for—and for love. And what love might grow into."

Liam, still seated below her, tried to place the ring on her left hand. "Shall we see how this fits, then?"

"No."

"Aw, Lydia. Surely you're not—don't cry, love."

"It's just that this reminds me of all the things I dreamed of for so long. I so wanted a ring. Ever since I was a teenager, and all the other girls seemed to get these—I don't know—rings, or a bracelet, or a locket even. From their boyfriends. And I never did. If I dated someone, he forgot my birthday, or broke up with me right before Valentine's Day, or said he thought anniversaries were commercial." Lydia stared up tearfully at the cavernous baroque ceiling of the empty salon and wondered why she was confessing all this to him. Don't make yourself out to be such a victim, he'd told her.

"Ah," Liam said. He seemed at a loss.

"Oh, shit. Shit! Here I am, living on my own—well, okay, with my brother for a roommate—and getting my act together, going back to graduate school, I've completely put romance on the back burner, and then you show up. And you probably think I sound like that cocker spaniel again."

"You're never going to forget I said that, are you?"

"Probably not."

Liam pondered. "I'm not just here for a short stay, you know. I'm trying to get my old job back. I figure I'm good for a few more years at it."

"Oh." Lydia found a tissue and wiped her nose.

"I can get you a better ring."

"Oh, please, no, I—"

"Please stop crying. Please."

Lydia made the sound again, and Liam gathered her into his arms. "What is it, then?"

"It's too late. Oh, Liam, we had a few days, a few hours, and that was a month ago. And in that time, I've been thinking—I've been trying—" Lydia bowed her head, stopped, then began again. "I've lost myself in romantic dreams for so many years. I even half-expected you to come after me before my plane took off. And then I realized what I was doing to myself. Liam, I have to start thinking about other things. There is a whole world out there that has nothing to do with whether or not I meet the right man."

"And here I thought you might have met him off on an island somewhere."

Lydia made a sound halfway between a laugh and a sigh. She touched his cheek. "Oh, my love, maybe I did. But it's such bad timing, don't you see? I need to become myself. I need to finish my degree and find a job and make a life. Otherwise, I'm just going to drag us down with the weight of too much expectation."

He held her against his soft cotton shirt and his hard chest, his hands tracing helpless patterns of longing on her back. He smelled of clean man and the streets of New York. There was no trace of Epiphany on him.

"What would you have done if I had gone after your plane?"

Lydia kept her cheek pressed to him. "I don't know."

"Have I blown it, then? Completely and beyond repair?"

She held him so tightly her arms hurt. "Please don't." She began to cry again, more softly than before.

"Shh. Shh. This isn't the way it's supposed to be. Do you have a sound system in here?"

Lydia nodded.

"Over there? Hold on a sec." Liam bounded up the stairs, withdrew a cassette from his inside jacket pocket, and then turned on the system.

The tune sounded oddly familiar. The xylophone and steel drums converted the melancholy samba into something lighter, something earthier and simpler than the original, but the singer's lilting voice conveyed the wistful promise of midnight conversation and emotion after the party is over.

"That's Baron and the boys," said Lydia.

"Yes. Care to dance?"

Lydia stared up at Liam's face. In his eyes, there was a strange, gentle, almost distant look, as if he were already commemorating an event that had happened long ago. A small smile played about his lips.

"What are we doing?"

"Replaying the end. It's carnival, and you're in the taxi leaving for the airport."

"Liam, we can't rewrite the past."

"We can."

"This is ridiculous. That moment in time is gone."

"Your taxi is waiting and I've pulled you out and your dad is glowering at me. I'm asking you to dance."

"There isn't time."

"Make the time."

The complicated, sensuous rhythm beckoned, and Lydia stepped back into Liam's arms for what she knew was the last time. He did not hold her particularly close; there was a dancer's tension in his arms, a small kingdom of space between them. She intuited, rather than felt, the movements of his feet and hips, and moved with him instinctively. When he turned her, it felt like a form of telepathy, Liam transmitting his intentions with the lightest of pressure at the small of her back.

The singer, who did not know all the words, fell silent, and Lydia whispered the lyrics he did not say: seeing someone out of nowhere, background fading, not knowing your destination. Avalon. She realized she was giving too much away. But Liam had chosen this song of Arthurian romance. He had given that away, too.

Liam's eyes never left hers. The half smile, secretive and unsentimental, never left his mouth. He brushed his thumbs across the tears spilling silently and continuously down her cheeks.

"Why are you crying, Lydia?"

Lydia choked on a laugh.

"Tell me." Liam stopped moving. Somewhere in the background, the music continued playing. Around them, a small wave of silence seemed to grow and gather force.

"Because it's all ending." Lydia lifted her chin. "Why are you laughing?"

"Because it's only the beginning that's ending." It took a moment for Lydia's mind to translate. Liam continued to smile down at her, as if bemused by his own intensity. And then the smile left his face, and he let the other thing show, the stark and naked thing that was not under his control. He looked like that when he was inside me, Lydia thought.

Liam bent his head and pressed his lips to her fingers, hard. "Don't leave me," he said, his voice hoarse with emotion. He held her hand captive beneath his, spreading her fingers out on his chest, over the quickened rhythm of his heart. Liam looked down at Lydia, and it seemed to her that at that moment, all the words they didn't speak crashed and broke over them, proposal and acceptance made without a gesture or a sound.

And because it was carnival, and because the lovers were, after all, on an island, the band played the melody on and on, the phrases of the song fading and falling, conjuring a place beyond Camelot's betrayal: a place where time stands still for the reckless and broken-hearted and there could yet be a happy ending for unrequited love. Liam and Lydia danced, sometimes smiling, sometimes not, their faces always close enough to kiss.